GAYLORD   PRINTED IN U.S.A.

THE MIDSUMMER ROSE

THE MIDSUMMER ROSE

Kate Sedley

This first world edition published in Great Britain 2004 by
SEVERN HOUSE PUBLISHERS LTD of
9–15 High Street, Sutton, Surrey SM1 1DF.
This first world edition published in the USA 2004 by
SEVERN HOUSE PUBLISHERS INC of
595 Madison Avenue, New York, N.Y. 10022.

British Library Cataloguing in Publication Data

Sedley, Kate
    The midsummer rose. - (A Roger the Chapman mediaeval mystery)
    1.   Roger the Chapman (Fictitious character) - Fiction
    2.   Peddlers and peddling - Fiction
    3.   England - Social life and customs - 1066-1485 - Fiction
    4.   Detective and mystery stories
    I.   Title   Fiction
    823.9'14 [F]   SEDLEY
                         miD
    ISBN 0-7278-6078-X   11·04

Typeset by Palimpsest Book Production Ltd.,
Polmont, Stirlingshire, Scotland.
Printed and bound in Great Britain by
MPG Books Ltd., Bodmin, Cornwall.

To my grandchildren,
Laura, Matthew and Katy.

One

I could see the house where the murders had been committed from where I was waiting, on the opposite side of the river Avon. It was visible because it was two-storeyed and stood some distance from the other cottages that formed the hamlet of Rownham Passage, on a muddy spur of rock that was washed by the river at full tide.

Surprisingly for one who was not a native of Bristol, I knew its history. It had been one of the stories told to me by my long-dead first wife, Lillis Walker, and for some reason it had stuck in my memory.

Fifty years and more ago, two women – a mother and daughter who had lived there – had hacked to death the tyrannical husband and father of the household, throwing his mutilated body into the river. Unfortunately for them, the corpse had been trapped by those underwater rocks that make the Avon such a treacherous river to navigate, and instead of being carried out into the Severn estuary on the receding tide, it had floated on the next *incoming* tide right into the heart of the city. In due course the two women had been arrested, tried, found guilty and suffered the horrible fate of being burned alive . . .

'You waitin' for this bleedin' ferry or not, then?' enquired an irate voice that made me jump.

The ferryman had returned from the opposite shore and beached his skiff on the narrow mudflat skirting the towering escarpment behind us – an escarpment that reduced human life to dwarfish proportions. Similarly, on the other side of the river, Ghyston Cliff made the huddle of cottages at its foot look like a handful of toys tossed down by a careless giant.

1

'You goin' to stand 'ere all bleedin' day?' demanded the ferryman, growing ever more frustrated by my lack of response. 'There's a storm brewin'.' He nodded towards a bank of dark clouds, marring the perfection of a warm, early-June morning.

'Sorry,' I apologized, heaving my pack and cudgel into the skiff and seating myself in the stern. 'How much?'

'Penny.' The ferryman took the oars, looking me up and down in a disparaging sort of way. 'Although for a chap as big and heavy as you, it ought to be more. You're a weight, you are.'

'Blame my wife. She feeds me too well.'

The man grunted as he pulled away from the Somerset shore and the Lordship of Ashton-Leigh.

'Leg-shackled, are you? You look married. Any children?'

'Three,' I admitted with a sigh. 'A daughter from my first marriage. She'll be five in November. And a stepson a few weeks older. Then there's Adam.' I tried to sound cheerful. 'He'll celebrate his first birthday at the end of this month. He's my child by my second wife.'

The ferryman looked sympathetic – or as sympathetic as his gnarled and weather-beaten features permitted.

'One, eh? That's a terrible age for any child to be. I should know! I've fathered six of the varmints. Girls ain't so bad, but boys!' He cast up his eyes to heaven, where they remained riveted. 'Them dang clouds, they'm blowing inland fast. There's going to be a real storm very soon.' He indicated my pack with a jerk of his head. 'You a pedlar?'

I nodded. 'I've been as far as Woodspring Priory and back. Now I'm heading home to Bristol. I intended to walk the landward way round to the Redcliffe Gate, but when I found myself close to the river, I thought I might as well take the ferry. So, here I am.' I gazed up at the cliffs rearing above us. 'Pity someone couldn't build a bridge up there,' I remarked idly. 'It would save travellers from Leigh to Clifton a great deal of time and effort.'

The ferryman snorted. 'Are you mad or what? No one could build a bridge at that height.'

He was right, of course, but I was reluctant to relinquish

my dream so easily. 'It might happen one day,' I argued. 'Centuries hence perhaps, when you and I are long dead.'

He showed me the whites of his eyes. 'You ain't one of them heretics, are you? Lollards, or whatever they call 'em?'

'I'm a good son of the Holy Church,' I protested.

But wasn't I being a little disingenuous? Weren't many of my secret beliefs and theories more in tune with the followers of John Wycliffe than with orthodox teachings? But I knew it was as well to keep a still tongue in my head on that score. Nowadays I was not only a family man, but also had the additional responsibility of being a householder, thanks to the almost unbelievable generosity of a sweet, dead friend who the previous year had left me her house in Small Street. Me! Roger the Chapman, who had never lived in anything better or bigger than a rented, one-roomed cottage in his life, and had never expected to do so until the day he died!

My good fortune had at first caused a lot of resentment in Bristol, particularly among my erstwhile friends, very few of whom had seemed happy for my wife Adela and me. Even Margaret Walker, my quondam mother-in-law and Adela's cousin, had been restrained in her congratulations, predicting that this result of my former (totally innocent) association with Mistress Cicely Ford would set the gossips' tongues wagging. But, ten months on, my wife and I had largely overcome all the unpleasantness by simply ignoring it and remaining our normal polite, imperturbable selves. Well, Adela had. And although I might have been forced to black Burl Hodge's eye in an effort to knock some sense into him, and to encourage my dog, Hercules, to bite the backside of a neighbour who openly objected to riff-raff such as my family and myself moving into Small Street, on the whole I had managed to behave with the propriety that became a man of property. And today, I could anticipate returning to a home that boasted not merely a hall, parlour, kitchen and three bedchambers, but also a buttery. Not that we needed such a room – only a modest amount of wine was drunk in our household, ale and small beer being cheaper – but the children found it useful for playing in, using the bottle racks as places to keep their toys.

3

The skiff scraped and bumped ashore at Rownham Passage and the ferryman berthed his oars, jumping out first in order to help me unload my belongings. I followed and paid him his fare.

'What did you mean,' I asked suspiciously, 'when you said I "looked married"?'

The man shrugged, paying more attention to the weather and the rapidly darkening sky than to me.

'Dunno,' he answered vaguely. 'But you can always tell ... 'Ere! I'm taking cover. Don't want to be caught mid-river in this lot.' A few drops of rain spattered the Avon's mudbanks as he spoke. 'An' if you've got any sense, chapman, you'll find shelter, too. This is going to be a nasty little squall.'

'Pooh! A shower doesn't bother me,' I boasted. 'I'm used to being abroad in all kinds of weather.'

The ferryman laughed and, with a rough word of explanation to his waiting fare – a fat woman dressed in grey homespun and carrying a large basket of eggs – hurried towards the alehouse perched just above the high-water mark and surrounded by the cluster of houses that was Rownham Passage. I, on the other hand, went in the opposite direction, along the narrow riverside track that skirted the base of Saint Brendan's Hill.

Suddenly the heavens opened and a violent gust of wind almost knocked me off my feet. The reeds fringing the river were lashed by spray and flurries of rain hit the path in front of me. In a few moments, everything seemed to have disintegrated into one deafening, wind-torn shriek.

I cursed my stupidity in not listening to the ferryman and for allowing my bravado to get the better of my common sense. But I had no time to dwell on the matter. I needed to take cover, and it was with relief that I saw, through the curtain of rain, a hovel of some sort, standing close to the track.

As soon as I opened the door, the pungent smell of horses greeted me, accompanied by the whinnying and shifting of two sets of hooves. Now, horses and I have never got on: they know I'm nervous of them and so they treat me with the contempt they think I deserve. Moreover, these two were obviously unsettled by the weather. I withdrew hurriedly, latching the door behind me.

The storm was at its height. I was soaked to the skin and my need for shelter was pressing. I was just screwing up my courage to take refuge with the animals after all, when I noticed a house standing a few yards nearer to the river bank than its attendant outbuilding. It was the 'murder' house, which had reportedly remained empty ever since the crime, but which was now showing a light in one of its downstairs windows.

At least, I thought I could see a light, and that was good enough for me. I dashed across the stretch of wind-bleached grass dividing the rocky promontory from the Saint Brendan's track, to discover that there was indeed a candle flame glimmering behind the parchment panes of a small back window. I fought my way around to the front of the house, which faced the river, and hammered as hard as I could on the door.

Somewhat to my surprise, my knocking was answered almost immediately by a woman who held the door open wide and urged me inside. I needed no second bidding.

I found myself in a short, narrow passageway with a flight of stairs at the far end and, to my right, another door which led into a small, barely furnished parlour. Indeed, one of the things I remembered later was the all-pervasive smell of must and damp indicative of a house little used and from which light and air are largely excluded. But at the time, events moved so fast and so unexpectedly that I was unable to register anything with clarity.

'We didn't think you'd be here just yet,' the woman said. She sounded edgy, nervous, as though the arrival of whoever it was she had mistaken me for was unwelcome. 'We thought you would have sought shelter during this storm.'

I was vaguely aware of movements overhead. Someone was upstairs. This accounted for the 'we' she had referred to.

I pushed my dripping hair out of my eyes, propped my cudgel against the wall, dropped my pack beside it and tried in vain to brush the rain from the front of my sodden jerkin.

5

'Look, I don't know who you think I am,' I began, but the woman ignored me.

As she brushed past to stare out of the window, I was aware of a pleasant-featured, strongly marked face and a well built figure, taller than average for a woman. Suddenly she uttered a sharp cry and beckoned me to join her.

'Come and look at this!' she whispered urgently. 'Hurry!'

Bewildered, I followed her to the window and peered through the dirty parchment which showed me nothing beyond the fact that it was coated with the grime of many years.

'What is it?' I demanded irritably. 'There's nothing there. And if there were, you couldn't see it through all this muck.'

The woman had left my side and was now behind me – again, something I realized later. Much later.

'There's something you must understand.' I tried again. 'I'm not—'

I can't even remember feeling the blow with which she felled me.

I had no idea how long I had been unconscious, but guessed it could not have been for any length of time; perhaps no more than a minute or two. I experienced no confusion of thought as I came to my senses, nor any difficulty in recalling what had happened or where I was.

I was lying where I had fallen, the dust on the floor tickling the back of my nose and throat and making me want to sneeze. I controlled the impulse, realizing that my best hope of eventually overpowering my assailant rested in the element of surprise. She probably thought she was stronger than she really was, and would pride herself on laying me out for some considerable time. But she would soon learn her mistake.

Meanwhile, I had a throbbing headache to contend with and, worse than that, the even greater pain of wounded vanity, for I had been struck down with my very own cudgel! Cautiously opening one eye, it was the first thing I saw, lying a couple of feet or so away. I cursed myself for every kind of a fool. It was all very well arguing that I could not possibly have foreseen what was coming; that I had no reason to suspect that danger lurked. But I had guessed from the start that I had been mistaken for someone else. That, if no other reason, should have put me on my guard. Furthermore, the unfurnished appearance of the house, coupled with the smell of damp and decay, should have alerted my senses to the fact that something was amiss. Instead, I had been preoccupied with my own discomfort. It served me right.

The storm seemed to have passed, in the abrupt way that such summer squalls so often do. The rain had ceased drumming against the window and a ray of sunshine was once more struggling to illumine the filthy panes. I could hear seagulls noisily foraging for food along the mudflats of the Avon.

Someone else had come into the room. Another woman. Presumably the person who had earlier been moving about upstairs. Opening my eyes the merest slit, I was just in time to see the hem of a blue brocade gown sweep past me and, beneath, the flash of red leather shoes. This was not my attacker, who was wearing a gown of much plainer, darker material, although I had had little opportunity to register it in any detail. But it had definitely not gleamed with the richness of brocade, of that I was certain. Who, then, was this?

Then a man's voice spoke from somewhere behind me. Whoever he was, he must have entered the house while I was unconscious.

'What are we going to do with him? Toss him in the river?'

It dawned on me with sickening clarity that I was in a far more serious situation than I had previously imagined. It was not just one woman I had to deal with. It was not even two. It was three people, one of whom was male and might be armed.

The thought had barely entered my aching head when he spoke again, confirming my worst fears.

'I'll use my knife. Finish him off.'

There was something foreign about his speech, some peculiarity that I could not quite place. French? Breton? Cornish? I didn't think so, but what the accent was, I was unable to say. In any case, there was no time for such considerations. I was in imminent danger of being murdered.

7

The first woman moved back into my line of vision and I hastily closed my eyes, but not before I had glimpsed several inches of brown sarcenet skirt and the end of a black leather girdle tipped with a silver tag studded with turquoises. Whoever she was, she was a woman of substance. Possibly also a woman of sense and education. I trusted that she was about to speak up in my defence.

'I suppose that might be the safest way to get rid of him.'

So much for the gentleness and mercy of the opposite sex! I should have known better; women can be far more ruthless than men. I tensed my muscles ready to sell my life as dearly as possible. I would not go under without a fight . . .

'The door was unlatched, so I just walked in,' announced yet another male voice. This one had an Irish lilt to it, the soft brogue of southern Ireland, around Waterford. I had heard it often during my years of living in Bristol.

There was an astounded silence. I can recognize total amazement even when my head is pounding fit to burst.

'Who . . . Who are you?' my assailant quavered as soon as she managed to find her tongue.

'Who do you think I am? I'm Eamonn Malahide of course. Who else are you expecting?'

Once more, I let my eyes flicker open. I could safely wager that no one would be looking at me.

Where there had been brown sarcenet and the hint of a shapely leg beneath, was now a huge pair of feet encased in worn but substantial leather boots with thick, hobnailed soles – excellent, I surmised, for kicking people to the ground and, afterwards, trampling them underfoot. Above the boots, a stout pair of legs were shrouded in thick frieze breeches such as seafaring men wear. I dared raise my eyelids no further for fear of revealing that I was awake, but the two hands dangling loosely by the man's side were as big as shovels, and one had a ship pricked out in woad on the back of it, with the word Clontarf underneath.

'C–Captain Malahide?' stammered the woman who had let me in. 'But . . . but we thought . . .'

'What did you think?' The seaman was growing uneasy.

I could hear it in his voice and could see it in the sudden shuffle of his feet on the dusty floor. At that point he must have noticed me for the first time. 'Who's this?' he demanded suspiciously.

I decided the moment had come to put the cat among the pigeons. It didn't take much brainpower to work out the situation, even when that brain felt as though it had been pounded to a pulp. I dragged myself up on to one elbow.

I heard someone curse, but whether a man or a woman I couldn't be certain: I was too busy trying to steady my swimming senses. I must have moved too quickly, or was weaker than I had thought. Whatever the reason, the room was revolving dizzily about me. But my powers of speech were still strong.

Fighting down a rising tide of nausea, I said as loudly and distinctly as I could, 'I'm just a poor pedlar who sought shelter here from the storm. Instead, I was knocked over the head with my own cudgel and my murder planned while these villains thought I was still unconscious.'

'But why?'

'Isn't it obvious?' I demanded. 'Use your common sense, man! They thought I was you!'

I was prepared for my seafarer to have some difficulty in working out the implications of this remark, but he didn't. Something he knew that they knew – or maybe guessed that they had guessed – made him accept my accusation without a second's hesitation. He gave a roar of anger and drew a wicked-looking knife from the sheath attached to his belt. He didn't falter for even a second, but went straight for the second woman in the blue brocade dress who, I now realized, had stationed herself just inside the parlour door. His intention was clear, and I desperately struggled to my feet in order to prevent murder being done. But I was too late – except that it was not the murder I had expected. It was the seaman who fell, stabbed to the heart by the expertly wielded short-handled, long-bladed dagger produced in a flash from the folds of the woman's blue skirt. Eamonn Malahide, if that were indeed his real name, dropped with nothing more than a grunt and was patently dead even before he hit the floor.

9

At the same time, I saw the first woman stoop and pick up my cudgel again. I divined her purpose without much effort and made a further frantic attempt to get to my feet. But it was hopeless. My knees buckled under me and I was violently sick just a moment before she dealt me another stunning blow to the back of my head, on almost exactly the same spot as before. For the second time that morning, I was knocked unconscious.

I moved uneasily in and out of a nightmare in which I was being pursued along a river bank by a whole posse of women, all of whom were brandishing knives and intent on murdering me.

The third time I recovered my senses, I was vaguely aware of being jolted across the rocky foreshore of the Avon, slung like an unwanted sack of flour between two people. My head and shoulders were being supported by someone I couldn't see. But the blue brocade dress, which I could glimpse from the waist down, was immediately familiar to me as the gown of the unheard other woman who had the murderous ability to wield a knife as well as any man. The skirt had been hitched up indecently high to reveal the occasional sight of a thin, but well muscled leg in a yellow silk stocking with a garter of fine buckled leather.

The lower half of my body was in the tender care of my attacker. She was grumbling and occasionally cursing under her breath as her shoes slithered on the wet stretch of rock separating the 'murder' house from the river. Just before I passed out yet again, I wondered where the third person, the man, was. Then I remembered the bulk and girth of the dead seafarer. It would need some strength to shift his carcass.

This time my dreams took me back inside the house, where I found myself locked in the parlour with two enormous horses, maddened by the storm raging outside. Just as one reared up on its hind legs, its evil-looking hooves flailing above me, the window flew open and I was drenched in water.

But that, at least, was no dream. I surfaced just as the two

10

women were rolling me into the Avon. And I saw the muddy waters close over my head as I lost consciousness for the final time. I remember thinking desperately of Adela. This was it, then. This was the end. I was drowning.

Two

I raised my eyelids just far enough to see the motes of dust dancing in the sunlight streaming through the open window. The heat lay as heavy as a fur across my knees. I was dry, warm and floating on a cloud somewhere between sleeping and waking. I suspected I must have died and gone straight to heaven . . .

But as my other senses began to revive, I realized that heaven could never smell like the Bristol streets on a hot summer's day. (And if it did, I didn't want to go there.) Nor would angels, playing their celestial harps, sound like street traders raucously vying with one another for customers. I therefore had to be at home in Small Street, in my own bedchamber, in my own bed.

Why I should find this idea so strange gradually became clear to me as unwelcome memories started to return, waving at me like discoloured rags from the corners of my mind. The house at Rownham Passage . . . The storm . . . The blow to my head . . . The sickness and nausea . . . The murder of the Irishman, whose name I could no longer remember . . . Above all, the two women, one in brown sarcenet, the other in blue brocade, who had tried to drown me in the river . . .

Something landed on my chest with all the force of a cart-load of turnips hitting a brick wall. I yelled, afraid I was being attacked again. Then my face was licked by a wet, enthusiastic tongue, and breath that could knock a grown man senseless at a dozen paces assaulted the back of my nose, making me sneeze.

My dog, Hercules.

I was definitely at home and I wasn't dreaming. But how

I had survived my watery grave and how I had got here were questions that I was unable either to answer or to cope with just at present. I lifted an arm that felt like lead and stroked Hercules's scruffy little head.

'Hello, lad. All right! All right! I'm as pleased to see you as you are to see me. But just shift a bit, will you? You smell as though you've been eating fly-infested meat.' (Which he probably had, from the drain in the middle of the street. Gnawing at putrefying carcasses was one of his less endearing habits, but also one of the greatest pleasures of his doggy existence.)

Hercules was not to be deterred, however, and at the sound of my voice grew even more excited, farting loudly to demonstrate his happiness at seeing me again.

The bedchamber door burst open and Adela came in, flour streaking her forehead, hands still partially caked with dough. She had obviously been in the middle of baking, and wiped them in a hurry. Her beautiful brown eyes, overflowing with anxiety, fixed themselves on me.

'Roger?' she asked in a whisper of painful intensity. 'Was that you calling out? Are you properly awake at last?'

I grinned weakly at her. 'You're not looking at a ghost.'

She threw herself on her knees beside the bed, pushing an indignant Hercules to the floor and embracing me in an all-enveloping hug. Her tears trickled down my face, mingling with my own. I managed, after a great deal of effort, to get both arms around her. This time it was like moving two dead weights.

How long we might have remained so – I was quite content to stay that way forever – is a moot point, but, as usual, our private moment was rudely interrupted. The room was suddenly full of people – my former mother-in-law and three children to be precise. But, as always with my nearest and dearest, it felt as if the hordes of Genghis Khan had invaded.

'A fine scare you've given us!' Margaret Walker upbraided me, standing at the foot of the bed, her arms akimbo. 'Falling into the river like that! You could have been drowned! Don't tell me! I suppose you were drunk!'

My feeble attempts at denial were frustrated by Elizabeth

and Nicholas, who clambered on to the bed, hauling Adam up after them. My son promptly gave a scream of delight and threw himself across my face in a determined endeavour to smother me.

'Ge'm off!' I mumbled.

Fortunately, Adela was able to interpret this anguished, but muffled cry, and lifted Adam on to the floor, setting him down alongside Hercules, where he immediately gave vent to a howl that could split the eardrums.

My daughter, ignoring her half-brother's tantrum with practised ease, said reproachfully, 'You didn't bring us home any presents like you promised. We know, 'cause Nick and I searched your jerkin pockets. Your scrip was empty, too.'

Her stepbrother nodded in agreement, then sniffed, wrinkling his nose. 'Why do you smell so funny?'

'Hercules has been licking me.' I tried not to sound as irritable as I felt, at the same time trying to remember where I had put the small gifts I'd bought for the children. Memory came flooding back. 'They're in my pack . . .'

My pack! Where was it? It must still be in that house. My cudgel, too! My money, thank God, the takings of a fortnight, had all been in my pouch. But where was that? Had it survived my immersion in the river? I propped myself on one elbow, dislodging Elizabeth and Nicholas. They started to grizzle.

'My pack, cudgel, money—' I began frantically, but Adela hushed me, laying a cool, if floury, hand on my forehead.

'Shhh! They're quite safe.' She turned to her cousin. 'Margaret, would you be kind enough to take the children away, my dear? And that flea-ridden hound.' Hercules gave her one of his looks. 'Roger needs rest and quiet. After a week in bed, his strength is bound to be at a very low ebb.'

But her words only started me off again. As Margaret ushered children and dog from the room, I raised myself on both elbows.

'A week?' I gasped. 'You mean I've been unconscious for a week?'

'Not totally unconscious, no. You've been extremely feverish, not knowing anyone, not knowing where you were, talking a lot of gibberish.' My wife leaned forward to kiss my cheek, but paused, grimacing. She reached for the ewer and a cloth, poured water into a basin and proceeded to bathe my face. 'There, that's better. You smell a bit less like a sewer and more like your normal self.' I wondered uneasily what my normal self smelled like, but decided not to ask.

She was trying to keep her tone light, but I could tell that she was still deeply anxious about me. I squeezed her hand.

'I'm all right. There's nothing to worry about. I shall be fit and strong again in plenty of time for the midsummer revels, you'll see. I just want to know what's happened.'

'We all want to know that,' Margaret Walker remarked with asperity, coming back into the room. She seated herself on the opposite side of the bed to my wife. 'Now then, Roger, how in the name of heaven did you come to fall in the Avon?'

'Never mind that for the moment,' I retorted peevishly. 'What I want to know is who pulled me out. And what are you doing here? Why aren't you at home, in Redcliffe?'

Margaret was offended, as she had every right to be. My rudeness was unpardonable, but her constant presence, when all I wanted was to be alone with Adela, was beginning to irk me.

'What do you think I'm doing here?' she snapped back. 'I came to help look after you, you ungrateful lump. How do you imagine Adela would have managed with you to care for as well as three children and that idiot hound?'

I tried to look suitably chastened. I must have succeeded, because Adela hid a smile behind her hand.

'Mother-in-law, forgive me. I'm not myself.' Margaret liked to be called mother-in-law, even though Lillis had been dead for almost five years. 'How did I get here? Who rescued me?'

'It was the Rownham ferryman,' my wife answered quietly, clinging to one of my hands as though she would never let it go. 'When he returned to his boat after the storm, he saw you in the water. You weren't very far out. It seems your leather jerkin had blown up like a bladder and prevented you from sinking, although the ferryman reckoned it wouldn't

15

have kept you afloat for much longer.' Her fingers gripped mine even more tightly. 'The passengers who were waiting for his boat helped him tow you ashore. Thanks be to God, you were still breathing. The ferryman recalled you'd said you were going home to Bristol, so he had you loaded into a farmer's cart that was coming this way. And, of course, once the farmer reached the city, there was no lack of people who could direct him here.'

Margaret Walker opened her mouth, no doubt to make some caustic remark, but thought better of it and closed it again. I suspected I looked more of a physical wreck than I cared to imagine.

'My pack! My cudgel! You said they were safe.'

'It appears they were lying on the mudbank, where you must have dropped them. Or so the ferryman told the farmer. He put them in the cart alongside you. Roger!' Adela leaned over and kissed me gently between the eyes, but she was frowning. 'How *did* you come to fall in? And somehow or another, you managed to hit your head. You've a nasty contusion on the back.'

Margaret, who was evidently still smarting from my earlier incivility, repeated waspishly, 'I suppose you were drunk. Sheltered from the storm in the Rownham alehouse, did you? Too much cider?'

'No,' I replied curtly, and said nothing more until I had a grip on my temper. Eventually I continued. 'If you don't believe me, ask the ferryman. He was in the alehouse. I started walking home along the Saint Brendan's Hill track.'

'But what happened?' Adela asked, puzzled.

So I told them. I told them everything, and perhaps a bit more than I could actually remember. Where memory was a little frayed around the edges, I filled in the details with what I guessed or thought must have occurred. Then I lay back on my pillows, exhausted, and waited for their horrified exclamations.

These, however, did not come. Instead, the two women looked first at me, then at one another; looks of such significance that I was hard put to interpret them. Finally, Margaret Walker raised two fingers and tapped her forehead, but when she saw me staring at her, pretended to brush aside a strand of hair that had escaped from her cap. I shifted my gaze to my wife, who was regarding me with concern.

'What's the matter?' I demanded. 'Don't you believe me?'

'Roger, dear!' Adela stood up, freeing her hand from mine and pressing it to my cheeks and brow. 'He's still a bit feverish,' she said anxiously to Margaret.

I pushed her away. 'I'm telling you the truth,' I shouted. 'You've seen the wound on the back of my head! You said so!'

'Hush, sweetheart, hush!' My wife tried to ease me back on the pillows, but I refused to budge.

'Why do you both think I'm lying?' I demanded furiously.

The women exchanged another of those significant glances, then Margaret said, 'The house that you're describing . . . It's the one where the murders took place half a century and more ago. I remember Lillis telling you about it one evening, when we were sitting round the fire, just before Elizabeth was born. She was a good storyteller, that girl of mine. She made things come alive. The two women knifing the man to death, throwing his body into the Avon . . . I could see it all so vividly, and so could you. I know you could.'

'You think I'm making this up!' I exclaimed wrathfully. I rounded on Adela. 'Is that your opinion, too?'

She looked uncomfortable. 'I think you've had a nasty knock on the head, Roger. Before you fell into the river, you were near the house where this murder took place and the story was probably in your mind. When you're more rested, you'll remember what really happened. Maybe somebody tried to rob you.'

'And left me my money and my pack?'

'Whoever it was must have been disturbed,' Margaret answered tartly. 'And there's no need to speak to Adela in that tone of voice. She's a saint, the way she's looked after you. Washing you. Shaving you. And other things.' She grimaced.

I closed my eyes, trying hard to subdue my ill humour. When women start conferring sainthood on one another, a man has to be in serious trouble.

17

'That'll do, Margaret,' my wife said gently. 'Roger's not himself. He needs rest.' She stooped and gave me another kiss. 'Try to sleep, sweetheart. I'll come and see you again when I've set the dough to rise. I'll bring you some wine and warm water. Are you hungry?'

'No!' It was a lie: I was ravenous. But at that moment I was so angry, I felt food would stick in my craw and choke me.

I refused to open my eyes when the two women tiptoed away, latching the bedchamber door behind them. There was the murmur of anxious whispering on the stairs before I was left to the cries of the street traders and my own uneasy thoughts.

I hadn't imagined it all, had I? It wasn't just a figment of my imagination? It really had happened? Of course it had, and there was a lump on the back of my head to prove it. My former mother-in-law had an explanation for that, as well, but it wasn't the true one. The two women, the foreign-sounding man and the Irishman really had existed. No one had attacked me for my money.

I tried to envisage what might have been the sequence of events after 'brown sarcenet' and her companion had rolled me into the water. Perhaps the unseen man had followed them down to the river's edge with my pack and cudgel. 'We can't leave these lying about,' he could have said. 'Throw them in with him.' But maybe one of the women decided it would appear more natural if they were found on the bank, where I might possibly have dropped them . . .

A dreadful lethargy was beginning to possess me. All I wanted was to sleep. I let myself drift, ignoring the various aches and pains of my body and the dull throbbing at the back of my head. Hercules must have escaped from some-where, because I felt him jump on the bed and snuggle up against my side with a contented sigh. The fleas would love it.

The next time I opened my eyes, it was early morning.

I could tell it was morning by the soft aureole of light rimming the shutters. And I knew it must be early because

18

Adela was still in bed, curled into my back, one of her arms, free of the bedclothes, flung protectively across me. The rest of the house was quiet. No one else was stirring.

Both feet had gone to sleep and I tried to shift them without disturbing Adela. But she was wide awake at the first movement, raising herself slightly on one elbow to smile down at me.

'That's better,' she said approvingly. 'You've some colour in your cheeks at last. I think you've almost recovered.'

I yawned and stretched my arms above my head until the bones cracked. Then, without warning, I lowered them, trapping her in a warm and meaningful embrace.

She laughed, then reluctantly surrendered. 'You've definitely recovered.' She pillowed her head on my chest. 'These last two days have made all the difference.'

I groaned. 'Oh, no! I haven't been asleep for another two days, surely?'

She raised her face to mine, looking guilty.

'I kept giving you infusions of poppy seed and lettuce juice each time you woke. The apothecary in Bell Lane advised it. He said sleep would drive away all the brain's ill humours.'

I relaxed my grip on her. 'You still don't believe my story.'

She kissed my cheek and looked even guiltier. I wondered what was coming.

'Don't be cross. I know that part of it, at least, is true.'

'Which part?' My suspicions were now fully aroused.

'I know you didn't go to the alehouse, so you couldn't have been drunk.'

I turned on to my left side, so that we were face to face. 'And how do you know that?' I demanded.

There was a confession coming that I definitely wasn't going to like. I knew Adela so well, I could sense it.

She ran a forefinger down my bare chest and avoided my eyes.

'I asked Richard to visit Rownham Passage yesterday and speak to the ferryman.'

Sergeant Richard Manifold, Sheriff's Officer! There was

little love lost between him and me. In the past, before Adela married her first husband, Owen Juett, and left Bristol for Hereford, Richard had been among her admirers. And when, two years ago, she had returned, widowed, to her native town, he had aspired to her hand yet again. I know he found it hard to understand why she had chosen me instead of him. I found it fairly hard to understand myself, although, of course, I would never admit it. He and I had never overtly been enemies and once he had even recruited me – albeit reluctantly – to help him solve a crime. But we weren't friends, either. We each rejoiced in the other's little discomfitures and disappointments, and were quite happy to serve one another a backhanded turn if we could.

To give him his due, however, Richard Manifold had not been amongst the many who begrudged us our stroke of good fortune in inheriting the Small Street house; something Adela was never tired of pointing out to me. Mind you, I had my own theory to account for the sergeant's lack of ill will. He had never married, and was happy to accept my wife's hospitality whenever it was offered. Moreover, a house boasting a hall, parlour and kitchen was infinitely preferable to the overcrowded, one-roomed cottage we had previously rented from Saint James's Priory in Lewin's Mead. And I found his frequent presence at my table less irksome, being able to avoid his company once the meal was done. All the same, a state of armed truce was the best that could be said for the relationship existing between us, and the idea of Adela inviting him to poke his nose into my affairs made me so furious I could barely speak.

'You . . . You asked *Richard Manifold* . . .' I was unable to continue.

Adela's face had drained of colour. She hated it when I was really angry. She wasn't afraid of me – she had no reason to be – but she hated us not to be friends. Not that that ever stopped her saying or doing anything she thought was right. She had more spirit than any other woman I had ever met, even Lillis, whose bravery had once saved my life.

She retorted now, a slight edge to her voice, 'You mentioned a murder. It was my duty, as a good citizen, to find out if

20

this were true or no. I reported the fact to Richard. He promised to investigate and rode out to Rownham Passage yesterday morning to make enquiries.'

'And what did our bloodhound discover?' I asked nastily.

'Don't be childish, Roger.' My wife reproved me in the tone she normally reserved for scolding the children. 'Richard spoke to the ferryman – whose name, by the way, is Jason Tyrrwhit – and he confirmed that you hadn't sought shelter in the alehouse during the storm, but set off along the St Brendan's track. He was utterly astonished to find you floating in the river half an hour later, and was completely at a loss as to how you came to fall in.'

'I did not fall in!' I shouted. 'I've told you what happened! You just won't believe me!'

'Hush!' Adela laid a warning fingertip on my lips. 'Let the others sleep for a while. Margaret is sharing Elizabeth's room, and that child is a very light sleeper.'

'So what else did Richard discover?' I demanded angrily. But I lowered my voice.

'Someone told him that the owner of the 'murder' house could be a James Witherspoon, nephew of the murdered man. When the two women were executed, the house passed to him.'

'And what did he have to say?' My heart was slamming against my ribs as my excitement mounted.

'Nothing. No one of that name lives in Rownham Passage any more. It appears the house has stood empty ever since the murder. As far as anyone knows, it hasn't been occupied for fifty years.'

'It's a lie!' I exclaimed furiously. 'There were two women and a man stopping in that house only last week. And there were a couple of horses in the hovel near the track! Why won't anyone take me seriously?'

'Sweetheart, we would,' my wife assured me soothingly, 'if there were any evidence to back up your story.'

'Then what really happened? Tell me that!' There was a pregnant silence. I waited grimly as realization dawned that my womenfolk had already concocted their own version of events. 'Well?'

21

'Richard . . .' My wife produced the name tentatively, rather like someone proffering a handful of truffles to a wild boar. She cleared her throat. 'Richard says that the ferryman told him you were talking somewhat wildly on the journey across from Ashton-Leigh. Something about building a bridge between the summit of Ghyston Cliff and the opposite heights. He thought maybe you'd got a touch of the sun. It was extremely hot the Wednesday morning of last week. He – we thought that perhaps you'd grown confused in your mind and wandered off the track down to the water's edge, where . . . where you became faint or dizzy – or both – and fell in.'

I was so taken aback that I was rendered speechless for at least half a minute. Finally, I forced out, 'It was raining! The heavens had opened! There was a violent summer squall! The weather conditions alone would have revived me if I'd been feeling faint.' I drew a deep breath, trying to contain my frustration. 'Adela . . . My love . . . I know what I saw and what happened to me. There were two horses, three people. They weren't figments of my imagination.'

'So what did these people look like?' she asked.

This was better. Here, I was on surer ground. I plunged confidently into a description of the woman in brown sarcenet.

'Tall, with a fine, big-breasted figure—'

'Trust you to notice that,' Adela grumbled, 'even in a dream.'

'About our age, maybe a little older, but not by much. Handsome face. I think her eyebrows were reddish in colour, which probably means she also has red hair. I didn't have time to notice her eyes. Spoke and moved like someone used to command. A mistress, not a servant. Her gown was made of silk. Oh, and she had a black leather girdle, tipped with silver tags studded with turquoises. Good, brown leather shoes.'

I could see that this detailed picture had impressed Adela more than she would admit. She was looking thoughtful. 'So, what about the other two?' she pressed.

There was silence for a moment, during which I realized that what I had been thinking was solid ground was really a quagmire.

'I . . . er . . . I didn't see the man who was with them at all,' I confessed reluctantly. 'Just heard his voice. But I can tell you that he spoke with a peculiar accent. Not one I know. I couldn't recognize it, if I'm honest.'

'And the other woman?'

'She . . .' I tried to sound confident. 'She had on a blue brocade gown – or skirt – and red leather shoes.'

'And that's all you can say about her?'

'That's all I saw.' The admission sounded damning, even to my ears. 'I was just recovering from a vicious blow to the back of my head,' I added defensively.

Adela said nothing, and I could see only too clearly what she and Margaret had made of my story. They had talked it over and reached the simple conclusion that I had been adversely affected by the hot weather. My reported remarks to the ferryman had made that a certainty, not only in their eyes, but also in those of Richard Manifold and this Jason Tyrrwhit himself. Later, approaching the 'murder' house as I walked along the St Brendan's track, I had been reminded of the killing and taken ill at one and the same time. I had wandered, not knowing what I was doing, down to the river's edge and there dropped my pack and cudgel as I lost consciousness, falling into the water . . .

Might it really have happened like that?

No! My womenfolk had got me doubting the evidence of my own senses.

'And the Irish sea captain?' Adela's voice cut across my teeming thoughts. 'What was he like? You haven't described him.'

The Irishman! Of course! How had I managed to forget him? I even knew his name. Well, I ought to have known his name; the man had proclaimed it loudly enough. Memory, however, was playing tricks on me – not surprisingly, I suppose, considering everything I had been through in the past week or more, but its loss was inconvenient at this juncture.

'He was a big man,' I said, 'from the south of Ireland.' I spoke with confidence. The southern Irish lilt was as familiar around the Bristol streets and Backs as our own west country

23

burr. 'He wore thick-soled boots, frieze breeches and had hands as big as shovels. He also carried a knife, but I've already explained that. Unfortunately, I didn't see his face.'

There was a protracted silence before Adela whispered, 'The man who was murdered in that house, all those years ago, was an Irishman. But I expect you know that. Lillis must have mentioned it when she told you the tale.'

Three

B reakfast was an uncomfortable meal.
I was in a foul mood and the children, sensing it, tiptoed round me with unusual caution. Margaret stated her intention to return to Redcliffe forthwith before lapsing into guarded silence. Even Hercules slunk off to some distant corner of the house that he had made his own. Only Adela made a brave attempt at conversation, although she soon gave up.

She had urged me to stay in bed, warning me that I would feel extremely weak after more than a week's inactivity. But I knew better. Of course I did. I was a man – one, moreover, who had experienced very little sickness in his life and who prided himself on his strength and resilience to any kind of illness. But Adela was right. Lying in bed I had felt fine. Getting dressed, washing at the pump in the tiny yard behind our house and forcing myself to swallow oatcakes and a thick collop of bacon, had been an altogether different matter. Quite apart from the fact that my legs didn't want to do as they were told, my head still swam from the effects of the potions administered to me over the past few days by Adela. But I wasn't going to let bodily weakness get the better of me.

When I announced I was going out after breakfast, my wife didn't argue. She merely advised: 'If you're going to Rownham Passage, hire a nag from the livery stable in Bell Lane. You're in no fit condition to walk all that way.' I scowled and Adela burst out laughing.

Her spontaneous merriment relieved the oppressive atmosphere and the children began to giggle. Even Margaret Walker managed the travesty of a smile. Adam, excitable as ever,

25

flicked a spoonful of porridge in my direction and scored a bullseye on my nose. I forced myself to smile at him reassuringly.

'You don't mean to go as far as Rownham Passage in your state of health, do you?' Margaret demanded, jeopardizing my newly restored good humour. 'Not just to prove this ridiculous tale of yours is true?'

'Roger must do as he sees fit,' my wife said warningly. 'He is the head of the household, after all.'

Margaret gave a derisive snort. 'If he believes that, he'll believe anything. And he's not the head of *my* household. I can tell him the truth.'

'Not under this roof,' Adela answered quietly, before adding, 'Besides, there just might be something in his story.'

'What do you mean? What's changed your mind?' I stuttered.

'You're humouring him,' Margaret accused.

'Nothing's changed my mind, and I'm not humouring him. But . . .' She paused long enough to encourage the children, who had finished eating, to run away and play. The elder two thundered upstairs, where they charged around like stampeding horses. The noise did my headache no good at all, but I did my best to ignore it. Adam performed his crab-like crawl and shuffled off to a corner of the kitchen, where he beat out a tune on the stone-tiled floor with his spoon. I ignored that as well.

'But?' I encouraged my wife, while Margaret looked sceptical.

'It's nothing, really.' Adela took a deep breath and clasped her hands together on the table. 'It's just that a week ago, while you were still on the road, Robin Avenel's widowed sister came to stay with him . . .'

Here, Margaret interrupted, anxious to fill in details which someone who had had the misfortune not to be born in Bristol might not know.

'Bess Avenel married into the Alefounder family. Her late husband's uncle is Alderman Gregory Alefounder. Well, you can't help but know who he is. Owns the biggest brewery in the city. But, more than that, her sister-in-law, that little fly-by-night Robin Avenel married, is Gregory Alefounder's daughter. Jeffery, Bess's husband, wasn't interested in the brewing business. He preferred to lead the life of a country gentleman. His father, Gregory's older brother, indulged him and let Jeffery live at home on the family manor near Frome. When he died, Jeffery inherited the house and lands, and Bess, in her turn, inherited them from him. She still lives there, no doubt queening it over her tenants and the local peasantry.' Margaret's tone was acerbic. Elizabeth Alefounder was plainly no favourite of hers.

'Thank you, Mother-in-law,' I said gravely and raised my eyebrows at Adela. 'So, what about this Bess Alefounder, sweetheart? What does she have to do with me?'

'As I was saying, she arrived in Broad Street to stay with Master Avenel while you were away. I think it was the Saturday before you were brought home. Her maid came with her and they must have been there now for almost a fortnight. I've seen Mistress Alefounder around on several occasions. It was Richard who first pointed her out to me.'

'Go on.' I nobly refrained from enquiring what she was doing in the company of Richard Manifold. (A chance meeting, of course. Really, I knew that without being told.)

Again, Adela hesitated. 'Oh, I don't know!' she exclaimed at last, with a shrug of her shoulders. 'It's just that your description this morning of the woman in brown sarcenet reminded me a little of Elizabeth Alefounder.'

'Aha!' I shouted, disturbing Adam, who stopped banging his spoon on the floor and shuffled across to embrace one of my legs in an iron grip.

'There's no "Aha!" about it,' my wife reproved me. 'I said it reminded me *a little*. Now, sweetheart, please don't go leaping to conclusions.'

'I should think not, indeed!' Margaret protested. 'What on earth would a respectable woman like Bess Alefounder be doing mixed up in a murder? What nonsense it is! Why don't you admit you were delirious, Roger, and simply dreamed it all?'

I could tell from Adela's expression that she was reluctant

27

to say anything further that might bolster my belief in my story, but her natural instinct to see justice done made her go on.

'You forget, Cousin,' she said gently, 'that for the past year, ever since last summer, the Sheriff's men have been keeping a close watch on Robin Avenel's household. He was suspected, if you remember, of Lancastrian sympathies. If it had ever been proved that the man we all thought was a Tudor spy really had been one, then there's no doubt, according to Richard Manifold, that Robin Avenel would have been arrested. As it was, with the stranger being murdered like that, nothing could be proved against him. Against Master Avenel, I mean.'

'But what has that to do with his sister?' Margaret demanded, rising from her stool. 'I'm surprised at you, Adela, encouraging that great oaf in this piece of arrant folly. He was exposed to too much sun. He fell in the Avon. And in his delirium, he dreamed he saw the re-enactment of an old murder, which he had recalled while passing the house where it happened. That's all there is to it. Now, I'm going upstairs to collect my things, and then I'm going home. You don't need me any longer, not now that Roger is up and about once more. And I've been away from Redcliffe for far too long. Goodness knows what's been happening in my absence. Maria Watkins and Bess Simnel will have been having things all their own way.'

Adela made a half-hearted attempt to persuade her cousin to stay, but I think, secretly, she was as anxious as I was to see her go. Margaret Walker was a woman with a heart of gold, an excellent friend in times of trouble, totally to be relied upon. But she was also domineering and liked to be in charge, whether at home or in someone else's house. A wearing woman whose strength of will necessitated constant combating with one's own.

I barely registered her decision to leave, I was so busy mulling over what Adela had said. I abandoned all thought of visiting Rownham Passage for the present. My first priority now was to try to catch a glimpse of Mistress Alefounder. I freed myself from Adam's hold and got unsteadily to my feet.

My wife observed me with a jaundiced eye. 'Still deter-mined to go out?' she asked.

I grunted. 'But not so far. At least, not yet.'

Adela smiled. 'Only as far as Broad Street, is that it?'

'The next woman I marry,' I retorted darkly, 'won't be able to read my mind. It's too unnerving.'

She laughed and gave me a swift kiss on one cheek. Friendly, but no more than that. 'Sweetheart, there's not a woman born who couldn't read you like an open book.'

I returned her kiss with interest and suggested there was nothing so urgent that it couldn't be postponed. But I was out of luck. She swore she had too much to do. When she had cleared the breakfast dishes, she must sit with the two older children in order to teach them their alphabet and numbers from one to ten. Their lessons, she said, had been sadly neglected during my illness. I sighed and began to pull on my boots.

'Tonight?' I whispered suggestively.

She shrugged and muttered something that sounded like 'maybe'. I was hurt, but said nothing. I cleaned my teeth with willow bark and found my jerkin, for although the sky beyond the open shutters gave every indication of another warm day, the early June morning was still chilly. And as one who had so recently been an invalid, I could take no chances.

'If you're really going round to Broad Street,' Adela said, 'would you call in at Saint Giles's and light a candle for me?'

I had a suspicion that some date around this time was the anniversary of her first husband's birthday, or his death, or some such thing, but I didn't enquire and she volunteered no explanation. We are all entitled to those secret places of the heart, those shrines to memory which are ours, and ours alone.

'Of course,' I said, kissing her cheek.

Until seven or eight months previously, when Adela and I had rented a cottage in Lewin's Mead, we had naturally worshipped at Saint James's Priory, the church being our landlord. Since the upturn in our fortunes and the move to Small Street, however, we had many more to choose from. Within a few minutes' walk were the churches of Saint Giles, Saint Stephen, Saint John, Saint Werburgh, Saint Lawrence, Saint Leonard and Saint Ewen, while slightly further afield were Christchurch and All Saints. Inside the city walls, between the rivers Frome and Avon, there were more churches than taverns, which should have made Bristol an exceptionally godly place. It wasn't. There was as much crime stalking its streets as in any other town in England.

Saint Giles lay at the Bell Lane end of Small Street, in the direction of the river Frome. These days, and for many years past, it had shared a priest with both Saint Leonard's and Saint Lawrence's, which meant that for much of every day it was deserted, except for the occasional private worshipper. The main entrance was on the quay side of the building, in Jewry Lane, but there was another, smaller door giving access from Bell Lane, and it was this, being the nearer, that Adela and I always used.

Saint Giles was not an old church compared with many others in the city. It had been built, so I had been informed, about a hundred and fifty years ago on the site of the old Bristol synagogue, which had fallen into disrepair following the expulsion of the Jews from England in the reign of the first Edward. Thrifty Bristol citizens had used much of the stone from the Jewish temple to construct Saint Giles; appropriate, perhaps, for a building in honour of a man whose life was dedicated to thrift, dwelling as he did in a cave and living on roots and the milk of a friendly deer.

The door creaked slightly as I pushed it open. The church was empty. I waited a moment for my sight to clear, then I cautiously made my way towards the altar where stood the saint's effigy, painted plaster hand resting on the head of a golden doe whose body was pierced by a silver arrow, the huntsmen of King Flavius, as you will recall, having tried to shoot it. Whoever had carved the face of poor old Giles – a mentor of Charlemagne – had made him appear very bad-tempered. But then, who wouldn't be, living on a diet of roots and doe's milk?

I made my obeisance, then searched around until I found a small store of candles on a shelf near the sacristy. I placed one among the previous day's dead offerings at the foot of the statue, but when I came to light it, I discovered I had left my flint and tinderbox at home in my pouch. Cursing, I was preparing to return to Small Street when a voice enquired, 'Do you need a light?'

I nearly jumped out of my skin. I had heard no one enter the church, in spite of the creaking door, nor noticed anyone's approach. Yet here was this young man standing beside me, smiling, genuflecting and offering me his flint and tinderbox at one and the same time.

'Where . . . where have you sprung from?' I asked, wishing there was something to sit on. My legs felt like jelly.

The young man laughed, but gave no explanation as to his sudden appearance.

'Is this your candle?' He nodded at the only fresh one amongst its burnt-out brothers, and, without waiting for my reply, proceeded to light it. 'There! Now you can say your prayer.'

I thanked him. I could see him better in the glow from the candle flame. He was, I judged, about nineteen or twenty years of age, of middling height – the top of his head barely reached two inches above my shoulder – with the straightest hair I had ever seen. Straw-coloured, there was no vestige of curl or even a kink anywhere in it, and it fell, like the proverbial yard of pump water, to just below his ears and was cut in a fringe across his forehead. His skin was as pale as his hair, but he was saved from anonymity by an enormous pair of sapphire-blue eyes, sparkling with life. Looking into them, I was suddenly and vividly reminded of what it meant to be young, to be just starting out on life's great adventure, when anything was possible, danger non-existent; when the words 'responsibility', 'wife', 'children' and 'family' were as alien as the moon; when these things belonged to other people, unfortunate souls; when the world lay before you for the taking.

Fighting down a surge of envy and nostalgia, I asked, 'What's your name?'

31

He bowed mockingly. 'Luke Prettywood, and I'm chief assistant to Alderman Alefounder at the Newgate brewery.'

Now there was a coincidence! Too much of one for comfort. I was seized with a sneaking suspicion that God was meddling in my affairs again.

'And what brings you to Saint Giles, Master Prettywood, so early in the morning?'

He was entitled to tell me to mind my own business, but he only laughed and said, 'I know who you are. You're Roger Chapman, the pedlar, who was left the old Herepath house in Small Street by Cicely Ford. You have a reputation for being nosy.' Which, of course, was just another way of saying the same thing.

The Bell Lane door creaked open again and we both turned to see a woman's figure outlined in the doorway. The noise and bustle of the street momentarily intruded on the quiet of the church; the sounds and smells of the nearby livery stables assaulted our ears and nostrils. Whoever it was hesitated for a second, as though taken aback by our presence, before stepping inside and closing the door. She drifted towards us across the rush-strewn floor, the skirt of a pale silk gown billowing in the draught, and I could see her eyes blink as they adjusted to the gloom of the nave.

'What are you doing here, Luke?' she asked in a light, fluting voice. 'I thought you'd returned to the brewery ages ago.'

I recognized her at once. Marianne Avenel, she who had been Marianne Alefounder before her marriage, had become a familar figure in the immediate vicinity since her marriage to Robin Avenel some sixteen months earlier. The couple had taken up residence in a house I had once known well, the late Alderman Weaver's house in Broad Street, bought for them by Robin's father, Peter Avenel, a soap manufacturer and one of Bristol's richest citizens.

Marianne was the sort of girl who would always be known as 'a pretty little thing' even when she was nearing thirty. At present, I guessed her to be a good ten years short of that, but her kittenish, heart-shaped face with its soft, pouting lips, wide-set, luminous grey eyes and peach-like cheeks would alter very little with the passage of time. Nor would the air of faint dissatisfaction that clung to her like a second skin. I've met many women like her throughout my life; women who think that their looks entitle them to the admiration of the world in general and of men in particular. I have never pandered to their delusion, however attractive they might be, and I had no intention of doing so with Marianne Avenel.

Consequently, I gave only the briefest of bows in answer to the brilliant smile she bestowed upon me, and remained unmoved by the seductive flutter of her charcoal-darkened eyelashes. Huffily, she turned back to my companion.

'I asked you what you're still doing here, Luke. My father will be wondering where you are and he'll blame me for delaying you. You have my answer to his message.'

'I came to say a prayer for the repose of my sister's soul,' the brewer's assistant answered, assuming a pious expression. 'You'll recall, mistress, that she died last year.'

I doubted this. Oh, not that his sister had died. He would hardly risk a lie if Marianne Avenel knew better. But his response had been altogether too glib, and I had so far detected no sign of any grief in his demeanour. Moreover, his thin, mobile mouth twitched with amusement as he clasped the little hand, impulsively extended to him, and raised it to his lips.

'Oh, Luke! I'm so sorry! How thoughtless of me not to remember! She's buried here, isn't she, in the crypt?'

He nodded, his pleasant face sobering as if he were indeed beset by memories of the dead girl.

'Would you . . . Would you care to see her coffin?' he asked tentatively. 'Would you let me escort you down to the crypt? The stairs are rather dark, but I have my tinderbox. I can light a candle.'

I half expected Mistress Avenel to refuse. I doubted if the crypt and the stairs leading to it were very clean, and she was wearing a gown of pale yellow sarcenet. Her little feet were shod in cream leather. But she nodded good-naturedly.

'Yes, of course, if you'd like me to.'

Luke smiled and once again bent over her hand, while she peeped up at him from beneath her long lashes. Her compliance, I reflected meanly, was easily explained. Her father's assistant was a good-looking young man and she couldn't resist adding him to her list of conquests – if she hadn't done so already.

Luke Prettywood fetched and lit a new candle, pocketed his tinderbox and gallantly offered her his arm.

'I'll wish you good day, then, chapman,' he said. 'I daresay you want to be off.'

It was almost as if he were anxious to see me gone. It made me wonder. Had the little scene recently enacted by the pair been solely for my benefit? Was there something more between them than I had so far suspected? Margaret had referred to Marianne Avenel as a fly-by-night, with an underlying suggestion that she was not as dutiful – or as faithful? – a wife as she should be. Or was I adding two and two together and making five?

I watched Luke Prettywood and Marianne Avenel disappear down the steps leading to the crypt, but made no attempt to be on my way. Instead, I lit another candle, gave the couple a moment or two's grace, then followed them.

The crypt of Saint Giles was an oppressive place, with a smell of damp and decay much more noticeable than in the church above. I was not normally so sensitive to atmosphere, but I suddenly had an overwhelming impression of unhappiness and suffering. I put it down to my weakened state and told myself not to be foolish. I looked around for my quarry, but saw nothing except tombs and rows of stone coffins lined up on shelves.

I held my candle higher, but its wavering light revealed only the dead. There was no sign of the living.

I moved forward cautiously, and as my eyes again grew accustomed to this greater gloom, I realized that the vault immediately below the church was not the full extent of the crypt. Ahead of me loomed an archway, and beyond that lay a second chamber, the only difference being that it was used, not as a repository for the dead, but as a storeroom. A number of chests, old and covered in cobwebs, were ranged against the walls, together with planks of wood and numerous pieces of furniture that had seen better days. I hazarded a guess that the priest was running a profitable little business on the side, augmenting his stipend by renting out space to those of his parishioners who had items they were loath to throw away, but no longer had room for in their houses.

To my astonishment, yet another archway beckoned, and I walked forward to find myself staring into a third, equally dusty chamber. This one, however, was empty. Empty, that is, except for the pale gleam of two figures at the far end, locked together in what was obviously a passionate embrace. Luke Prettywood and Marianne Avenel, without a doubt. Who else could it be?

I was uncertain whether I should announce my presence or withdraw discreetly. In the end, as they seemed not to have noticed me, discretion won. I tiptoed back the way I had come and was just about to mount the steps to the church when the amorous pair reappeared, looking hot, dishevelled and, when they clapped eyes on me, distinctly guilty.

'Ch–Chapman? I . . . We . . . What are you doing down here? I thought you'd gone.' Master Prettywood was plainly disconcerted.

I assumed my blandest expression. 'Once I'd finished my prayers, I decided that I, too, would like to pay my respects to your sister.' It sounded a pretty lame excuse, so I hurried on. 'But when I got down here, I couldn't find you anywhere. Where were you?'

I saw Marianne Avenel glance sideways at Luke as she surreptitiously let go of his hand. But her swain, having regained his composure, was up to the challenge.

'Mistress Avenel,' he lied smoothly, 'has never been in Saint Giles's crypt before, but of course she's heard of the great cellars that run beneath the church, almost as far as Saint John's-on-the-Arch. She asked me to show them to her.'

I was intrigued to know about these cellars myself. 'I did peep into the next chamber,' I admitted, adding innocently, 'Are there others beyond that?'

Luke, taking this as proof that I had seen nothing that I shouldn't have done, gave me a relieved smile.

'There is a third one. These are the cellars of the Jewish synagogue that once stood on this site. Do you know about that?' I nodded. 'Well, when Saint Giles was built, the cellars were left. But only the first room, this one, is needed as a crypt. So local people have always used the second as a storeroom. The third one's empty.' He laughed. 'My grandfather told me that *his* grandfather, as a boy, used to come down here with his friends searching for a way into the secret vault that people swore had been built by the Jews in order to house their hoard of gold and silver. In those days, everyone thought that as the Jews had been forced to leave in such a hurry, they must have gone without their treasure.' Luke laughed again. 'But no one ever found it – the entrance to the secret vault, I mean. If, that is, it ever existed outside of people's imaginations.' He turned to his companion. 'And now, Mistress Avenel, I must get back to the brewery. Thank you for coming down to see my sister's coffin. It was kind of you. But first, may I have the pleasure of escorting you home? Broad Street is on my way.'

Four

I said swiftly, 'I can escort Mistress Avenel home. You must be wanting to return to the brewery.'

Luke Prettywood smiled triumphantly. 'I'm not returning to the brewery, chapman. I'm on my way to the market to buy grain, but I can't do that until the market bell has been rung. It's one of the city's laws,' he added in answer to my look of scepticism, 'written down in Bristol's Great Red Book. It's so that one brewer shan't have the advantage over another by buying up all the best grain just because he's an early bird and his rival has overslept. All very commendable, but it's a scramble once the bell has gone and the bidding starts.'

'Well, then,' I argued, 'shouldn't you be off at once in order to make sure of a place at the front of the crowd? Mistress Avenel will be perfectly safe in my company, I assure you.'

But Luke wasn't prepared to forgo his mistress's company except for a very good reason. He offered Marianne his arm, which she accepted with an alacrity that would have been positively insulting had I not known how things stood between them. I wondered if they were cuckolding Robin Avenel, or if matters had not yet gone that far.

I let them reach the steps leading up to the nave. Then I called after them. 'Mistress Avenel! I wanted to speak to your sister-in-law. Is she at home this morning?'

The lady turned, her delicate eyebrows arched in surprise. 'Do you know Mistress Alefounder, sir?'

I thought quickly. 'I'm not sure. I think I might do. But I shan't be certain unless I see her. Is she at home?'

Marianne frowned. 'She may have gone out; she rises

37

early . . . Her companion might be there, however. Are you acquainted with Mistress Hollyns?'

'Not that I know of. On the other hand,' I went on hastily, before Marianne lost interest, 'I could be. Does Mistress Hollyns by any chance own a blue brocade gown?'

'She may do,' my informant conceded doubtfully. Her tone implied that, as mistress of the house, she had better things to do than notice the attire of her sister-in-law's maid.

'I think, then, that I must try to see either Mistress Alefounder or the other lady for myself,' I concluded.

Marianne Avenel gave her companion an apologetic glance and sighed. 'In that case, you'd better come home with me.'

Luke Prettywood made no comment, but I could well imagine his thoughts as we left Saint Giles and proceeded along Bell Lane, he and Marianne walking decorously side by side, with me only a pace or two behind. He must have wished me in Hades.

A few yards further on, we turned into Broad Street. The house that had belonged to Alderman Weaver, and which I had once known so well, was a little over halfway up on the left-hand side. And judging by the growing babel of noise, the market around the Tolzey was getting under way, leaving Luke Prettywood no choice but to abandon his companion and take himself off. In silence, the lady and I watched him walk rapidly up the street and disappear into the rabble of people heading for the market. Only then did she turn her attention back to me.

'Wait there,' she ordered, 'while I find out who's at home. Who do I say is calling? Roger the Chapman?' There was the same slightly contemptuous note in her voice that I had noticed earlier, when she had been speaking of her sister-in-law's maid.

I hesitated, suddenly a prey to misgivings. If Mistress Alefounder was not the woman I had met at Rownham Passage, what excuse could I offer for calling on her? As for Mistress Hollyns, unless, by some lucky chance, she was wearing a blue brocade gown, I shouldn't even recognize her. As so often in the past, I had rushed into a situation without carefully considering all its ramifications.

'Perhaps I'll leave my visit until another time,' I said, backing away and treading on the toes of several indignant passers-by. 'Yes, that's what I'll do. Let me wish you good day, Mistress Avenel.'

She shrugged, plainly thinking me an idiot, and, having knocked for admittance, vanished inside the house. But instead of returning home, I crossed the street, nearly getting run down by one of the refuse carts clearing the central drain, and took refuge in the mouth of an alleyway almost directly opposite. Here, I propped myself against the wall of a house and waited.

And waited. Half an hour or more passed and still no one had emerged from the Avenel dwelling. Either Marianne had kept her own counsel, or her story had provoked little or no curiosity among the inmates. No one had considered it worthwhile to find out if I might still be loitering in the vicinity.

After my lengthy wait, my legs were again beginning to feel as if they were stuffed with sawdust. The morning was getting steadily hotter as the sun rose in a sky of unrelenting blue. I removed my jerkin, but the heat burned through the linen of my shirt until I could feel it scorching my skin. My head swam and once or twice I had to swallow hard to prevent the bile from rising in my throat. Moreover, I was afraid I was becoming conspicuous. Several people who had noticed me on their way up Broad Street stared even harder on the return journey, obviously wondering why I was still skulking there. Those who recognized me shrugged and no doubt decided that I was living up to my reputation for nosiness. And, of course, there were others who were not even as charitable as that.

'Snooping again, Roger?' A familiar voice sounded in my ear.

'Hello, Jack,' I said, none too pleased at being accosted.

Jack Nym, the carter, gave me his broken, black-toothed grin. He was wearing his customary greasy, food-stained leather jerkin and wrinkled hose, and even in the height of summer his nose was running. He wiped it on one of the empty sacks he was holding. Adela and I had once spent an entire week in his company, on a journey to London, and a kinder, more considerate person it would be hard to find. (Moreover, he had never been one of those alienated by my stroke of good fortune.) But he wasn't a man whom anyone with a sensitive nose would choose to get too close to, particularly on a warm summer's day.

'I hear you haven't been well,' he continued, sniffing prodigiously. 'Fell in the Avon, I was told. Mind you, it happens to most of us sometime or another. Drop too much at the Rownham inn, was it?' He gave me no chance either to offer an alternative explanation or to reflect how every detail of one's private life became common gossip in this city, but went on, 'I trust you'll have recovered enough for the midsummer revels.' Almost at once, his face fell. 'How do you count the petals on a rose, chapman?'

I laughed. 'You go out into the hedgerows and pick a dog rose, Jack. It's no good trying to do it with one of those fussy, frilly things you buy from the street vendors. Even so,' I sighed, my mood suddenly matching his in despondency, 'with a wife as clever as mine, she knows I've already counted the petals and made certain there's an odd number. So instead of starting off: 'He loves me, he loves me not', she reverses it and I end up accused of not loving her.'

'That's the trouble with women,' the carter agreed morosely. 'They're that artful, you can never win. Silly custom, anyway! The Midsummer Rose, I mean.'

'Indeed it is! However hard you try, it's nigh on impossible to convince even a sensible woman that picking the petals off a rose doesn't prove your affection for her.'

Jack nodded glumly, then raised his eyes to my face.

'You feeling all right, lad? You're looking mighty pale. What you need is a sit down and a draught of the Green Lattis's best ale. Come on! I'll pay. Here, lean on me.'

I refused his offer of assistance – he was too short to make a comfortable crutch – but accepted his invitation. I suddenly realized that I was indeed in urgent need of refreshment and rest, but I didn't want to return home yet and face my wife's triumphant. 'I told you so!' At the same time, the idea of the Green Lattis failed to appeal, it being one of the city's most popular taverns, frequented by many of my friends and acquaintances. I couldn't stand the thought of their jokes at my expense or their probing questions concerning my recent dousing in the river Avon.

'Couldn't we go somewhere else?' I proposed, as we made our slow way up Broad Street, elbowing a path through the crowds.

'Why?' Jack Nym demanded reasonably. 'The Lattis is nearest, and you don't look to me like you want to go dragging all over town, especially in this heat. I'm bloody sure I don't.'

'There are a couple of alehouses in Marsh Street,' I suggested.

'You are joking, aren't you?' the carter asked grimly, grabbing my arm as my footsteps faltered momentarily. 'Marsh Street is where the Irishers drink, and they don't care for strangers.'

I knew this. I had visited one of the alehouses there many years ago, when I had been trying to find out what had happened to Margaret Walker's father. It was not an experience I had been eager to repeat, although I had received a polite, if frosty reception. But now I was in a truculent mood.

'They're the strangers. I live here.'

Jack Nym tightened his grip on my elbow.

'Don't be more of a fool than you can help, chapman! You know as well as I do what trade goes on in those alehouses.'

Of course I did. I hadn't lived in Bristol for six years without learning some of the city's darker secrets. Centuries after papal intervention to ban the trade, and centuries after royal decree had made it illegal, slaving between Bristol and Waterford, Bristol and Dublin still continued. Did you have an unmarried daughter who had brought disgrace on the family by getting herself pregnant? Did you have an aged parent who was an interfering, or incontinent, old nuisance? Did you have a son who was in trouble with the law and ripe to become gallows meat? Did someone owe you money and wouldn't pay up? If you were a Bristolian, you knew exactly what to do in those circumstances. You did a deal with the Irish slavers. And the place to do that deal was in the Marsh Street alehouses. I decided perhaps it was better not to go there, after all.

Luckily, the Green Lattis was less than a quarter full, most folk preferring to postpone convivial drinking until after the ten o'clock dinner hour. A hasty glance confirmed that there were few people I even knew by sight, and a mere handful whom I knew well. Jack Nym sat me down in a quiet corner while he went in search of a pot-boy and ordered us both some ale. He had offered to buy me wine, tipping a shower of coins from his purse into one hand and jingling them in an affluent sort of way. But, much to his obvious relief, I had declined. Like me, being common and low-born, he preferred ale.

A group of men at the next table were having an animated discussion about an expedition they were preparing to launch the following year; a search for the fabled island of Brazil which, as everyone in those days knew, lay somewhere beyond the west coast of Ireland. The moving spirits of this enterprise seemed to be a Welshman and a native Bristolian who went by the name of John Jay. I thought I had heard him mentioned by Margaret and Adela. So, until Jack returned, I let my mind drift on a tide of strange and, to me, meaningless nautical phrases until I fell asleep, my head resting against the wall behind me.

'Roger! Wake up, lad!' I opened bleary eyes just in time to see Jack plonk a mazer of ale in front of me before sitting down on the stool beside mine. 'Sorry I was so long, but I met an old friend and stopped for a chat. Never mind. You were well away in the land of Nod.'

'Just a quick doze,' I excused myself, unwilling to admit how tired I still felt after more than a week in bed. I swigged my ale gratefully. It was the best the Green Lattis had to offer and a brew I could rarely afford. 'You're very flush with money today,' I accused him. 'What's happened? Someone died and left you a fortune?'

'We work damned hard, me and my horse and cart,' he answered, righteously indignant, as he had every right to be. Everyone in Bristol knew him for one of its most industrious citizens. Then he grinned. 'Matter of fact, I managed to fit in an extra job last week, in between carrying a load of sea coal up to Gloucester and a cartload of soap, for the older Master Avenel, as far as Chipping Sodbury. It was when I got back from the first jaunt and went to the soapworks, to get instructions for the second, that I ran into Robin Avenel. He asked me if I could spare him some time to shift an old bed and some other unwanted bits and pieces round to Saint Giles's crypt. I dunno if you know about the crypt, you not being born here . . .'

'By coincidence,' I interrupted, 'I saw it, and learned its history, for the first time this morning. I understand the church was built on the foundations of the old city synagogue.'

'That's right. The Avenels have always had a close connection with the place. It was old Peter Avenel's great-grandfather, or great-great-grandfather, or some such, who had a hand in helping to build the church on the ruins of the Jewish temple. Not literally, you understand, but he gave generously to the project. Consequently, the Avenels think they own it. Saint Giles, that is.' Jack regarded me thoughtfully. 'You really don't look well, lad. Finish your ale and I'll take you home.'

But by early the following morning, after another night's undisturbed sleep, I was wide awake long before cockcrow. By the time Elizabeth and Nicholas stormed into our bedchamber and heaved themselves astride my chest, I was ready for them. I had shoved a pillow between myself and the counterpane to prevent myself becoming the most flat-chested man in Bristol.

'What is he today?' my stepson asked.

'A log!' Elizabeth shouted. 'Wake up, Father! You're a log and we're floating on you down the river Frome!'

Her penetrating tones woke Adela, who groaned and rolled on to her back, throwing out an arm and hitting me in the face as she did so. My two young limbs of Satan laughed so much they fell off the bed, so I wriggled into a sitting position before they could climb back up again. Inevitably, we were joined by Hercules, who tore upstairs, uttering short, ecstatic barks, while Adam stood up in his crib and roared to be lifted out.

43

'He's had me dancing attendance four times in the night,' Adela announced ominously, struggling up from our goose-feather mattress in order to comply with her younger son's wishes.

I didn't know. I hadn't heard. I'd slept (and no doubt snored) throughout everything, and that could mean trouble. So, being so much stronger and better in every way than I had been the day before, I hastily made plans to remove myself as far as possible from Adela's neighbourhood once breakfast was over. And if that meant riding to Rownham Passage rather than hanging around Broad Street for a glimpse of Elizabeth Alefounder or Mistress Hollyns, so be it, I decided.

It occurred to me, while eating a second bacon collop, washed down with a third beaker of ale, that a resolution made the previous evening to have nothing more to do with this case – if, indeed, a case it was – had been completely overlooked in my urgent need to get out of the house. Not that Adela often reproached me for my shortcomings, and she knew how much I had been in need of that afternoon and night's healing sleep. But, as so often happened, she was overtired and overworked and, consequently, short-tempered.

While she washed the breakfast dishes, the children and dog went out to play in the small back yard. This was not large, and most of the space was taken up by our very own pump and lean-to privy – both undreamed-of luxuries in either of our lives until now. Add to these things an apple tree and a little flower bed where Adela had started growing herbs and simples, and the envy of many of our former friends was understandable. This was the town house of a gentleman – which I most definitely was not.

Once the contents of Cicely Ford's will had become common knowledge, there had, inevitably, been speculation concerning the exact nature of my friendship with this young woman, several notches above me on the social scale. Margaret Walker had warned us that there would be gossip, and she had been right. All I could do was assure Adela that there had never been anything more between myself and that lovely, sad, young creature except gratitude on her part – for proving, too late, that the man she had loved was innocent of murder – and a carefully suppressed affection on mine. Adela had accepted this with her usual generosity of spirit, even though she was fully aware of my susceptibility where fair hair, blue eyes and soft, peach-bloom complexions were concerned. The fact that she herself was the exact opposite, with dark, almost black hair and liquid, deep-brown eyes seemed to convince her that my love for her was real and abiding. And that was indeed the truth. Nevertheless she also knew that I was a man, with a man's appetites and a roving eye, and was easy prey to flattery and admiration.

I began to inspect the contents of my pack, which had not been replenished since my illness. But there must have been something in my attitude, in my indifferent glance as I turned the remaining items over, that made my wife say sharply, 'If you're fully recovered, I hope you intend getting on the road again as soon as possible. We need the money, Roger.'

I turned and made a grab for her, managing to get an arm about her waist and trying to steal a kiss.

'You are in a bad mood! I know! I know! You've had a rotten night while I was snoring my head off. So let me put a smile back on your face. While the children are outside, let's go upstairs for a while.'

She pushed me away, almost violently. 'I can't be doing with all that just now, Roger!' She sounded exasperated. 'Men never have any sense of time, how short a day is or how much a woman has to do. Cleaning, cooking, going to market, preserving, mending, teaching the children their lessons.'

I knew that her protest was justified, but I felt hurt and angry at her rejection.

'If that's how you feel, then I'll be off.' I shouldered my pack and grabbed my cudgel from the kitchen corner.

'Sweetheart! I'm sorry! I didn't mean to be so abrupt,' Adela began, but she was still flushed and angry.

'I know,' I said lightly. 'You're busy. I understand.' And so I did, but I allowed my tone to imply the opposite. 'Well, I'll be off. Don't expect me back much before curfew.'

'Roger! Wait!'

I pretended I hadn't heard, and let myself out of the kitchen into the flagstoned passageway beyond. I hadn't even bothered to summon Hercules, but had left him, along with the children, to be an additional burden on Adela.

By the time I began to feel ashamed of myself, I had walked as far as the Tolzey, where I managed to purchase a number of small goods – laces, needles, ribbons and suchlike – at very reasonable prices, and which I would be able to sell in the surrounding villages and hamlets for a slightly increased sum. Then I walked down to the Backs and the ships moored along the quayside of the river Avon to see if I could pick up any merchandise of a more exotic nature. Some of the masters were not as scrupulous as they should have been, and had no compunction in stealing and selling various items from the owners' cargoes.

With my pack now three-quarters full, I decided to set out for Rownham Passage without further delay. I needed to find out for myself what had happened eleven days earlier, when I had been left for drowned by that murderous pair of women. This need was made all the more urgent by the discovery, since I awoke this morning, that my own belief in my story was beginning to falter. Ironically, with renewed health and strength had come increasing doubts about what I actually remembered. Had the 'murder' house and all that had happened there really been part of a delirium caused by my immersion in the river? Yesterday, I would have sworn not. Today, I was less certain.

But first, conscience dictated that I go home to make my peace with Adela; apprise her of my plans. I could also relieve her of Hercules's unwanted presence. In addition, I could leave my pack, admitting that I had no intention of doing any work that day, and trusting that my recent purchases would be sufficient to convince her of my good intentions for the day after next, Monday.

Consequently, I once more directed my feet up High Street, giving the time of day to those of my acquaintances who chose to acknowledge me, and ignoring those who did not. But at the top, close to the High Cross, I ran into someone I would have given much to ignore, but who,

46

unfortunately, was only too happy to welcome me with outstretched hand and a supercilious grin.

Richard Manifold.

'I'm glad to see you up and about again, Roger,' was his greeting. 'You gave Adela and Mistress Walker a rare fright, falling into the Avon like that. You were delirious for days, they told me.'

I released his hand after the merest shake.

'I was not delirious,' I said, vexed. 'I simply explained what had happened. Adela and Margaret chose not to believe me, that's all.'

'That's not quite true,' he objected, his grin broadening to insulting proportions. 'In fact, Adela was so worried that your story might be genuine, she sent me to Rownham Passage to make enquiries.'

'So she informed me,' I answered shortly, taking exception to his choice of words. The idea that my wife would send him anywhere, rather than make a polite request, argued a degree of intimacy between them that I knew, in my heart of hearts, did not exist, but which raised my hackles nonetheless. 'Of course, you didn't discover anything.' It was my turn to sneer.

'There was nothing to find out.' He smiled in his maddeningly superior fashion. 'Well, I won't keep you.' He nodded at my pack. 'I see you're anxious to be off about your work. I fancy that house must be something of a millstone around your neck, eh? Anyway, I have important business to attend to.'

I wondered unkindly how many pockets had been picked, how many purses snatched and how many little old ladies beaten up while he had been standing chatting to me. But I remembered Adela wanted us to be friends, so I said nothing, merely hitched my pack higher on my shoulder and prepared to depart. But just at that moment, Burl Hodge's son, Jack, came running up High Street and, seeing Richard, stopped in full flight, catching him by the arm.

'Sergeant! You'd better come. They've just fished a body out of the Avon.'

Five

'A body!' Jack repeated, clutching his side. 'A man.'
Richard Manifold frowned. 'A drunk, I suppose, who's fallen in the river and drowned. Nothing to get excited about. There are at least two such every week. Get a couple of men to carry the corpse to Saint Nicholas's Church, then spread the word. Whoever's missing a husband, son or father will turn up to claim the body eventually.'

'You don't understand!' Jack shook Richard's arm. 'This man wasn't drowned. He's been stabbed through the heart.'

Richard cursed. There was now no way he could avoid going down to the Backs to take a look.

'Very well,' he said grudgingly. 'There's no need for you to come, Roger. You'd best be off home.'

But I had no intention of doing any such thing. I gave him and Jack Hodge a moment or two's start, then followed them.

A crowd had begun to gather near Bristol Bridge, everyone looking at something – or somebody – lying on the ground. Richard Manifold shouted as he approached – 'Make way for the law!' – and the people fell back to let him through. He dropped to one knee and rolled the corpse on to its back, when the depredations caused by over a week in the river became horribly apparent.

I knew the body must have been in the Avon for over a week, because I recognized it without difficulty. I recognized the unnervingly thick-soled boots, the seaman's stout frieze breeches, the hands, or what remained of them, as big as shovels. And I recognized the tattoo on the back of the left one: a ship and what had once been the word Clontarf. I noticed, too, a rent in the left breast of his leather, salt-stained jerkin, surrounded by a darker mark that had to be blood.

48

I touched Richard Manifold on the shoulder. 'He's an Irish sea captain called Eamonn Malahide.' The name had suddenly come back to me.

The sergeant's face, when he glanced up and realized who was speaking, was the picture of frustration.

'I thought I told you to go home, chapman! This is none of your business. It's strictly a matter for the law!'

'Even the law needs witnesses and information,' I snapped.

'That's right, it does,' a voice from the crowd agreed.

Richard got slowly to his feet, looking as though he might be about to burst a blood vessel. His face was a brighter red than his hair. His blue eyes sparkled furiously.

'And what would you know about anything?' he asked me angrily. 'Unless, of course, you're the murderer.' He sounded hopeful.

I repeated, 'This man's name is Eamonn Malahide. He was at the house at Rownham Passage. Adela must have explained how I saw a man murdered by one of the two women who were present. It was the reason you rode out there.' I indicated the waterlogged corpse. 'That is the man I saw killed.'

Richard's features relaxed. 'You're not back at that nonsense, are you? Go home and lie down, Roger. You haven't been well.'

'I'm telling you—' I began hotly.

But I was ignored. The sergeant was already directing two of the men in the crowd to carry the body to Saint Nicholas's Church and give it temporary lodging in the crypt.

'I'm telling you the truth, you dolt!' I shouted. But instead of reacting angrily, as I had expected, Richard merely smiled in a nauseatingly patient and long-suffering way. 'Why won't you believe me?' I went on desperately. 'Why not, when the evidence is right there, in front of your eyes?'

'Lad,' he said, in such a condescending tone that I could barely keep myself from hitting him, 'I've been to Rownham Passage. I've made enquiries. Nothing happened. No one saw or heard anything at all suspicious. Now, enough's enough. Off you go and leave me to get on with the Sheriff's business.'

I wasn't sure that he was as unconvinced by my identification of the corpse as he was pretending to be. The trouble was that he couldn't resist taking me down a notch or two in public, any more than I could have withstood a similar temptation. Adela was right: the rivalry between us had reached absurd proportions, especially as we both knew the true state of her affections. But Richard resented me, while I was unable to rid myself of an irrational jealousy of him.

I shrugged. 'Let me know when you need to pick my brains again,' was my parting shot. 'Because you will, when you find out I'm telling the truth.'

The crowd had begun to disperse even before the corpse was removed. Violent death was too much of an everyday occurrence to engage people's attention for long. I turned to resume my broken journey back to Small Street, and blundered into a young woman standing just behind me, catching her as she staggered and nearly fell beneath my weight. My first thought was that although she looked strained and somewhat troubled, she was extremely pretty. My second, as I was hit by a painful jolt of recognition, was that I knew her – had, indeed, once fancied myself more than a little in love with her.

'Rowena Honeyman!' I gasped.

It struck me later that she was nothing like as surprised to see me as I was to see her. But then, as it transpired she was staying in Bristol, I suppose she had already guessed that we might meet at some time or another.

I must have been goggling, open-mouthed, like a stranded fish. She smiled faintly and released herself from a clasp that had become more of a support for me than for her.

'Rowena Hollyns,' she corrected me. 'The *Widow* Hollyns, to be precise.'

'H–Hollyns?' I croaked stupidly. 'Widow Hollyns? Are you sure?'

But even as I realized the crassness of my question, memory stirred. I was transported back two years and more to the village of Keyford, near Frome, where I had gone, not only in pursuit of one of my investigations, but also in the hope of meeting Rowena Honeyman, who lived there with an aunt. I had been desperate to engage her affections, but before I could make a fool of myself, a neighbour had informed me of her betrothal to a young man whose name was Ralph Hollyns.

But another memory was jostling for position. Only yesterday, Marianne Avenel had told me that her sister-in-law's companion was a Mistress Hollyns. It would be too great a coincidence to have two women of that name take up residence in the city together. They had to be one and the same person.

It might mean nothing at all, of course. I had yet to clap eyes on Mistress Alefounder, and until I did, there was little to connect her to the murder at Rownham Passage. I found myself hoping that Adela was wrong; that there was no similarity between the woman in the brown sarcenet and Robin Avenel's sister.

'Allow me to escort you home, Mistress Hon – er, Mistress Hollyns,' I offered.

She was as beautiful as ever, with soft, rose-petal skin, eyes as blue as cornflowers and a full, gently curving mouth. And she disliked me as much as ever; I could see it in the hard, set lines of her face. She still held me responsible for her father's death.

'No, thank you,' she replied coldly. 'I am quite capable of looking after myself. I've had to since my husband died.'

'You weren't married long, I think? Indeed, I know you could not have been.'

She refused to rise to my bait and ask how I knew.

'Ten months. Ralph died of the plague last summer.'

'You . . . You didn't catch it too?' I asked anxiously.

'He was away from home when it happened.' She did not enlarge on the subject, but added, 'Mistress Alefounder has been very kind to me and given me employment as her companion. We are here, in Bristol, on a visit to her brother.'

I nodded. 'Yes, I know . . . You decided against returning to live with your aunt, then?'

She gave a mirthless smile. 'Dear me! What a lot you seem to know about me, Master Chapman. But why are you so interested? Does your conscience bother you?'

'About your father? I've never lost a moment's sleep on his account, I do assure you.' I was angry at the mere suggestion.

For a few seconds, she gave me back stare for stare, then dropped her eyes and turned away, indicating that our conversation was at an end. I looked around for Richard Manifold but he had disappeared. The life of the quayside was back to normal; the momentary excitement had passed like the shadow that it was, the dead stranger already half forgotten. By tonight, he would not even be deemed worthy of a mention in the alehouses. I hoisted my pack higher on my shoulder.

'Mistress Hollyns! Rowena!'

Someone was calling to my erstwhile companion who, meantime, had set off towards the bottom of High Street. I saw her pause and scan the crowds. Then Robin Avenel appeared, pushing his way through the workmen and sailors who were impeding his progress. I gained on him and Mistress Hollyns rapidly, and was soon close enough to overhear their conversation.

'What's happened?' Robin demanded, hurrying to meet her. 'Someone told me that a body's been dragged out of the Avon. A man! Murdered! Is it true? Is it . . . Is it anyone I know?'

Rowena smiled and my heart gave an uncomfortable lurch. She was even lovelier when she wasn't frowning.

'My dear sir, how can I tell? Our acquaintance has been so short.' She laid a hand on his sleeve. 'I heard it said that the poor fellow was a sea captain. An Irishman . . . Master Avenel, you're looking very unwell. But it's hardly surprising, the sun is so hot. Please take my arm. I'm returning to Broad Street now that I've finished my errand for Mistress Alefounder.'

Robin Avenel may have been suffering from the heat, or from anxiety, perhaps – as yet I wasn't sure which – but it didn't prevent him from taking full advantage of Rowena's invitation. He leaned against her so heavily that she had to support him with an arm about his waist. Keeping a few yards behind them, I eyed him malevolently and recalled that I had always disliked him, ever since the days when

52

he and I had both fancied ourselves in love with Cicely Ford.

He was about a year younger than I was, with auburn hair cut in a fringe and curling to his shoulders. He had a cherubic, florid face, was a dandy who adopted every passing fashion, regardless of whether or not it suited him, believed himself to be irresistible to women, and, above all, oozed the sort of self-confidence that came from being the son and heir of one of Bristol's richest citizens. I loathed him, and was greatly cheered by the thought that his wife of a mere eighteen months was playing him false with her father's brewery assistant.

I was hoping, as we entered Broad Street, that I might be rewarded by a sight of the elusive Mistress Alefounder, but I was to be disappointed yet again. As they reached Alderman Weaver's old house, Robin Avenel produced a key, letting both himself and his companion in without having to knock for admittance. I was unable to loiter and so proceeded on my way, knowing that if I were to visit Rownham Passage that day, I was already pressed for time.

Adela had not been expecting me, but was pleased to see me nevertheless. She professed herself suitably impressed by my (almost) full pack and by much of the merchandise I had bought from the ships along the Backs. It was now ten o'clock and dinnertime, so I was able to sit down at the kitchen table with her and the children and share their rabbit stew.

While we ate, I told her of the man pulled from the Avon, and who he was.

'Did . . . Did Richard believe you?' she asked uncertainly, her spoon arrested halfway to her mouth.

'He said he didn't, but I was none too sure it was the truth. Do *you* believe me?'

'Yes, I think I do. I think I have to. I don't suppose you'd invent a thing like that.'

'Thank you,' I said and meant it, although my tone may have sounded a little caustic. I looked steadily across the table at Adela, engaging her eyes with mine. For once, the children were quiet, intent on emptying their bowls. 'I also met Elizabeth Alefounder's maid down on the Backs. The

Widow Hollyns.' I took a deep breath. 'When I knew her, she was still Rowena Honeyman. I told you about her.'

I had indeed told Adela about my unrequited passion, and it had been her sympathy and understanding that had led to the completely unexpected revelation that I was not really in love with Rowena at all, but with herself. And I was still in love with her, which she knew. Unfortunately, she also knew that I would always be a little in thrall to those ladies who had once engaged my affections. She had had the experience of Cicely Ford the previous year. Now here was Rowena come out of the past to haunt us. But she gave no sign of any unease.

'Of course,' was all she said, 'if Mistress Honeyman – or Mistress Hollyns as I suppose I must now learn to call her – lives in Keyford, she must know Elizabeth Alefounder well. Two widows drawn together by loneliness, one rich, one poor, what could be more natural than that the former should offer the other employment?' She placidly resumed eating, leaving me to my own self-reproaches, until she was struck by a sudden thought. 'Roger! Does this mean that Mistress Hollyns could be the woman in the blue brocade dress? The one who killed the Irishman?'

The idea had already crossed my mind, but I wasn't about to admit as much.

'Firstly, I haven't yet established that Mistress Alefounder is the woman in the brown sarcenet,' I pointed out. 'Secondly, Rowena Hollyns gave no indication that she recognized Eamonn Malahide.' I added slowly, 'Though Robin Avenel, now . . . He did seem perturbed, even though he hadn't seen the body.'

'You think he might be the man whose voice you heard?'

I smiled at her. 'Why are you suddenly so certain that my story's true, and not the result of delirium?'

'Because you gave me a detailed description of the man who was killed. At least, the part of him that you could see. It seems to tally in every respect with the man pulled out of the Avon. And I've only to visit Saint Nicholas's crypt to check that you're not lying . . . Will you still go to Rownham Passage?'

'I must.' I pushed aside my empty bowl and rubbed my overfull belly. If I weren't careful, I should grow fat. 'I still have to convince that dunderhead, Dick Manifold, of the truth of my story. There must be some evidence *somewhere* of what happened. Someone must have seen something, heard something, but I wouldn't trust him to winkle it out. Mind you, I don't suppose he tried very hard because he didn't believe me.'

My wife looked guilty. 'That was my fault, I'm afraid. He knew I wasn't convinced by your story. As for Margaret ...' Adela broke off, laughing.

I grinned in reply. 'She'll be most upset if it can be proved I'm in the right of it, after all.' The children had finished eating and were beginning to get restless. It was time to be off before I was captured to be a horse or a donkey and give them rides around the kitchen, crawling on all fours. As well as being the man with the flattest chest in Bristol, I was also on the way to becoming the man with the knobbliest knees. 'I must go if I'm to get to Rownham Passage and back before dark.'

'Then do as I suggested the other day,' Adela said. 'Hire a nag from the livery stable in Bell Lane.'

I've never been much good on horseback, although I have ridden, and for quite long journeys. I grew up in Wells and the surrounding countryside, but my chief pastime was playing football, trying to kick a blown swine's bladder between two upright sticks. I was good at it, too. But with the time at my disposal I couldn't afford to hire the slowest nag in the stables. The liveryman, therefore, apprised of my dilemma, recommended a solid brown cob; a good little mover, he assured me, but blessed with an even temper. I also paid for the hire of a saddle and duly mounted, feeling strangely unencumbered without either pack or cudgel, both of which I had left at home. I clutched the reins, urged the beast towards the Frome Gate and prayed that I wouldn't make an idiot of myself by falling off.

The gatekeeper let out a whoop of laughter when he saw me.

'What you doing perched up there, Roger?' He grinned. 'You look pretty stupid. I'd stick to my own two legs if I were you.'

'I'm going to Rownham Passage and I want to get back before curfew,' I answered tartly, not sharing in his mirth.

I knew all three of the Frome gatekeepers well, but this man, Edgar Capgrave, was the one I liked least. A little butterball of a man, almost as broad as he was long, with small, shrewd eyes set under beetling brows, he had an aggressive manner that many people besides myself found offensive. Nevertheless, he had an intelligence that his fellow gatekeepers lacked. He signalled me to pass through the arch with a dismissive jerk of his thumb, but instead, I reined in the cob and sat looking down at him.

'Can you remember who was on duty here last Wednesday week?'

'Last Wednesday week? That's a bloody tall order, chapman.' He puckered his fat little face in a travesty of concentration. 'How's anyone supposed to remember that far back?'

'It was the day of the storm,' I reminded him.

'So it was.' I could tell by the smirk on his face that he already knew that. 'I might remember,' he admitted. 'Anything in it for me if I do?'

'A groat?' I suggested through gritted teeth.

He leered up at me. 'Make it two. A rich man like you, a house owner, should be willing to help out his poorer fellow citizens.'

By this time, there were at least a couple of carts lined up behind me and the cob was growing restless. It moved suddenly, almost unseating me. The gatekeeper let out a guffaw, while one of the carters yelled, 'Will you get a move on, please?' Well, that was undoubtedly what he meant.

I gave the horse the office to start. I couldn't waste any more time: it would soon be midday judging by the position of the sun. But as the cob clattered on to the quayside and, guided by me, headed towards the Frome Bridge, Edgar Capgrave called out, 'I was the one on duty that day. Wait a few moments until these fools have cleared the archway, and then you can ask me whatever it is you want to know.'

He got a mouthful of well deserved abuse from the carters for his rudeness, but it didn't seem to bother him. Indeed, the fouler the imprecations, the more they made him chuckle. He was a man who throve on confrontation.

I dismounted and led the cob back towards the gate. Even after less than quarter of an hour in the saddle, it was a relief to have both feet on the ground again. The two carts rattled away and there was a sudden lull in the amount of traffic passing in and out of the city.

'All right,' Edgar said, as though we had come to some unspoken agreement. 'A groat.'

I towered head and shoulders above him. Even on foot, I still found myself looking down at him, a fact which many small people resented, but which didn't seem to disconcert Edgar in the least.

'You may not be able to tell me anything I want to know,' I cavilled.

He shrugged. 'That won't be my fault, now will it? Just your bad luck. I'm more than ready to answer your questions. If, that is, you really have something sensible to ask me.'

'Very well. A groat,' I conceded grudgingly. 'Were you on the gate all that day? The day of the storm.'

'From dawn until curfew. Right! That was easy. Anything else?' Pleased with his own wit, he guffawed again.

'Do you know Robin Avenel's sister?' I asked. 'She's been staying with him, so I understand, since the end of May.'

'Bess Alefounder? Of course, I know her,' was the scathing response. 'Known her since she was knee-high to a grasshopper. You forget, chapman, it's you who's the stranger in these parts.' He proceeded to reminisce, as people will when they want to prove how much more they know than you do. 'Handsome girl, she was. Older than Robin by about three years, but always treated him like she was his mother. Still does, I reckon, given half the chance, although she doesn't see him so much nowadays, not since she got married and moved away to Keyford. Her husband was Gregory Alefounder's nephew, first cousin to Master Avenel's wife.'

Edgar Capgrave grinned lasciviously. 'Reckon my fine Cock Robin's bought himself a packet of trouble there.'

'Oh?' I endeavoured to look innocent.

The gatekeeper tapped his nose. 'I know what I know. I've seen sweet little Marianne mooning after that Luke Prettywood. Never wanted to marry Robin in the first place. At least, that's the word in the taverns. Arranged by the two old men.'

'The day of the storm, last Wednesday week,' I said, dragging the conversation back on course. 'Can you recall if Mistress Alefounder and her maid left by this gate during the day?'

Edgar Capgrave replied without hesitation.

'Oh, yes!' he said. 'Bess Alefounder was the first person through the gate that morning. Curfew had only just been lifted. It was barely light. She was wearing a light woollen cloak, grey in colour, as I recall, and riding that roan mare of hers. Looked down her nose at me, she did, just as if we hadn't known one another since we were children. Mind you,' he added viciously, 'the Avenels were always like that. High and mighty, thinking themselves better than any one else.'

'Was her maid with her?' I asked.

The gatekeeper shook his head. 'No. There was no one with her, not then. But now you put me in mind of it, she did have that Mistress Hollyns alongside her when she came back. That would have been ... let me see ... sometime around midday, I reckon. About an hour after her brother returned and about an hour and a half before they brought you home, half-drowned, in a farm cart.' He laughed even louder than before at the recollection.

'Master Avenel had been out as well?' I queried.

'Left by this very gate some two hours after his sister, also on horseback, if you want to know. But, as I told you, he was back after three hours or so.' Traffic was building up again on both sides of the arch, waiting to be let through. 'So, if there's nothing else you want to ask, I'll have my groat and be about my work.'

I took the money from my pouch. 'One other thing,' I said, continuing to hold it in my fist. 'Did you happen to notice what colour of gown Mistress Alefounder was wearing?'

Edgar shook his head. 'She still had her cloak on when she returned, because the rain hadn't quite cleared away. But that maid of hers, I did happen to see what she was wearing. She had a cloak on, too, but it blew back in a gust of wind. Her gown was blue brocade.'

Six

'Blue brocade?' My voice shook a little. 'Are you sure?' 'I'm sure. I remember thinking it was a pretty fancy gown for a maid to be wearing.' Edgar Capgrave eyed me curiously, then shrugged. 'Don't know where they'd been or what they'd been up to, but they both looked like drowned rats. Their skirts were soaking wet for ten or twelve inches above the hem. Leastways, Mistress Hollyns's was. Didn't get a proper look at the other's. Reckon they'd been caught proper by that storm.'

Or been wading in the river, up to their knees, trying to drown some poor sod they'd previously bludgeoned unconscious!

'Are you absolutely certain that Mistress Alefounder's companion was Mistress Hollyns?' I asked all the same.

By this time, there were growing protests from both sides of the archway, where two fresh lines of traders and honest citizens waited to pay their tolls.

'Who else could it have been?' the gatekeeper demanded irritably. 'Bess could have met up with her somewhere and they rode home together. Mind you, Mistress Hollyns must have left by another gate. She didn't pass through this one on her outward journey. I'd stake my life on it.'

I believed him. Edgar Capgrave's powers of observation seemed phenomenal. I asked about the red shoes, but he answered that he hadn't noticed, and that, in any case, they would probably have been too wet for him to say anything with certainty about their colour. I gave him the groat, remounted the cob and rode off across the Frome Bridge, leaving him to deal with his irate customers. I had no doubt at all that he could handle them.

60

Once across the bridge, I rode sedately along the quayside of Saint Augustine's Back, past the abbey, to the confluence of the Frome and Avon. There, I turned towards Rownham Passage and the ferry, skirting the steeply rising ground to the north of the city, which culminated in the high plateau of Durdham Down and Lord Cobham's manor of Clifton.

It was another beautiful day. The sky was blue; little clouds, fragile as blown glass, danced to the tune of a following breeze; sailors and dockers were mostly stripped to the waist, bronzed and fit and enjoying the summer sunshine. But my mind was elsewhere, trying to reconcile Rowena Hollyns with the role of a ruthless killer. Instinct and a knowledge of human nature denied the possibility. But then I remembered whose daughter she was and conviction wavered.

Nevertheless, I still felt uncomfortable with the idea, although I now felt sure that she was the woman in the blue brocade gown, and so, by natural corollary, that Elizabeth Alefounder must be the woman in the brown sarcenet. As for the motive behind the whole murderous episode, now that I knew Robin Avenel might have been involved, I was certain it must have something to do with that perennial thorn in the English Government's side, the Lancastrian faction's last and very forlorn hope: the exiled Henry Tudor.

As Adela had reminded me, it was less than a year since Master Avenel had come under suspicion of being a Lancastrian supporter, but nothing had been proved against him. And unless I could prove some connection between him and the old 'murder' house at Rownham Passage, there would be no evidence of wrongdoing this time, either.

My mind reverted to Rowena Hollyns, and from her it was but a short step to thinking about Adela. It would have been an exaggeration to say that there was something amiss between us, but I couldn't deny that there had been a certain constraint this past year, since Adam's birth. Three months ago, Adela had ceased feeding him at the breast, and from then on had been anxious to avoid conceiving another child. Ironically, for the first time in our lives, we had a bedchamber almost to ourselves, and all the privacy any married couple with three small children could reasonably hope for.

I understood, but still resented, Adela's lukewarm acceptance of my bedtime advances. She was much more God-fearing than I was, and therefore far more inclined to abide by the Church's regulations. For me, as, I suspect, for many other people, there are some rules which are simply made to be broken. For instance, according to the Church, married couples should refrain from carnal pleasure on Sundays, Wednesdays and Fridays, for forty days before both Easter and Christmas, and for three days before going to Mass. I worked this out once, and it totals at least five months of enforced abstinence every year. Enough to make any red-blooded male resort to the nearest whorehouse!

Of course, wise women can always offer remedies against conception, but, frankly, most of their ideas make my hair stand on end. One we consulted advised Adela to eat bees (presumably dead ones, although we didn't bother to enquire). Another recommended that the wife drink a pint of raw onion juice just before the act itself (on the assumption, I suppose, that no man could possibly perform at his sparkling best whilst being asphyxiated by his wife's breath). A third tried to convince us that a foolproof method was for the woman to eat a whole cabbage as soon as she got out of bed. (Adela hates cabbage.) So there we were, left with using less traumatic, but more frustrating ways of assuring we had no more children just at present, and with a relationship every bit as loving, but not nearly as carefree as it was of yore . . .

I realized that my musings had brought me to Rownham Passage. I was abreast of the 'murder' house on its rocky promontory, overlooking the slimy grey mud that forms the Avon's banks on both sides of the river. In the distance, I could see the ferryman plying his trade, but for the moment he was rowing towards the opposite shore. I dismounted, looped the cob's reins around the lower branch of a stunted, wind-blasted tree and crossed the patch of coarse, dry grass to the 'murder' house.

I had half expected the door to be locked, but it wasn't. As I cautiously pushed it open, I was met once again by the same strong smell of must and damp that I recalled from my first, ill-fated visit. I stood on the threshold, straining my ears for any sound that might indicate occupation, but apart from the inevitable scurrying of mice, all was silent.

I advanced a pace or two along the narrow passageway and entered the parlour. Nothing. Nobody. Yet something was different. The room was much gloomier, and the shapes of its meagre furniture loomed oddly menacing in the darkness. The shutters, previously open, were now closed, blocking out what little light had been afforded by the grimy parchment panes. Someone had been here.

I returned to the passageway. Dust lay in drifts across the floor, but there were no footprints apart from my own. There were, however, other marks which I recognized as strokes made by a broom. Someone had thought it worthwhile to erase as far as possible all traces of occupation. A sensible precaution, I thought, smiling grimly.

I went upstairs. Here, there was just one room, a little larger than the parlour below. Even so, it was cramped and, remembering the family who had once lived here – daughter, mother and tyrranical father – I found it hardly surprising that their story had ended in tragedy. The only piece of furniture was the bed and it took up most of the space. Made of oak and with carvings of angels decorating the headboard, it was, however, devoid of bedding except for a mattress, its covering of grubby, once-white linen torn in several places and goose feathers protruding in handfuls. I walked around it and peered underneath, but there was nothing to be found, not even a chamber pot.

I brushed the dust from the knees of my breeches and was conscious of a sharp pain in the back of my head. I was also feeling a little dizzy, another indication that I was not yet as fit as I pretended to be. I sat down on the bed. The room spun once or twice, then steadied. I felt a little better.

The house was beginning to get on my nerves. The knowledge of what had happened there fifty years earlier, and also ten days ago, was making me jumpy. All the same, I would make a further search of the downstairs before I left.

It was at that moment that my right hand encountered a small, hard lump in the mattress. Through the ticking, and embedded in goose feathers, it wasn't easy to say exactly what it was, but it felt suspiciously like a ring. The pain in my head and my uneasiness both forgotten, I slewed round to examine the mattress more closely and saw that the location of the lump was about the length of a man's forearm from a large rent in the covering. Hanging on to my prize with my right hand, I cautiously inserted my left arm into the tear until my fingers met with solid metal. A few seconds later, I was staring at a heavy gold signet ring lying in the palm of my hand.

I brushed the fleas aside and inspected my trophy. It was a man's ring, there was no doubt about that – it would have fitted easily on any of my fingers. There was no jewel, just a richly chased band and a roundel deeply engraved with the insignia of its owner, whoever that might be. I held it up to the light, but the carving was too elaborate to decipher. I could see that there were two capital letter As entwined, but another concave motif behind them was less distinct.

I debated what to do with my find. If there was an owner of the 'murder' house, and there must be somewhere, did it belong to him, by right of having been discovered on his property? On the other hand, it might belong to the unseen man whose voice I had heard, in which case, should I hand it over to Richard Manifold? A third alternative was that it had been the possession of the original owner of the house, but somehow I didn't think so. The mattress was certainly torn and filthy, but I doubted very much if it were fifty years old.

And someone had used it recently. There was a definite hollow in the middle of the mattress where a body had lain not too long since. And the man, whoever he was, must have been up here: he wasn't in the parlour when I was first admitted – unless he had come in through the front door while I was unconscious . . .

My head was starting to ache again, and I was no nearer a solution as to what to do with the ring than I had been ten minutes ago. For the time being, then, I would do nothing. I would let the course of events and my instincts guide me. Whether the ring had been deliberately hidden in the mattress or accidentally lost was another question altogether. But for the moment, it was not a problem I was prepared to cope with. I dropped the ring into my pouch and went downstairs again.

I opened the shutters, letting in a shaft of sunlight that slabbed the floor with gold, and when I scuffed aside some of the dust near the door, a large dark stain was visible. Blood, I had no doubt, belonging to the Irish sea captain. A sudden vivid picture flashed into my mind of the man falling, the dagger thrust through his heart after his attack on the woman in blue brocade. Rowena? But why would she have been carrying a knife? And it must have been a beautiful stroke, clean, swift, unerring. If only the scope of my vision had been greater instead of confined to a mere few feet above the floor!

I was certain that the man whose voice I'd heard in the background had not been Robin Avenel. Firstly, according to Edgar Capgrave, Master Avenel had returned to Bristol too early for him to have been present during the attack on myself and Eamonn Malahide. Secondly, I remembered thinking that the man's accent was slightly foreign, or, if foreign was too strong a word, then strange – not the broad, diphthong-vowelled speech of the west country. That was the way in which the woman in brown sarcenet had spoken, but try as I might, I could not recall the voice of the woman in blue brocade. She must have remained silent throughout the entire episode.

I prowled around the parlour once more, but found nothing else. I closed the shutters again before emerging into the sunshine with a feeling of relief. Then I remembered the outhouse where the horses had been stabled, but on inspection this, too, was empty except for a large besom, propped against one wall. I searched for signs of dung or wisps of hay, but there were none. I was up against a thoroughly disciplined, orderly mind, not easily panicked by unforeseen circumstances.

I unhitched the cob's reins and glanced towards the river. The ferryman had by now accomplished his return journey and was pulling into shore. By great good fortune, no one was yet waiting to cross to the manor of Ashton-Leigh, so I led the horse forward and, remembering that I had been told his name, shouted 'Master Tyrrwhit!' as loudly as I could.

The Rownham Passage alehouse was as small and shabby inside as it was out, but the landlord served excellent ale. I handed a mazer to Jason Tyrrwhit, then squeezed in beside him on a dirty corner bench that accommodated two. I had chosen it deliberately as a place where we were less likely to be interrupted by one of his many friends.

The tiny room, with its sanded floor and row of barrels along one wall, was crowded to suffocation. Seafaring types of all shapes and sizes were crammed together around a long, central table or seated on rickety stools or lying prone on the ground, having drunk themselves into a stupor. The stink of the place was enough to knock a grown man senseless, and I felt the bile rise in my throat as soon as we entered. Not so my companion, who was obviously very much at home there; a frequent visitor if the general chorus of greeting from all sides was anything to judge by. A few sips of the landlord's brew, however, were sufficient to settle my stomach, and I was able to devote my full attention to the ferryman.

'You're looking well,' he observed, 'for a man who cheated death by inches and gave his head a nasty knock into the bargain.'

'You were the good Samaritan who rescued me, I believe. This,' I apologized, 'is the first chance I've had to come back and thank you.'

'Think nothing of it! I'd've done the same for a dog.' He slewed round on the bench to look at me. 'But how in Hades did you manage to fall in? You were striding out along the track to Bristol last time I saw you. Mind you,' he went on, without waiting for a reply, 'I thought as how you'd got a touch of the sun, the way you were going on about building a bridge between the top o' Ghyston Cliff and Ashton rocks. Sun's addled his brain, I remember thinking.'

I let it go. There was no point in trying to explain; it would only confuse him further.

'When you found me in the water, did you see anyone on the bank? Anyone walking or running in the direction of the old 'murder' house?' I asked.

He shook his head. 'I was too busy rescuing you, weren't I? You're a big fellow. I didn't have any passengers that crossing, and hauling you into the skiff was hard going fer a little chap like me. Specially when you was waterlogged. It was only air gettin' in under that jerkin of yours kept you from sinking. First, I thought you was a bundle of old clothes someone had tossed in the river. That's why I rowed over to take a look. I've had some decent finds from the Avon one time and another. These 'ere boots, fer example.' He lifted a skinny leg, proudly displaying a foot encased in a brown leather ankle boot of surprisingly good quality. 'See what I mean?'

I didn't know whether to feel insulted that I could be mistaken for a bundle of old clothes, or grateful for the fact that I had been. In the end gratitude won.

'You're sure you didn't notice anyone – anyone at all? A woman, perhaps, or maybe two, in the neighbourhood of the 'murder' house when you fished me out of the water?'

He paused to consider. I regarded him hopefully.

'Well, I can't say I saw anyone, no. Oh, I know why you're asking. That red-headed Sheriff's man, who came snooping around a day or two later, told me what you'd been saying. It was all nonsense, he reckoned, caused by the pain in yer head. Mind, 'e described you as a pain in the arse!' The ferryman roared with laughter at this witticism, took another swig of ale and wiped his mouth on his sleeve. 'All the same, I've been thinking about it since,' he went on, 'and there were a couple o' people waiting for the ferry this side of the river. That's why I rowed over empty from Ashton-Leigh. It was still raining a bit and I didn't want 'em getting wetter'n necessary. Course, I have me back to the Rownham shore while I'm rowing in this direction, so I wouldn't have seen anything. But they might have done.'

'Who were they?' I demanded excitedly. 'Do you know?'

Jason Tyrrwhit scratched his scanty grey locks. 'There were a man and a boy. Didn't know them. Come from the other side. But I knew the woman. Lives in one o' them cottages along the foreshore. Goody Tallboys, I think they call her. Got a sister at Ashton-Leigh, so crosses regular.'

'Do you know which cottage? Could you take me to see her?'

He grinned. 'Fancy a bit o' dalliance, do you?' His sense of humour was easily tickled. 'All right. But finish yer ale first. This stuff's too good to waste.'

I agreed with him. In fact it was good enough for me to treat us both to another beaker apiece. While we drank, I asked him how long he had been the Avon ferryman.

He shrugged. 'Ten year, p'raps. Maybe more. I was a sailor fer most of me life.' His puny chest swelled with pride. 'I was with Warwick's fleet when we beat the Spaniards in '58. Keeper of the Seas he was, and never a man before nor since deserved the title better. Twenty-eight men-o'-war them Spaniards had. All we had were three carvels, four pinnaces and five forecastle ships. Outnumbered by more'n two to one! But we drove our little fleet in amongst them and taught 'em a lesson they won't forget in a hurry! Six hours that battle lasted, but we beat 'em hands down in the end. Over two hundred Spanish were killed, hundreds more wounded. We sunk two of their ships and captured six others. The rest limped back to the Flanders ports, their tails well and truly between their legs. Those were the days!' He sighed regretfully. 'Then, when I was too old to go adventuring any longer, I came home. The job of ferryman had just fallen vacant, so I took it. It's a living. Can't complain.'

'You must know a lot about the sea,' I said respectfully.

'I know a lot about a lot of things. Fer instance, I know that from Bristol boundary stone to Rownham is a mile in length, two if you measure from the city's High Cross. I know Ghyston Cliff is sixty fathoms high. I know from here to the Hungroad is near on two mile—'

'What's the Hungroad?'

He gave me a withering glance. 'You ain't no Bristol man, I can tell. If you were, you'd know that out there, in a direct line with Ghyston Cliff, are the Leads – great, jagged rocks

68

on the bed of the Avon. If you try to navigate up this river into Bristol at low tide, the Leads'll rip yer vessel open from bow to stern. So ships anchor in the Hungroad and wait for the incoming tide.'

'Which side of the river is this anchorage?' I asked.

My companion jerked his head towards the window. 'Ashton-Leigh,' he said.

I thought about this. 'If a ship was anchored in the Hungroad, and the captain wanted to be put ashore over here, would he be rowed across by his own crew? Or would he use the ferry?'

Jason Tyrrwhit grinned. 'You're a landlubber all right. 'Course he wouldn't need to use the ferry. Chances are, he'd row himself. Partic'ly if he wasn't sure what time he wanted to return aboard. Mind you, don't know why anyone'd want to visit Rownham Passage; leastways, not if he was sailing upriver to Bristol. Who're we talking about, anyway?'

'Does the name Eamonn Malahide mean anything to you?'

The ferryman shook his grizzled head. 'No. But sounds like an Irisher to me.'

'He is. Or rather was. He's dead. Knifed through the heart. He was the man I saw killed in the "murder" house last week.'

'Oh, him! The Sheriff's man said you was having delusions.'

'No delusion,' I answered tersely. 'His body was fished out of Bristol docks this morning.'

'Drowned?'

'He'd been stabbed.'

'Had he now?' Jason Tyrrwhit whistled through broken teeth. 'Seems like you could've been telling the truth, after all, chapman. Wait here a minute while I ask around. Somebody might have some information worth knowing.'

He got up from the bench and began moving amongst our fellow customers. Some he merely slapped on the back or exchanged a cheery word with. But beside others, he paused for a confidential chat. There was no way, from where I was sitting, that I could hear what passed between them: the noise in the alehouse was deafening. But I could tell from the expression on his face, as he resumed his seat on the bench, that he had learned something worth the telling.

'Old chap in the corner,' he said, 'the one with the broken nose—'

'Next to the young lad who's just been sick?'

'That's the one. Lives in the manor of Ashton-Leigh. Just comes across for the ale. He says there was an Irish ship, the Clontarf, anchored in the Hungroad sometime last week.'

'The Wednesday,' I suggested.

'Dunno. Probably. He can't recollect for sure. But here's the interesting bit. He remembers it dropping anchor, but it didn't go on upriver on the next high tide. Stayed in its berth three days before slipping its moorings and tacking about.'

'You mean it never went into Bristol. Just sailed for home?'

'Seems like it. And old Josh there had an idea there was some trouble on board. Didn't know what. Didn't ask. But the landlord –' he indicated a tall, cadaverous-looking man in a leather apron '– said there were a couple of Irish seamen in here a week ago yesterday – that'd be the Friday – nosing around. Asking a lot o' questions without really saying what they wanted. He reckoned they were looking fer someone, but wouldn't admit it right out.'

That made sense if their captain had gone missing and the crew was on some secret mission that no one was supposed to know anything about. I stood up.

'Thanks for all your help,' I said. 'Now, if you'd just point me in the direction of this Goody Tallboys's cottage . . .'

My voice tailed off as I stared, transfixed. Once on my feet, I could easily see across the crowded taproom. In the corner, on the far side of old Josh, sat another, smaller man, wearing a tattered, wine-stained jerkin, who glanced up and caught my eye, then hurriedly looked away again, coyly trying to pretend that he didn't know me, but I could see annoyance shadow his sharp little features as he recognized my unwelcome face.

His shoulders hunched and his whole body tensed as I moved towards him, just to give him a fright. But he needn't have worried. I'd play his game if that was what he wanted.

70

I followed the ferryman outside and listened to his simple directions for getting to Goody Tallboys's cottage.

All the same, I would have given a great deal to know what Timothy Plummer, the Spymaster General, was doing in Rownham Passage.

Seven

Goody Tallboys's dwelling was the end one of a row of four that teetered on the edge of the riverside track. A small, fenced-in patch of ground beside the cottage was home to five or six hens, all clucking noisily or pecking greedily in the dirt.

The woman who answered my knock seemed familiar to me, and I thought I recognized her as the passenger who had been waiting for the ferry on the day of the storm – the fat woman with the basket of eggs. When I asked if this were indeed the case, she acknowledged the fact with a cheery, gap-toothed grin.

'And well soaked I got,' she complained, 'old Tyrrwhit pushing off to the alehouse like that. Although, to be fair, there wasn't much else he could've done, the storm was that bad. So I came home and dried myself, then went across later. Anyway, who are you? And why do you want to know?'

I explained that I was the man Jason Tyrrwhit had rescued from the river and she was immediately all concern, inviting me in and offering me a seat at her table.

The cottage was of the single-roomed variety that I had been used to for most of my life. A mattress was rolled up against one wall, a pillow on top of it. A hearth, on which a small fire burned, occupied the central floor space beneath a blackened hole in the roof, while a table and two stools stood close to the tiny window. A spinning wheel, a water barrel and a cupboard, where, presumably, she kept her meagre store of food, comprised the rest of the furnishings. A solitary shelf was sufficient to hold her tinderbox, a couple of tin plates, a knife and two beakers. These last, she reached down and filled with elderberry wine, which she poured from a cracked pottery jug.

'So,' she said, seating herself on the second stool, 'you're the young man Jason pulled out of the river, are you? We thought you were dead. You'd hit your head a nasty blow on something or other when you fell in.'

'*I* thought I was dead,' I answered with feeling. 'But I hadn't hit my head on anything. Someone did it for me. Tell me,' I added, 'from where you were standing, did you see anyone else on the shore before Master Tyrrwhit fished me out of the Avon?'

'What are you saying?' she asked. 'That someone deliberately threw you in?' I nodded. 'That's a very serious accusation.'

'It's a very serious crime,' I retorted, 'and one I take great exception to. Let me explain what happened.'

She listened carefully to my story, which was patently new to her. It was obvious that Richard Manifold hadn't paid her a visit; had probably not even been aware of her existence. He had accepted the ferryman's assessment of my condition – a touch of the sun – and enquired no further. Typical!

'And you say that all this happened in the old Witherspoon house?' Goody Tallboys sounded doubtful. 'Impossible! That place has been empty these fifty years and more. Ever since Silas Witherspoon was murdered by his wife and daughter.'

'I know that,' I said, irritated. 'But that's not to say the house couldn't have been occupied for a night or two. Or even for a few hours. Who does it belong to now?'

My companion rubbed her cascade of chins. 'I think it was the nephew who inherited. Old Witherspoon's brother's son. What was he called, now? John? James? That was it. James Witherspoon. He was a young man back then, but he must be getting on by now. Might even be dead, for all I know. He was an apothecary, if I remember rightly. Had a shop in Bristol, near the castle somewhere. Never came to live in Rownham Passage. Said his wife couldn't bear the thought of the house, not after what had happened there. Or so my mother told me. Tried to sell it, but no one would buy it. So it's just stood empty, rotting away.'

I thought about this. If James Witherspoon was married, he might well have a son who had continued in his father's calling. It was a long shot, but worth a try. An apothecary's shop near the castle, if there was one, shouldn't be hard to locate. But I still hadn't had an answer to my original question.

'Do you recollect seeing anyone on the shore before I was rescued from the river?' I persisted.

Goody Tallboys shook her head. 'Let's see now. I recollect the storm coming on. I was taking a basket of eggs, to my sister who lives over on the Somerset side. I saw you get out of the boat with Master Tyrrwhit. He went off to the alehouse, so I took myself back here until the rain should stop. I don't know what happened to you. I didn't notice. By the time I'd got myself dry, the weather was on the mend, but when I looked out of my window, Jason was halfway across the river again. So I stayed where I was and waited for him to return. He was about mid-way across when I left the cottage and walked down to the shore. A man with a little boy was there and we got talking. Said he'd crossed from Ashton-Leigh earlier in the day to see his mother, who'd been unwell. He was going to give me details of her illness, but just then we heard old Tyrrwhit yelling and shouting. When we looked round, he was rowing off course towards something floating in the river. That was you.'

'And you didn't see anything or anyone further along the bank? No one running towards the Witherspoon house?'

Goody Tallboys shook her head. 'I'm afraid not. Until that moment, I was looking away from the house, you see. And the man, the stranger – I didn't ask his name – was looking at me. Although, now I come to think of it . . .' She sipped her wine slowly, frowning.

'Yes?' I asked eagerly, hope reviving.

'Now I come to think of it,' she repeated, 'I do recall the child kept tugging on his father's sleeve, trying to attract his attention. He was facing in my direction, but not looking at me, if you follow what I mean.'

'He was looking beyond you? Upriver?'

'That's right, dear. Eyes all over the place, bored by the

adults' conversation, as children are. Perhaps he saw something. Perhaps that was what he wanted to tell his father.'

'He didn't mention anything later on, after I was safe
ashore? He didn't say anything then?'

'Oh, as to that, lad, I couldn't rightly tell you. Not that I
know of, at any rate. Might have done to his father. Jason
and I were too busy trying to decide if you were alive or
dead and thinking up the best way to get you home to
Bristol.'

'And you don't know the boy's name, or where he lives?'

She shook her head sadly. 'Only that he and his father
come from the other side of the Avon. Somewhere in Ashton-
Leigh.'

That was that, then. I thanked her for her time and trouble,
and apologized for bothering her.

'No bother, dear. I was glad of the company.' She was
struck by a sudden thought. 'What's today? Saturday?' I
nodded. 'Ah, well then! He might be over here, that man.
Told me he and the boy usually visit his mother on a Saturday.
He'd only made a visit on the Wednesday that week because
the old lady had been poorly, and had sent a message across
by a neighbour.'

'Do you happen to know where the stranger's mother
lives?' I enquired eagerly, but without much hope.

My companion shook her head. 'But don't look so down-
hearted,' she encouraged me. 'Rownham Passage ain't that
big. Not above a score of cottages all told. Walk around a
bit. Most windows'll be open in this weather. Pop your head
inside. You'll find him and the boy somewhere. Sure to.'

I was less optimistic. I took her advice, however, having
first begged a bucket of water for the cob, still patiently
awaiting me. Then I stabled him in the cool of the outhouse
belonging to the old Witherspoon dwelling.

It was by now very hot indeed. I removed my jerkin, slung
it over one shoulder and retraced my steps towards the main
group of houses, Goody Tallboys having assured me that
none of her immediate neighbours was a sick, solitary, elderly
woman. I had no real expectation of finding my quarry, even
when the the hamlet was so small. Goody's estimate of a

75

score of cottages was on the generous side; by my reckoning there were no more than fourteen. But not all of them had their shutters open, and I could hardly knock on each door demanding to know who was inside.

A brief conversation, however, with a little girl sitting in the dirt and trying to mend a broken hoop with an inadequate piece of string, elicited the information that a certain Goody Longstaff was an ailing widow whose son and grandson came to visit her every Saturday. My informant pointed out the hovel, I parted with half a groat, much to her grateful surprise, then set off at a trot to the other end of the village.

A thin-faced man with a watery, defeated eye answered the door. He was accompanied by an equally thin child, about ten years of age, whose white slip of a face beneath a thatch of dark, curly hair registered a lively curiosity and a determination not to be left out of whatever it was that might be going on. It took me some time to explain what I wanted because of frequent, querulous interruptions from the old lady in the bed on the far side of the room; but when the gist of my enquiry eventually sank in, the boy, without waiting for permission from his father, caught hold of my hand and dragged me indoors.

'I saw them,' he said, hopping up and down on one sticklike leg. 'I saw them.'

'Who did you see?' I asked, crouching down beside him and gripping him by his bony shoulders in an effort to make him stand still. It was like holding a little bird.

'What's that? What's going on, John?' chirruped the voice from the bed. A cane thumped the bare beaten-earth floor.

'I'll tell you later, Mother. Just lie still,' begged her harassed son, turning his attention back to me and the child. 'Henry, what are you saying? You didn't see anything. You're making things up again. Don't tell lies.'

'I did see them!' Henry stamped his feet in their worn, but carefully mended little boots. 'I tried telling you, but you were too busy talking to that fat woman with the eggs. After, it was too late. There was no point in wasting my breath.'

The elder Master Longstaff made a threatening move,

hand raised, towards his offspring, but this had no effect whatsoever on the ebullient Henry, who wriggled from my grasp and danced out of reach, waggling his fingers in his ears.

'Henry,' I pleaded, straightening up, 'tell me what you saw.'

'Two women,' he answered excitedly. 'One of 'em had her skirts hoisted right up round her waist.' His eyes sparkled lasciviously at some secret recollection. (I could guess what. I'd once been ten years old myself.) 'They were dragging something across the mud. I couldn't see what exactly, 'cause it had started to rain again, but I thought it might be a bundle of old clothes they didn't want.'

I made no comment, but I was tired of being mistaken for a parcel of old rags. There was no help for it: I should have to sharpen up my sartorial image.

'What did the women do with this bundle?' I asked.

'They towed it into the river until they were nearly up to their knees in water, then they shoved and prodded it as far out into the current as it would go before wading back ashore. The one who'd hitched up her dress, well it had worked loose from her girdle and fallen down by now.' Henry sounded disappointed. 'She was as soaking wet as the other one.'

'Was there a man with them? Or anywhere about?' He regarded me blankly. 'Right,' I said, taking his silence to mean no. 'And after that, what happened?'

The boy shrugged. 'Dunno. They vanished. Into the house, I reckon. I'd given up trying to tell Father what I'd seen by then, so I lost interest. It wasn't until the ferryman began shouting and waving and dragging you out of the river that I realized what they must really have been up to.'

'What's he saying? What's he been up to?' the old lady demanded agitatedly, brandishing her cane to the danger of life and limb.

Her son ignored her and, making a lunge at the boy, roared, 'Why in the Virgin's name didn't you tell me all this at the time, you stupid little brat? Didn't you stop to think it might have been important? You need a good leathering, that you do!'

Henry skipped behind me as I was the biggest object in the room and therefore afforded the greatest protection. His one aim was to avoid physical chastisement; otherwise, he was not at all put out by his parent's disapproval.

'I'm fed up with talking to you when you never listen to me,' he piped. 'Ever since Mother died, you take no notice of anything I say. I might as well not be here.'

The fight went out of the older man. His hands dropped to his sides. Tears welled up in the dark eyes.

'He's right,' he admitted sadly. 'I always confided everything to Margery. I miss her. Henry's just a child.'

I drew Henry out from behind me.

'Oh, he's more than that,' I said. 'I think you'd find him rewarding enough to talk to if only you'd make the effort.' I smiled down at the boy, who grinned back cheekily. 'Thank you, Henry. You've proved the truth of a story no one else believed in. If I asked you to repeat what you've just said in front of a Sheriff's Officer, sometime or another, would you be willing to do so? You wouldn't be frightened?'

'Of course not.' His thin chest swelled with self-importance.

I looked for confirmation to his father.

Jack Longstaff nodded. 'He doesn't know the meaning of fear . . . We live on the other side of the river, in the manor of Ashton-Leigh. Anyone over there'll tell you how to find us.'

I thanked both him and his son, then turned towards the old lady in the bed, who was regarding me malevolently.

'My gratitude for your hospitality, ma'am,' I said.

'What?' she screeched in frustration. 'Who is it? What's he saying? Why doesn't anyone tell me what's going on? I'm not deaf and dumb, you know! I'm not a fool!'

I took my leave, having pressed my remaining half groat into Henry Longstaff's receptive little fist, and made my way back towards the 'murder' house. I must think about returning home if I were to reach Bristol in time for a belated supper. I was tired: it had been many long hours since I had replenished my pack. And I was yet to clap eyes on Elizabeth Alefounder, although I now had no doubt at all that she was the woman in the brown sarcenet. But at least now I had a witness to the fact that I had been set upon and nearly murdered. Richard Manifold would have to listen to me – he could no longer afford to discount my story. I should be completely vindicated in the eyes of the law and in those of my womenfolk.

I whistled tunelessly to myself as I walked along the track.

Someone was lying in wait for me. Someone who was trying to look as inconspicuous as possible behind the stump of wind-blasted tree. I slowed my step and grinned.

'Come out and show yourself properly, Master Plummer,' I called as I got within hailing distance. 'You're getting too fat to hide behind a tree trunk of such meagre proportions.'

'Will you keep your voice down,' he hissed as I drew nearer. He made no attempt to come into the open.

'What in heaven's name are you up to?' I demanded, rounding the tree to confront him. 'I saw you in the alehouse, trying to look like a part of the furniture. It doesn't work, you know. In spite of that noisome jerkin and two days' growth of stubble, you still look what you are. A King's man.'

'That's only because you know who I am,' he snapped. 'I've a reputation at court as a master of disguise.' I tried to maintain my gravity. 'Moreover,' Timothy added, deeply affronted, 'I am not getting fat.'

'Of course not,' I soothed. 'Just a little bit plumper than you used to be. A plumper Plummer, shall we say? Now, do you want to speak to me for some reason?'

'Yes, but not here, where every fool in creation can see us.'

This was a gross exaggeration. Even on a hot summer's afternoon, Rownham Passage was hardly West Cheap on a festival day. Nor even on a wet Sunday morning, if it came to that. But I curbed my impatience with such posturing.

'All right,' I humoured him. 'There's a hut just behind you, where I've stabled my horse. We can go in there.'

'A horse?' he queried as I led the way. 'You have a horse? But, of course! You've come up in the world since last we met. Or so I've been told.'

'I've inherited a house,' I answered shortly, pushing open the door and leading the way inside. The cob whinnied, evidently pleased to know that he hadn't been forgotten. 'But no money to go with it. I still have to earn my daily bread by the sweat of my brow. And the horse is hired from the local stable.'

'All right! All right!' Timothy groped his way forward, temporarily blinded by the transition from bright sunshine to near total darkness. 'No offence intended. Your good fortune doesn't bother me. Although I don't suppose it's delighted too many of the good folk of Bristol.'

'True,' I agreed glumly, thinking of former friends like Burl Hodge, who were now little more than polite acquaintances. 'So, why do you want to see me? And why the secrecy? You're not usually this coy about advertizing your presence.'

'I am when I'm engaged on a highly sensitive job that requires diplomacy and finesse,' he retorted.

Once again, I restrained a smile. I'd forgotten just how pompous Timothy could be.

'Well? And what has that to do with me, pray?'

'This.' He prodded me in the chest. 'Keep your nose out of things that don't concern you, Roger!'

'What are you talking about? What things? And if you mean what I think you do, let me tell you that it's very much my concern. I was nearly murdered.'

'I know all that,' was the irritable rejoinder. 'But keep your nose out, all the same.' Timothy sighed. 'It was just one of fate's dirtier little tricks to land you right in the middle of this affair. I couldn't believe my eyes when I saw you in the alehouse. After you left, I got in conversation with your friend, the ferryman. A couple more beakers of ale soon loosened his tongue enough to learn the whole story. Fortunately, he still isn't completely convinced by your version of events.'

'Well, he should be,' I barked triumphantly. 'I've found a witness to what really happened.'

'Who?' Timothy's eager question instantly made me wary.

'Never you mind. That's my secret.'

I saw him clench his fists. The cob stirred uneasily.

'Now, look, Roger, I'm warning you! Go home and forget any of this ever happened. You haven't discovered a witness to your story. You're beginning to think it may all have been a dream . . .'

'Oh, no! I'm not admitting to anything of the sort,' I roared. 'I'm sick of being thought a fool!'

'Keep your voice down,' he begged, his own sinking to little more than a whisper. 'Try to forget what's happened. Stop talking about it. Stop discussing it with all and sundry. If anyone mentions it, just say you're bored with the subject. It's over. You're not interested. And, above all, stop prying and poking around this village. Stop asking questions. Because if you don't, I won't be answerable for the consequences. And I don't want anything to happen to you, Roger, I really don't. I've grown fond of you over the years, strange as that might seem. And Duke Richard would be most upset . . . No need to look like that. This has nothing to do with him. He still lives retired on his Yorkshire estates. I'm working for the King. Pity, but there it is. The quiet life and I don't mix.'

'That's all very well,' I said. 'But if Robin Avenel and his sister are involved, it's easy enough to guess that it has something to do with Henry Tudor.'

The Spymaster General managed both to nod and shake his head at the same time, quite a remarkable feat.

'Yes and no,' he grunted. 'There's more to it than that, my friend. You'll just have to take my word for it. It's not that I don't trust you,' he continued hastily, recalling past services that I had rendered the Crown, 'but you might inadvertently let something slip. You wouldn't mean to, but you might.'

'Have I ever, in the past?'

'Not wittingly, no. But you just can't keep your nose out of trouble. When you scent a mystery, you're like a dog after a rabbit. I daren't risk telling you. Be content with that.'

I was hurt, even though I had to admit the truth of what he said. But I was angry, too. It was my life, after all, that had been put in danger.

'I think I have a right . . .' I began hotly, but Timothy interrupted me without compunction.

'You have no rights at all where the safety of the realm is concerned. I'm warning you, Roger. Forget this entire episode ever happened. Go home to that wife and family of yours and, like I said, pretend it was all a dream.'

'Or?'

'Or you might get hurt. Or one of your children might get hurt. Or Adela – is that her name?'

I was beyond anger. I was furious.

'Don't you dare threaten me or mine, Timothy Plummer!' I could scarcely spit the words out fast enough. 'If necessary, I'll go to London and appeal to the King!'

The Spymaster laid a placatory hand on my arm.

'Calm down. Be sensible. You must realize as well as I do, that King Edward wouldn't lift a finger to protect you or yours if he thought his throne was in danger. Do as I ask, I'm begging you, and no one will get hurt.'

My temper cooled a little. 'Like that, is it?'

'Like that.'

I chewed my bottom lip. 'Very well,' I said after a pause for reflection. 'But I shall tell Adela the truth. She'll say nothing, particularly if she knows that doing so would jeopardize my life or those of the children.'

Timothy hesitated, then nodded. 'All right,' he agreed. 'I've met her. She seems a sensible woman. Far too sensible for you,' he added with gratuitous insult, but then grinned affectionately and squeezed my shoulder. 'Off you go now, lad, and take care.'

I led the cob outside and mounted. 'Take care yourself,' I told him.

He grinned and slapped the horse's rump. At the bend in the track, I slewed round in the saddle, but, as I had expected, he was nowhere to be seen.

I rode home through the softly shimmering landscape, watching the shadows lengthen and the grasses blacken in their path. It was cooler now, a soft breeze floating inland from the river. But my curiosity was on fire. Something was going on, but I wasn't allowed to know what it was, in spite of having, albeit unwittingly, become a part of it.

As I rode towards the Frome Bridge, someone was

approaching, also on horseback, from the opposite direction. With a jolt to my stomach, I recognized her directly. She was actually wearing the same brown sarcenet gown, while, behind her, rode Rowena Hollyns, demure in grey homespun and a white linen coif.

'Good evening, Mistress Alefounder,' I said through gritted teeth.

She inclined her head, but did not answer. From her demeanour, it would seem that she had never seen me before in all her life.

Eight

I would have made love to Adela that night – God knows I wanted to! – but she held me off, reminding me that tomorrow was Sunday and we should be at church. So, I had to content myself with holding her in my arms while I recounted my day's adventures.

This was the first chance I'd had since returning from Rownham Passage to be alone with her. Now, at last, the house was quiet, humans and animal exhausted by their own high spirits, asleep in their respective beds; Hercules snoring away in the kitchen, Elizabeth next door, Nicholas and Adam in the small chamber just above ours, for it had been decided during my absence, that our youngest child should join his half-brother on the thick goose-feather mattress that occupied most of the floor of the attic. Adela was tired of getting up each night to attend to his wants, and considered that removed from my snoring, his nights would be less disturbed. What Nicholas made of the arrangement, I didn't dare ask.

Adela was as alarmed by my intelligence as I had known she would be. She stared anxiously at me through the gloom.

'If those were Timothy Plummer's instructions, then promise me, Roger, that you'll stop your incessant meddling. I won't have you put anyone's life at risk. Do you understand me?'

'I don't suppose for a minute—' I began, but she interrupted me with a hand across my mouth.

'I'll leave you,' she threatened, 'if you endanger your own life or the children's.'

I tried insinuating a hand inside her nightrail. 'The Church doesn't approve of disobedient women.'

She permitted me to cup her breast, but made it plain that tonight that was as far as I was going to get.

'The Church doesn't approve of husbands who jeopardize the lives of their families, either,' she answered tartly.

She fell asleep quite quickly. I, on the other hand, lay awake for a long time, turning over the day's events in my head. The house was quiet, the noise and bustle of the streets stilled at last, the silence broken only by the occasional 'All's well!' of the Watch or the ululating cry of an owl. It was uncomfortably warm, and I envied Hercules the cool of the kitchen.

I knew I had to respect Adela's wishes. I was responsible for lives besides my own: it was the penalty for marriage and fatherhood ... Did I really mean penalty? But I was uneasily conscious that the sight of Rowena Honeyman had stirred old bachelor yearnings that I had long thought dead.

The word 'dead', however, brought me up short. The woman was a cold-blooded murderess. She would have helped her mistress drown me – had in fact aided and abetted Elizabeth Alefounder to that end. And under attack from Eamonn Malahide, she had retaliated with a dagger thrust that would not have disgraced a professional soldier. Once again, I recalled Gilbert Honeyman, a man of few, if any, moral scruples; yet somehow, the same description did not seem so apt when applied to his daughter. But what did I know of her? Nothing, except the manner in which Gilbert had spoken of her, and his concern for her welfare after his death.

The shadows of the room broke up and reformed as I drifted towards the edge of sleep. Rowena's face and figure swam mistily before me. She was wearing the blue brocade gown and red shoes. She reached out a hand to grasp one of mine, but just as I was about to take it, I realized she was clutching a dagger, whose evil-looking blade was dripping blood ...

I was suddenly wide awake, sitting bolt upright. I could swear that something had woken me ... Some movement ... Some noise ... And there it was again! The creaking of a stair.

I slid out of bed, trying not to disturb my wife, and reached for my cudgel. I tiptoed as quietly as possible towards the door, and, easing it ajar, was at once aware of a blast of air which must have originated from an open door or window downstairs. I crept on to the landing and began, stealthily, to descend.

The flight led down to a narrow passageway outside the kitchen. I could hear Hercules's snuffling and whining which, at any moment, would culminate in a series of ear-splitting barks. After that all hell would break loose as he protested against his incarceration, while an intruder invaded his home.

But I had no wish for my nocturnal visitor to be alerted and escape before I had time to see who he was. I knew the squeaky tread was near the bottom of the stairs, so I crept down as fast as I dared, but to no avail. By now, Hercules was making sufficient noise to waken the dead, and it was therefore only a matter of minutes before Adela called out to ask what was happening. Adam was screaming, and that intrepid duo, Elizabeth and Nicholas, were thundering down to join me. As I turned the bend in the staircase, I was just in time to see a cloaked and hooded figure disappear through the street door, and although I ran out, barefoot, he had already vanished. The Watch was nowhere to be seen. Are they ever, when you need them?

I returned indoors and, ignoring the questioning of my loved ones, knelt down to inspect the lock, peering into its mechanism.

Adela now appeared. 'Roger, what's going on?'

I straightened up. 'We must get a bolt for this door. Someone has managed to pick the lock.'

'How do you know?' My wife gave a sudden scream as she sighted Adam, who was negotiating a perilous descent of the stairs entirely on his own, his yelling having attracted no attention. He was unused to such treatment.

'Well, for a start,' I answered acidly, 'I locked this door before I went to bed and now it's open. And it hasn't been forced. So, someone managed to pick it. With what purpose, I'm unable to guess, but I suspect it wasn't to kiss us all goodnight. And secondly, I'm an expert at picking locks, myself. Nicholas Fletcher, a fellow novice at Glastonbury, taught me how. This one would have been easy.' The question is, who did it and why?'

'That's two questions,' Adela retorted huffily, preparing to shepherd the children back upstairs and settle them down again. 'And I must say that lock-picking is hardly an accomplishment I'd have expected you to acquire during your novitiate . . .'

She didn't continue, but made her way upstairs for the second time that night, carrying Adam, with the other two children trailing in her wake. I was aware that her bad temper, like mine, stemmed from acute anxiety as to why our home had been broken into. It was well known that we had nothing valuable enough to steal . . .

I almost shouted aloud, but restrained myself in the nick of time. The ring that I had found in the 'murder' house and subsequently forgotten all about! How could I have been so absent-minded? I could have – and probably should have – given it to Timothy Plummer, to whom it might have meant something.

But my moment of euphoria was short-lived as common sense reasserted itself. There was no way anyone could know that *I* had the ring. No one had seen me find it, and there was a good chance that its owner had no idea where or when it had been mislaid. The ring couldn't possibly be the reason for our intruder.

Hercules, who had been sniffing around the front door, whined suddenly and prodded something with his front paw.

'What is it, lad?' I stooped to examine his discovery, which he presented to me with all the air of an intelligent and highly trained bloodhound. He dropped it in my outstretched hand.

I was looking at a shoe made of very soft, scarlet leather.

I slept fitfully for the rest of the night; a sleep broken by dreams in which a blue brocade gown swept past me as I lay on the floor of the old Witherspoon house, revealing a glimpse of scarlet leather shoes.

Adela had been dead to the world when I finally crept

back to bed, so I had not woken her with the news of Hercules's find. But I showed it to her the following morning as we sat in bed, adjusting our minds and bodies to the rigours of the day ahead.

'A shoe?' She was incredulous. 'How could anyone lose a shoe? Unless it was too big, of course. But surely no one would set out to rob a house in shoes that were too large. Loose shoes can cause all sorts of difficulties. And accidents.'

'Precisely. But suppose a person removed the shoes in order to make less noise, placing them just inside the door—'

'Which he'd left open—'

'For a quick escape should he need it—'

'Which he did, thanks to Hercules!'

I felt somewhat annoyed at being denied my share of the credit. 'So, having been discovered, our thief turns and runs, grabbing his shoes, dashes outside only to find that, in his haste, he's left one behind. Does that make sense?'

Adela leaned against my shoulder. 'You're quite clever,' she conceded, 'when you want to be.'

I let that go, although I felt like the prophet in his own country: I didn't always get my due. I picked up the shoe from where it lay, like a drop of blood against the white counterpane, and handed it to my wife.

'Could that belong to a woman?' I asked.

'Do you really suspect the intruder might have been a woman? I thought you said it was a man.'

I tried to conjure up a mental picture of the figure I had seen disappearing through the door. An all-enveloping cloak and hood viewed from the back – what could that tell me with any certainty? In different circumstances, I would have sworn it was a man. Something in the general bearing, in the economy and decisiveness of movement seemed more masculine than feminine. But I had seen red shoes on one of my attacker's feet: Rowena Hollyns.

'I can't swear it was a man. So, what do you think? Could this shoe belong to a woman?'

'Too big for a woman. Oh, I know there *are* women with

big feet. My own aren't exactly dainty. But this is far too large.'

She frowned suddenly and bent to scrutinize the shoe more closely. I kissed the nape of her neck in a suggestive manner, but I could have saved myself the effort. I doubt if she even noticed. She turned her head abruptly, so that her nose nearly collided with mine.

'I know who this shoe belongs to,' she breathed excitedly. 'I've seen him wearing them. It's one of a pair belonging to Robin Avenel.'

'Are you sure?' I frowned. 'His shoes are usually far more fashionable than this. You know what a dandy he is. He likes those ridiculously long pikes. You can't even walk in them unless the toes are fastened round your knees with fancy gilt chains. The pike on this thing can't be more than half an inch.'

'Not all his shoes are the same,' Adela argued. 'It stands to reason that someone as wealthy as he is has a number of different pairs. But I recollect seeing him in these some months ago, when I met him one day in High Street. He was wearing them with particoloured hose in purple and green. Robin never has had any taste in clothes. Why are you doubtful?'

'One of the women who attacked me was wearing red shoes.'

My wife shrugged. 'That proves nothing. Lots of people have red shoes, women as well as men. Another reason I recall this pair is that they have gold embossing around the toes. Look!'

She held up the shoe for me to make a closer inspection, and, sure enough, beneath the accretion of dirt and staining, I could see the glint of gold pressed into the leather. I got out of bed and carried it over to the window, where I opened the shutters. As the morning sunshine flooded the bedchamber, I plainly saw the embossed gold Greek key pattern. There seemed no further room for doubt that it belonged to Robin Avenel.

But I had no time to consider the matter further, as the arrival of Adam and Nicholas from upstairs, followed almost immediately by Elizabeth, debarred Adela and me from any further private conversation. The two elder children, far from being upset by the events of the night, were only too anxious to discuss such an unlooked-for adventure, while Adam, still deeply reproachful about his banishment to the attic, tried to clamber back into his crib, which remained standing against one wall.

Although I had not opened the windows as well as the shutters, the noise of the city's church bells, all tolling at once – but not in harmony – penetrated the room with deafening clarity. They were ringing for Prime, warning us that the day had begun. I put the shoe away in a small wall cupboard near the head of the bed before any of the children saw it and demanded to know to whom it belonged and where it had come from. Later, when Adela had shooed them back to their own rooms and gone downstairs, I took the ring out of my pouch and placed it inside the shoe. Then I locked the cupboard and removed the key, which I hid in my secret place, beneath a loose floorboard under the window.

That morning, it was the turn of Saint Giles to be graced by the presence of our parish priest and the nave of the church was crowded. Adela, the children and I arrived just as the five-minute bell ceased tolling and consequently had to stand right at the front, close to the altar. Throughout my life, I have frequently observed this phenomonen: the later you are, the more prominent your position. The truth is that the majority of people prefer to herd to the back of churches, of courts – of any place, in short, where being at the front means being under the eye of Authority.

There are, of course, glaring exceptions to this general rule; persons who consider themselves so important that they assume the rest of the world cannot wait to obtain a glimpse of them, and the Avenels were just such people. Gregory Alefounder, Marianne Avenel's father and Elizabeth Alefounder's uncle by marriage, was another. Gregory was a big man of florid complexion, who always carried the scent of the brewery with him in his clothes. It was not unpleasant; indeed, I knew some men who positively liked to stand beside him just to inhale the smell. The only feature he had in common with his dainty, kittenish daughter was a pair of fine grey eyes; other than that, there was no physical resemblance between them whatsoever. Marianne apparently favoured the distaff side.

That morning, Gregory stood beside his son-in-law's father, Peter Avenel. The soap manufacturer was somewhat dwarfed in size by the brewer, but he was plainly unaware of any other inferiority. Like Robin, Peter was always dressed in the height of fashion, regardless of whether it suited him or not. Today, both father and son wore doublets that were almost indecently short, the elder in peacock blue, the younger in jade green, revealing codpieces decorated with dangling laces in one case and bows of ribbon in the other. I saw quite a few men in the congregation sniggering behind their hands, numerous ladies and goodies carefully averting their eyes, and was unsurprised to note the look of contempt on Luke Prettywood's face as he surveyed Marianne's husband and father-in-law.

But the sight of Robin Avenel had aroused all my former uneasiness. I had never liked him, and knew him to be vain and self-important, but I nevertheless found it hard to imagine him creeping into anyone's house in the middle of the night, intent on some felonious purpose. I could well imagine him ordering or paying someone else to do so, however, feeling sure that his conceit would prevent him from undertaking so risky or so criminal an act himself. Robin might be dipping his toes in treasonable waters, but he would take all necessary care to cover his back.

And, although I had said nothing to Adela, nor had any intention of doing so, a cold certainty was beginning to grip me that last night's intruder had been bent on murder. Mine. And with equal conviction, I knew he had to be the man whose voice I had heard, but whose face and involvement in this affair remained a mystery. He had come to finish what his two accomplices had tried, but failed to do.

How I had reached this conclusion, I was unsure, but certainty was growing. As for the shoe, I accepted Adela's word that it belonged to Robin Avenel, but could only think that he had lent it and its fellow to the stranger for some reason. For, whatever was going on, Robin was in the thick of it – that, at least, seemed obvious.

Braving the indignant and reproachful stare of the priest, I glanced around to see who else was present, and was rewarded with the sight of Rowena standing quietly behind Elizabeth Alefounder. She wore a simple blue homespun gown – definitely not brocade, but blue, nevertheless – and her coifed head was bent devoutly in prayer. Her mistress was more flamboyantly dressed today, having abandoned the brown sarcenet for green velvet and an even more elaborate girdle: sapphire-blue leather studded for its entire length with what looked like tiny emeralds. It spoke of money; a lot of money. The sort of wealth that can sometimes engender boredom, when there is nothing left to want or to strive for. (The sort of boredom, needless to say, that Adela and I would never experience.) Was that the reason Elizabeth Alefounder had decided to embroil herself in politics? Or were the Avenels a family of convinced Lancastrian sympathies? I had never heard them named as such in a strongly Yorkist city such as Bristol, where it would surely have been noticed, but many supporters of the late King Henry had learned to dissemble their feelings and bide their time.

Though bide their time for what, I could never make out. Henry Tudor's claim to the crown, as I think I've mentioned before, was tenuous indeed, descending as it did through the bastard line of John of Gaunt. And rumours lately coming into Bristol, disseminated by the many Breton sailors whose ships tied up along the Backs, suggested that the Tudor was of a sickly constitution, recently suffering from several bouts of a debilitating illness, the cause of which his physicians found hard to diagnose. A situation doubtless worrying to his adherents, however much it might have cheered the rest of us.

The Mass was over. The miracle of transubstantiation had taken place: the bread and wine of the Eucharist had been transformed into the Blood and Body of Christ within each member of the congregation. (The Lollards would have us believe that this is impossible, a heresy I half subscribe to myself, although I have always kept such ideas strictly private:

I shall be dead when these records are read. If they ever are.) As we turned to make our slow way out of Saint Giles, Adela was waylaid by a neighbour's wife, a pleasant enough soul who seemed not to begrudge us our good fortune, and I found myself standing to one side, ignored, waiting for the conversation to come to an end. Adam was held in his mother's arms, while the other nosy pair were listening with rapt attention to what their elders were saying.

Glancing round, I saw that I was standing close to the steep flight of steps leading down to the crypt. On a sudden impulse, and as no one appeared to be even slightly interested in my movements, I descended to the vault below. The same smell of must and decay that I had noticed previously met my nostrils as my eyes grew accustomed to the gloom. Cautiously, I inched my way forward, past the coffined rows of Christian dead and on into the second chamber of what had once been the synagogue cellars. Here, everything was as I remembered it from Friday morning, with all the parish's unwanted bits of furniture and other rejected items ranged along the walls. Suddenly, I recollected what Jack Nym had told me – that the preceding week he had brought a bed and some other bits and pieces here for Robin Avenel.

Now, beds were as valuable a commodity in my young days as they are today, in my dotage. I was intrigued, therefore, to discover what sort of bed it could be that even a rich man could discard with impunity, especially with a household as large as Master Avenel's. But although I looked long and hard amongst the rickety chairs, bales of rags, stools with two legs that were meant to have three, handle-less pots and pans and all the rest of those things that 'might come in useful one day' and so were hoarded rather than actually thrown away (to the greater profit of Saint Giles), I could find no bed of any shape or size, broken or dismantled.

To begin with, I thought I must have missed it in the gloom, but a second search, after my eyes had adjusted to the crypt's dim light, convinced me that there was nothing there that resembled a headboard or a mattress or the empty wooden frame of a bed. So I walked forward, under the second archway and into the third chamber of the synagogue

93

cellar, where I had seen Luke Prettywood and Marianne Avenel embracing the day before yesterday. But even though it was darker than ever in there, I could see that it was empty. The dust, rising in little clouds wherever I put my feet, made me sneeze violently.

I had turned to look behind me, back the way I had come, when a sudden noise made me spin round sharply. But the chamber was deserted except for myself. I was alone. There was nothing or no one there. After a few seconds, during which I stood stock still, almost afraid to move, I regained my courage and prowled around the room's perimeter, trailing one hand along the rough stone walls that oozed with damp and slime. I tried to recall the nature of the noise I'd heard, the quality and density of the sound, but, as always in such cases, it grew more difficult to recapture the more I thought about it. In the end, the best I could say was that it had had a kind of hollow resonance – a thump and yet not a thump.

Something – a door, perhaps – closing? I remembered the story of the Jews' secret chamber, and the local belief that had persisted for so many years after their expulsion that it had contained their abandoned hoard of gold and silver. Prompted into fresh action, I started rapping the walls, but all I got for my pains were bruised and bleeding knuckles, which, I felt, served me right for being such a credulous fool.

The silence now was all-encompassing. I could no longer hear even the distant murmur of voices from the church above. There was no living being down there except myself, only the sad ghosts of a long-gone past to keep me company and play tricks with my imagination, mocking me with phantom noises made by the dead.

I turned on my heel and strode the length of the crypt, ascending thankfully into the sunbeamed quiet of the nave.

Nine

For the next ten days I schooled myself to follow my own advice; to keep my nose clean and not to meddle in matters that were not my concern.

But they *were* my concern. I had been assaulted, nearly murdered, and the two women responsible were living quietly in the next street, going about their business, the model of two well-respected citizens. Still, as I say, I taught myself to ignore their existence; and on those occasions when it was impossible to do so, I touched my forelock with all the humility that was expected of a humble pedlar whose material good fortune had in no way enhanced his social status. (And he had better not forget it!)

All the same, it lifted my spirits to note the inconspicuous, but assiduous attention being paid to the Avenel household by Richard Manifold. It was heart-warming to remember the number of times in the past few days that I had met him either sauntering up or meandering down Broad Street, apparently looking at nothing in particular, but in actual fact keeping a close watch on the comings and goings in Alderman Weaver's old house. And once, I ran into – literally – a heavily disguised Timothy Plummer on the corner of Broad Street and Corn Street. Well, he thought he was heavily disguised. I recognized him instantly. I apologized for stepping on his foot; he glared and called me a name I prefer to forget, but I remained faithful to my promise and pretended we were strangers. But I had no doubt as to his purpose in being there: he was observing the Avenel house on the opposite side of the street.

Fortunately for my peace of mind, I had other things to think about. We were approaching Midsummer Eve and Midsummer's Day, with all their attendant jollifications.

On June 22nd, the day before Midsummer Eve, the rose sellers were out in force on the streets of Bristol, peddling their overblown wares. But, as I had told Jack Nym, the Midsummer Rose needs to be a flower of simple proportions. The outcome of 'He loves me, He loves me not' should never be left to chance. In the past it had not worried Adela when I brought her a dog rose from the hedgerow. Last year, it was true, she had mischievously started off with 'He loves me not', thus altering the desired resolution, but she had done so laughingly, teasingly, and had been prepared to demonstrate her affection afterwards. This year, however, I was not so sure of her reaction to any overture on my part. We seemed to be drifting further apart with each passing day, while our nights, when we weren't sleeping, were spent in a constant passage at arms, with me attacking, she defending. In the past, I would have taken my troubles to Burl Hodge and received sound advice in return, but Burl's jealousy had come between us. We were no longer friends.

Instead, I found myself confiding in, of all people, Luke Prettywood.

June 22nd that year, as I remember, was extremely hot, with a hint of thunder in the air. I had had a long, tiring day and was making my way homewards through the broad meadows below the castle, carrying, as well as my almost empty pack, a bedraggled and tattered-looking bunch of dog roses. As I sat down for a well-earned rest on the banks of the Frome, Luke Prettywood arrived. He was in charge of a handcart laden with barrels and pulled by half a dozen stout and sweating young apprentices. These youths set to work filling the barrels with water from the river, while Luke sat down beside me and watched their labours with the malevolent enjoyment of the foreman.

'What's going on?' I enquired.

Luke grinned. 'It's the city's Great Red Book again, isn't it? Bristol brewers ain't allowed to draw water from the public conduits for fear of upsetting the supply to our beloved private citizens, who might not be able to wash, or even take a bath, as often as they'd like.' He roared with laughter. 'So we take water from the Frome. It's what gives Bristol beer its special taste.' He regarded me with interest. 'What's wrong? You look like you've lost a shilling and picked up a groat.' He added shrewdly, 'The wife I'd guess, by all the signs.'

'What makes you say that?'

He smiled the insouciant smile of the carefree bachelor. 'When men look as glum as you do, it's never anything else.'

'Never?'

'Well, hardly ever. Want to tell me about it? The lads'll be some time yet.' And he shouted a word of encouragement to the toiling apprentices. They glowered at him in return.

I hardly knew him. I should have said nothing. But I needed to unburden myself to someone. When I'd finished, he nodded understandingly.

'Avoiding children is always a problem,' he acknowledged with the world-weary air of a man twice his age. 'I'm not married myself, but as you know I'm not celibate, either.' He gave me a nudge and a wink before fishing in the leather pouch attached to his belt. 'Ever seen one of these?' He held out his hand.

On his palm lay what appeared to be a sheath for a knife blade, except that it was made from very fine skin or, more likely, a membrane. A calf's or pig's bladder, I reckoned after a closer inspection. I had heard about these things, but had never seen one. All the same, I could guess its function by its shape. I also knew that generally they were for use only by the nobility, and not for the likes of Luke Prettywood or me. The proliferation of peasant stock was necessary for the successful running of the country. Who else would perform menial tasks, or be sent as common foot soldiers in time of war?

I asked Luke where he'd got it and how much it had cost.

He grinned. 'There's an apothecary that makes them. For a price, naturally. He has a shop near the castle, on the corner of the Pithay and Gropecunt Lane.' Handy for the brothels, then. 'Funny little humpbacked fellow called Witherspoon.'

Witherspoon! An apothecary with a shop near the castle! I really should have to take myself in hand. Goody Tallboys had told me of Witherspoon, and I had forgotten all about him. Of course, I had promised Timothy Plummer and, more importantly, Adela, not to pursue any enquiries that might have to do with the events at Rownham Passage. But this was different. I needed to visit the apothecary, I told myself, on a personal matter.

'Does it work?' I asked. 'Or wouldn't you know?'

Luke chuckled. 'Oh, I know all right.'

I quirked an eyebrow. 'Mistress Avenel?'

The chuckle slid into a self-conscious laugh. 'Now why should you think that?'

'I saw the pair of you in the crypt of Saint Giles that day. Besides, it's general gossip.'

He looked uneasy. 'Master Avenel knows nothing, I'll swear.'

The apprentices had finished filling the barrels and loading them back on to the handcart, and were now taking their ease on the river bank. I lowered my voice to a whisper.

'Then you and the fair Marianne had better be more careful.'

Luke gnawed his thumb, looking troubled. 'You wouldn't say anything to Master Avenel, would you, chapman?'

'Of course not!' I exclaimed, revolted by the very idea of myself in the role of informer. 'You and the lady aren't planning anything foolish, are you?'

He gave what was meant to sound like an amused, man-of-the-world laugh, but which sounded somewhat hollow to my ears.

'No, no! In truth, I rather fancy that maid-companion of Mistress Alefounder. And I rather think she favours me.'

'A very beautiful woman,' I agreed, subduing an impulse to punch him on the nose. I saw my opening. 'Do you see much of her and Mistress Alefounder?'

'Mistress Alefounder calls in at the brewery now and then. Her late husband was Master Alefounder's nephew, you know.'

I nodded. 'And what do you think of her? There are rumours that she and her brother are loyal to the Lancastrian faction.'

Luke Prettywood shrugged. 'I wouldn't know about that. I'm not interested in politics, myself. Although, now you mention it, I did hear Master Gregory the other day telling her to guard her tongue, and he wouldn't have that sort of seditious talk in his brewery.'

'And Mistress Hollyns?'

He looked puzzled. 'What about her?' He had already forgotten his vaunted interest in Rowena and was pulling petals off a daisy like any lovelorn youth. 'She loves me! She loves me not! She loves me . . .'

I remembered my wilting dog roses and proffered one. 'It's Midsummer's Day the day after tomorrow,' I reminded him. 'An occasion for the women to play at that game.'

He turned up his nose at my offering and glanced over at the apprentices, two of whom had fallen asleep. 'Time we were getting back,' he said, jumping to his feet. 'I hope things go well for you at home, chapman.'

'And you take care!' I warned him, but he merely laughed.

'Oh, I can look after myself,' he assured me, waving a hand in farewell.

I hoped he was right. As for me, I threw away the almost dead dog roses and decided that this Midsummer's Day I would live dangerously and buy Adela a rose from a street seller, waiting with baited breath while she denuded it of petals. 'He loves me! He loves me not!' The answer would be unknown to both of us.

But now I had another visit to make before returning home.

It would have been easy to miss the entrance to the apothecary's shop on the corner of Gropecunt Lane, so discreet was it. Indeed, I walked the entire length of the street without noticing it, and it was only on the return journey, steadfastly ignoring the invitations of the madams seated at the doors of their respective whorehouses, that I found it, just where Luke Prettywood had told me it would be.

The shop was as dark and dingy inside as it was outside, the light which filtered through a single, dirty window augmented merely by two miserable tallow candles standing on the counter. There was a peculiar smell about the place, too, like a very old, very dead rat. I gagged and wished I still had my roses.

Once my eyes had adjusted to the gloom, I was aware of being watched. A small man, about half my height, with a bowed back and a disfiguring hump, was regarding me from behind the counter with a pair of bright, shrewd eyes. When he spoke, his voice was low and cultured. Not at all what I had expected.

'Did you want something, young man?'

'Er . . . Master James Witherspoon?'

'No. I'm Silas Witherspoon. James was my father. He's been dead these fifteen years. What would you be wanting with him?'

'Ah! Well . . . Nothing really. Not if he's dead, that is. But you may be able to help me.'

I approached the counter. The unpleasant aroma became stronger. Silas Witherspoon saw me wrinkle my nose and laughed.

'I'm boiling up my winter remedy for chilblains. A rather evil-smelling concoction of different fungi which, when it cools, is very much more efficacious than spiders' webs. Not so cheap, of course,' he added with a smile, 'but it works faster. Can I persuade you to buy some? No? Ah well! It is rather difficult to think of winter in this heat, I agree. So! As I say, my father's dead, but if I can be of any assistance . . .'

I hesitated for a second, then asked, 'Are you the present owner of the old "murder" house at Rownham Passage?'

'I am.' He frowned. 'This is most strange, you know. That place has been like a millstone around the neck of both my father and myself. No one has wanted to know about in half a century. Now you are the third person to enquire about it in the past few weeks.'

'The third? Who was the first?'

'I'm afraid I not at liberty to tell you that. I was sworn to secrecy.'

'Then let me guess. Was it Master Avenel of Broad Street?'

He looked disconcerted. 'I . . . No . . . I mean, I can't say. I told you, I promised secrecy.'

'That means yes then. What did Master Avenel want with the house? Did he want to rent it? How long for?'

'Please! I've explained. I can tell you nothing.'

'Did it have to do with a woman? A man? Or both?' I persisted.

'Both,' the apothecary answered involuntarily, then bit his lip. 'Damnation! Look, will you please go away! I've already said too much.'

'But not enough.' I rested my elbows on the dusty counter. 'All right! Who was the other person asking about the house at Rownham Passage?'

Silas Witherspoon sighed. 'I don't know. And that's the truth. A little fellow, not a great deal taller than myself. He's not from hereabouts, judging by his speech. London, I reckon. He had a thin, straggly beard that he kept fingering, as though unused to finding it on his chin, and a pair of those "scissor" spectacles that you perch on the bridge of your nose. They kept falling off.' Timothy Plummer, master of disguise! It could be no other! 'He was dressed like an out-of-work wool comber, but had a gold ring set with a very fine agate stone.' Typical!

'And what did he want to know?' I asked, adding with heavy sarcasm, 'Or are you sworn to secrecy about that, as well?'

'No.' Silas Witherspoon gave me a blinding smile that transformed his ugly little face into something close to beauty. 'But I don't suppose he could foresee that some long-nosed pedlar would be making enquiries about him, or he, too, might have instructed me to hold my tongue.'

'But as he didn't . . .'

'He simply wanted to know the same as you. Had my house at Rownham Passage been let to anyone at any time in the past few weeks. I told him what I told you. I'm not at liberty to say.'

'Did he ask about Master Avenel by name?'

'He did. And got the same answer.'

Well, Timothy was no fool. Like me, he could work out how many beans made five. And unlike me, with his superior knowledge of what was going on, he could complete the picture.

'I'm sorry,' Silas Witherspoon added, without much sign

101

of regret, 'that I can't be of greater assistance. Are you desirous of hiring the house yourself, perhaps?'

'No, no! Heaven forfend!' I replied, rather more rudely than I'd intended. 'I do have reasons for asking about it, but I'm afraid I'm not at liberty to divulge them.' He gave his lopsided smile again, acknowledging a hit. 'However,' I went on uncomfortably, 'there is something else I understand you might be able to help me with.'

I glanced over my shoulder to make certain that no one had entered the shop behind me, then leaned even further forward across the counter.

'Indeed?' he queried, but there was an expression in his eyes that told me he already guessed what I was going to say.

I explained my present domestic predicament as quickly as I could in a sort of embarrassed mumble. 'So you see,' I concluded, 'neither my wife nor I wish for another child for some while yet. Maybe not for a considerable time. I've seen a sample of . . . of your work. The . . . the sheath. I wondered if you . . . er . . . would make one for me?'

'I can make you one, certainly,' he agreed. 'But they are not easy to sew. It will cost you a lot of money.'

'How much?'

He named a sum that would normally have kept me and my family in food for a week or more. I thought about it, but only for a moment. Unknown to Adela, I had a small store of money which I had salted away for emergencies. The question was, could this count as an emergency? I decided that it could.

'Very well,' I agreed. 'I'll pay on receipt.'

'That's understood. Do you require small, medium or large?'

'Large, naturally,' I said, affronted.

'I thought you might,' was the enigmatic response. 'When it's ready, do you want it sent? Or will you collect it?'

'Oh, I'll collect it,' I answered hurriedly.

'This day next week, then.' He half turned towards a rickety shelf behind him, on which reposed what seemed to be a small stack of parchment, curling at the edges.

'I have a very good love manual, if you should need one. It contains splendid advice from a number of well known people. Arnoldus de Villanova, for example, writing in the last century, advises a lover to always be sensitive to his woman's needs, and suggests only caressing her breasts while she sleeps, to save her embarrassment.' What a spoilsport! 'Then, in our own time, the eminent physician, Anthonis Guainerius, recommends men should kiss with "sweet sucking of lips".' I could go along with that. 'And Hildegard of Bingen describes making love like "a stag thirsting for the fountain, the lover racing swiftly to his mate, and she to him. She like a threshing floor, pounded by his many strokes and brought to heat when the grains are threshed inside her".'

I croaked, 'Hildegard of Bingen? Are you sure?'

Silas was emphatic. 'Oh, yes. She didn't just write sacred music and verse, you know.'

Obviously not! But it left me wondering what on earth they got up to in those foreign nunneries three and a half centuries ago.

'Well, do you want it?' The apothecary lifted the folio off the shelf and, holding it by its rotting laces, shook it free of dust and dead flies.

I refused as politely as I could. Silas looked disappointed and returned it to its former resting place.

'That's up to you. But I think you'd have found it useful. I'll see you in a week's time, then.'

I tottered out into the brilliant sunshine and the stench of the summer streets.

I went home, confident that the weight of my purse would guarantee me the warmest of welcomes. Not that Adela was mercenary, you understand, but with the midsummer festivities almost upon us, there were bound to be extra expenses. But although I received a kiss and several words of commendation for my day's efforts, there was a hint of coolness in Adela's general attitude that I found difficult to explain.

Difficult, that is, until she said frostily, 'She's been waiting to see you. I've put her in the parlour. I'll bring you both in a drink.'

103

'Who's waiting to see me?' I asked. But suddenly I could guess. My wife's chilly demeanour suggested only one name. 'Mistress Hollyns. She called about half an hour ago. I told her I didn't know how long you'd be, but she insisted on staying in the hope of your early return.' Adela gave a small, tight smile. 'It seems she's in luck.'

'I didn't ask her to call,' I protested.

'No?'

The monosyllable conveyed a world of disbelief. I could see that it would take time and skill to appease my wife and convince her of the truth. But my first priority was to get rid of Rowena.

The parlour was a smaller, snugger room than the hall, but both were considerably less well furnished than when the house had belonged to Edward Herepath. In the hall, the only thing of any opulence was the big, open hearth with its intricately carved stone mantel, picked out in shades of red and blue paint. Otherwise the room remained empty. But for the parlour we had managed to buy a carved armchair – second-hand – and rescued a flat-lidded linen chest from the central drain in High Street, where it had been thrown to rot along with the maggot-infested meat and decaying vegetables. Some people have always had more money than sense. Adela had brightened up both pieces with hand-woven green and yellow tapestries, and made sure that the floor rushes were changed daily. The broad window seat was clean, but bare. I could still remember a time when it had been adorned with velvet cushions, and when the floor had boasted rugs, not reeds.

As I entered, Rowena rose from her perch on the very edge of the chair and made me a slight, formal curtsey. She gave no indication that we had ever met before, either in the distant or the more recent past.

'Master Chapman?' she asked.

My patience snapped. 'You know very well who I am. I was talking to you only the ten days or so ago. You didn't seem to have any difficulty recognizing me then.'

The colour surged up beneath the delicate skin.

'I . . . I'm sorry,' she stammered. 'I didn't . . . I mean . . .'

She broke off and, to my horror, the blue eyes brimmed with tears.

'No! I'm sorry,' I apologized. 'Forgive me! That was unpardonably rude. Please . . .' Almost without realizing what I was doing, I stepped towards her and embraced her gently. 'Don't cry,' I murmured.

It was inevitable that Adela should walk into the parlour at that precise moment, carrying a tray with two beakers of her elderflower wine.

I stood there like the miserable fool I was, knocked sideways by the realization that I had just put my marriage in jeopardy, and that my long-dreamed-of ambition to hold Rowena Honeyman – Hollyns – in my arms meant absolutely nothing to me now that I had finally achieved it.

Adela made no comment. She put the tray down on top of the chest and left, closing the parlour door quietly behind her. She hadn't looked directly at me or our visitor, but she could not have avoided seeing us, nevertheless.

Rowena angrily released herself and refused my offer of refreshment. She had stopped crying, and now had her emotions well under control. I didn't delude myself for a second that I was responsible for her unhappiness, but undoubtedly my abruptness had been the immediate cause of her distress.

'So? What can I do for you, Mistress Hollyns?' I asked, motioning her to take a seat again.

She declined, standing stiff and straight beside the chair, one hand resting lightly on its arm.

'I am here merely as an envoy for Mistress Alefounder,' she said. 'She would be pleased if you would call on her this evening, sometime after supper and before curfew. She feels she owes you an explanation.'

'And you? Do you feel that you owe me an explanation, also?'

She stared. 'I don't know what you mean.'

I sneered. 'Not so honest as your mistress, eh? Very well! Tell Mistress Alefounder I'll wait upon her after supper, between five and six o'clock, at Master Avenel's house in Broad Street.'

There seemed nothing more to be said, so I escorted her to the street door and stood watching as she turned in the direction of Bell Lane. Then I went back inside and made my way to the kitchen in search of Adela.

Ten

We made our peace, after a fashion.

I grovelled. Adela admitted that she had not been as affectionate as she might have been of late. In short, we both blamed ourselves rather than each other.

Supper was in preparation. Adam, seated in a corner, was unusually quiet as he investigated his bare feet with studied concentration. Elizabeth and Nicholas were upstairs re-enacting the Battle of Hastings, if the shouting and stampeding feet were anything to judge by.

'So what did Mistress Hollyns want?' Adela asked, dropping chopped vegetables into a pot of boiling water. But when I told her of Mistress Alefounder's invitation, she turned to look at me, genuinely worried. 'You won't go, of course,' she said.

'Why ever not?'

'Because it's obviously a trap of some sort.' She came across and put her hands on my shoulders, giving them a little shake. 'For heaven's sake, Roger, the woman has tried to kill you once already.'

'She isn't going to murder me in her brother's house!' I protested. 'Especially when she must realize that I would have told you where I'm going.'

'She could have you waylaid somewhere. Bell Lane, perhaps? The houses there are closer together than most.'

'In that case, I'll go by Corn Street. There's always plenty of activity there of an evening on account of the Green Lattis.' I put my arms around her, half expecting a rebuff. But none came, although she made no move to respond. 'I have to find out what she wants, sweetheart. You must see that.'

107

Adela sighed. She would not attempt to dissuade me further. That was not her way of doing things. She was far too shrewd for that.

Supper was a quiet meal, the two older children having exhausted themselves with playing. Adam, tied into his little chair, was niggly but not obstreperous, as he so often was. And Adela and I were both preoccupied with our own concerns. The memory of Rowena Hollyns, and of my arms about her, still lay between us.

We discussed the coming festivities of the next two days, and my wife reminded me that we had to be up before dawn the following morning, Midsummer Eve, in order to gather the necessary herbs with which to ward off midnight's evil spirits. I groaned inwardly, as I frequently did, at the practice of these ancient customs, whose origins were lost in the misty past of our Saxon and Celtic forebears. But I acquiesced meekly, knowing how much their observance meant to Adela.

It was well past five o'clock before I made my way to Broad Street and knocked on the door of Robin Avenel's house. While I stood waiting, I reflected it would once have been Marjorie Dyer, then Dame Pernelle, Rob Short or Ned Stoner who answered my summons, or perhaps even Alison Weaver herself. But Marjorie and Alison were both dead, Rob and Ned had found new masters and Dame Pernelle had gone to live with her sister, Alice, in London. This evening the door was opened by a young maid who was a stranger to me.

'I wish to see Mistress Alefounder,' I said politely. 'She's expecting me. I'm Roger Chapman.'

The girl eyed me up and down, rather suspiciously I thought. Then she sniffed and held the door wide.

'You'd better come in,' she conceded reluctantly.

I reflected that I must be losing my touch; my irresistible boyish charm had failed to work its magic.

I was left to kick my heels in the hall while the girl went in search of Mistress Alefounder. I looked about me. How familiar it all was; the windows, giving on to Broad Street, shuttered below but the top halves fitted with rare and expensive glass panes; the doorposts and the ends of the roof beams carved in the likenesses of birds and flowers and picked out in red and gold; and the beautifully carved staircase spiralling upwards to the floor above. The two armchairs, which had stood on either side of the fireplace, had given way to a single, elaborately decorated, high-backed settle, while rushes and dried flowers had been discarded as floor covering in favour of crimson and blue woven rugs.

'Oh! It's you!' exclaimed a voice. 'What are you doing here?'

I spun round to confront Marianne Avenel. She was dressed for going out, with a light cloak clasped around her shoulders over a dress of emerald-green sarcenet and a jewelled belt that served to emphasize her slender waist and hips. Her winged headdress and veil were also made of silk, and I noticed for the first time that her eyebrows had been modishly plucked. Unlike her husband, however, she was sensible enough to avoid the extremes of fashion and had refused to shave her forehead or to ruin her complexion with applications of white lead.

'I'm waiting for Mistress Alefounder,' I said. 'She's asked to see me. Mistress Hollyns brought the message this afternoon.'

Marianne looked puzzled and would plainly have liked to question me further, except that she was in a hurry to be gone. She hesitated for a second or two, then wished me a hasty, if somewhat unwilling, farewell and vanished through the door.

She was not a moment too soon. As it closed, Robin Avenel descended the stairs, shouting, 'Marianne!' He pulled up short at the sight of me.

'What are you doing here?' he demanded, echoing his wife.

I was growing tired of this.

'Why don't you ask your sister?' I snapped. 'She's the one who sent for me.'

'Oh.' He seemed as nonplussed as his wife had been, but a great deal more worried by the information. 'Why?' he asked.

'I have no idea.'

We stared at one another, me in my dirty working hose and jerkin, he a particoloured vision in orange and white. It made my eyes hurt just to look at him.

'Oh,' he said again, then enquired, 'You haven't seen Mistress Avenel by any chance?'

'She's just gone out. Didn't she tell you?'

'No,' he answered with a scowl that boded no good for the absent Marianne.

'Gone to visit a friend,' I suggested.

I could guess which one. And by the look on his face, so could he. But then Master Robin proved me wrong by exclaiming angrily, 'It's that Jenny Hodge! I've told Marianne, I won't have her associating with the low-born wife of a tenter. I warned Burl Hodge about it, too. Told him to put a stop to it, but all I got was a mouthful of abuse. Said his wife was quite good enough to be the friend of a brewer's daughter and the daughter-in-law of a sudsman. He called my father a sudsman!' Robin strode towards the door. 'I shall go and see Hodge at once to know why he hasn't obeyed my instructions.' Then he paused, remembering that I was there to visit his sister. He turned, anxiety once again creasing his face. But he was saved the trouble of interrogating me further.

'Ah! Master Chapman!'

A voice sounded behind me, and Elizabeth Alefounder emerged from the kitchen quarters, as cool and unruffled as ever.

'What do you want with the pedlar?' her brother demanded before she could speak again.

She gave Robin an icy stare. 'That is between him and me. Come into the parlour, chapman. We can be private there.'

She was evidently fully at home in her brother's house and had no compunction in acting as though she were its mistress. I could see by Robin's expression that he resented this attitude, but also that he was afraid of her – or afraid of what she had dragged him into. His voice rose squeakily when he addressed her.

'I'm entitled to know what's going on in my own home. I won't be ignored. If it's about—'

'Be quiet, you fool!' Elizabeth Alefounder spoke quietly, but her tone would have chilled Lucifer in his inferno. 'Leave this to me. You'd better go and look for that wife of yours. The saints alone know what she's up to.'

But her brother was not to be fobbed off so easily. His overstretched nerves suddenly broke and he screamed, 'This is all your fault, do you hear me?' And he threw himself at her, violently pummelling her shoulder.

I was so astonished by such infantile behaviour in a grown man that it was a second or two before I moved to go to her assistance. But Elizabeth Alefounder had no need of help from me. She reacted so rapidly that I could not really see how she managed it, but the next moment, Robin's right arm was twisted up behind his back and he was whimpering in pain. She was a very formidable woman. But then, I already knew that.

Mistress Alefounder released her brother and he fell to the floor, sobbing wildly. She gave him an enigmatic glance that I found hard to define; a considering look, as though she were coming to some sort of a decision about him. I found it quite unnerving.

She turned to me. 'This way, Master Chapman, if you please.' And she led me into the parlour.

Here again, the furnishings had changed since the last time I had stood in this room, but it was still the same stuffy and airless little chamber that I remembered, especially in summer. I could feel the perspiration starting to course down my back.

My companion indicated a joint stool with a carved, acanthus-leaf edging, so I folded up my tall frame and sat down, feeling awkward. She herself took the armchair opposite. She was now higher than I was, putting me at a disadvantage, which, of course, was what she had intended. I stared at her defiantly, waiting for her to begin.

This, to my surprise, she was finding difficult to do.

'You're . . . You're not a rich man, Master Chapman. Or so I believe,' she managed at last.

'No,' I answered coldly, 'but I'm a live one. No thanks to you and Mistress Hollyns.'

111

She looked startled at first, presumably by my plain speaking, but then smiled with relief that I had brought the subject into the open. She lifted a green satin purse that I had noticed earlier, dangling from her girdle, and shook it. It chinked richly, and when the drawstring was released, a stream of gold coins cascaded into the palm of her hand.

'This is all yours,' she said, 'if, from now on, you can remember nothing of what happened at Rownham Passage.'

I regarded her thoughtfully. She had no idea that I had already been warned against remembering anything further. She only knew that my initial accusations had not been taken seriously and, accordingly, felt safe.

But not safe enough, apparently. After more than two weeks of mulling things over, Elizabeth Alefounder had decided to offer me a bribe.

I watched her jingling the gold pieces in her hand, but said nothing. My silence annoyed her.

'Well?'

'The price of treason?' I asked.

'I don't know what you mean,' she answered sharply. 'What you witnessed . . .' I raised my eyebrows mockingly and she continued. 'Oh, all right, then! What you accidentally became embroiled in, when I mistook you for someone else, was nothing more than a private, family feud . . .' Her voice tailed away as she confronted my stare of naked disbelief.

I clicked my tongue. 'I expected better of you than this, Mistress Alefounder. Are you unaware that your brother has been watched by the city's law officers ever since last summer, when a man suspected of being a Tudor spy was seen leaving this house? Fortunately for Master Avenel, the man was murdered before anything definite could be proved against him.'

She returned me look for look. I had to hand it to her. She was not a woman to lose her nerve.

'No, I was not aware,' she replied coolly. But there was a glint in her eye that suggested her brother would be hearing more from her on this subject.

'So, I repeat, is this the price of treason?'

'Surely that depends on your definition of treason?'

She was right, of course, up to a point. To an ardent follower of the House of Lancaster, supporters of the House of York were the traitors. But, like many others of my persuasion, I happened to believe that the sons of York were the rightful occupants of the English throne, being descended from King Richard II's legitimate heir, who had been illegally set aside by the usurper, Henry Bolingbroke, when he seized the crown as King Henry IV. But even had I been less assured in my convictions, there would still have been an insurmountable obstacle.

'Henry Tudor!' I mocked. 'How can anyone support Henry Tudor? A scion of the bastard line of John of Gaunt! A whey-faced nonentity, who, by all accounts, jumps at his own shadow! Sickly, too, I understand. What sort of loyalty can he inspire compared with King Edward?'

'The golden boy?' she sneered. 'Although not so golden these days, according to what I hear. Running to seed. Too much food, too much wine, too many women. But in any case,' she added, almost as an afterthought, 'there are other contenders for the English throne.'

I was instantly alert, especially as her expression told me she was afraid she had said too much. But if there was someone else, it would surely explain Timothy Plummer's presence in the city and his interest in what was going on.

But I pretended to be sceptical. 'Other contenders? What other contenders? The Lancastrians had to scrape the bottom of the barrel to come up with Henry Tudor.'

Elizabeth Alefounder flushed with anger and I stood up abruptly. The flush receded and she gave a forced smile, indicating with a slight wave of her hand that I should resume my seat. When I refused to do so, she dropped the coins, one by one, chink by chink, back into the green satin bag.

'You don't accept my offer, then?'

'Did you expect me to?'

She made a little moue of impatience. 'I didn't think you a man of many convictions. Certainly not political ones.'

'You should have enquired more thoroughly, Mistress. Almost anyone in Bristol, including your brother, could tell you that I have worked on several occasions for His Grace, the Duke of Gloucester; that I regard myself as his man.'

'But you're still poor,' she mocked. 'Oh, I know you have a house in Small Street, but that, as I understand it, has nothing to do with Crookback Dick.'

That was the first time I ever heard him called that; a description so widely and commonly used today that it has become almost a part of his name. I was astounded. It was as scurrilous as it was untrue. He had no deformity that I had ever noticed. There might have been a slight thickening of the right shoulder muscles and sinews, as there so often is with many fighting men, but that was all.

'My poverty,' I answered furiously, 'is no one's fault but my own. I have never wished to be obliged to anyone, not even to Prince Richard, who has all my loyalty. *All* my loyalty,' I stressed through clenched teeth. 'I have always refused his frequent offers of reward. I am my own man. But make no mistake about it. He is as generous with his purse as he is great in spirit. Which is more than can be said for the skinflint you and your brother serve!'

Her eyes narrowed to the merest slits, but she answered me levelly enough. She had her emotions well under control by now.

'I don't remember admitting that I and my brother *serve* anyone. And if you think back over our conversation, I'm sure you'll have to agree. I told you that your unfortunate embroilment in my affairs came about because of a family feud. It had nothing to do with Henry Tudor.'

'True. But you may also recollect what I told you about your brother having been under suspicion since last summer. Sergeant Manifold might take my word in preference to yours.'

'That idiot!' I only wished Richard could have heard her uncompromising opinion of him. She once more jingled the bag of coins. 'Are you sure you won't accept my offer? A small recompense for the . . . er . . . the discomfort you had to endure.'

I laughed. 'I've never heard attempted murder called "discomfort" before. And tell Master Avenel that the next time he tries to break into my house, he won't find it so easy. I've had bolts fitted to the top and bottom of the street door.' Elizabeth Alefounder's startled face told me that the incident of the break-in was something she had not known about. 'He left one of his shoes behind,' I added. 'He was in a hurry to be gone once his presence had been discovered. He really should get better-fitting footwear if he's to make a habit of sneaking into other people's houses uninvited.'

'This is calumny,' she answered coldly, but I could see a nerve twitching at the corner of her mouth. She was not as calm as she pretended to be. I smiled at her and her eyes met mine, dark with dislike.

'I make a bad enemy,' she warned me.

'But, in this case,' I pointed out, 'it would be unwise to do anything about it. I told my story and wasn't believed. That should suffice you. But if something were to happen to me, the Sheriff and his officers might begin to take my accusations seriously. Moreover, I have a witness who saw what really happened.'

'Who?' The word rapped out like a hailstone hitting tiles.

I laughed. 'You don't honestly expect me to tell you that, now do you?'

'You're lying,' she replied, but without conviction.

'Maybe. Maybe not.' Suddenly I was tired of this cat-and-mouse game, of saying things and not saying them, of fencing around one another but landing only glancing blows. 'Look, Mistress! I'm prepared to forget everything that took place at Rownham Passage if you're willing to leave me and mine alone. So, what do you say? Do you agree?'

She gave no hint of the relief she must have been feeling, but she was suspicious.

'Why would you be prepared to do that?'

'Because I'm sick of people thinking me a fool or a liar.'

She thought this over. 'Very well.' She half proffered the purse again. 'You're certain . . .?'

'I'm certain, Mistress,' I told her harshly. 'I'll wish you good evening.'

I found my own way out. Robin Avenel was still lurking in the hall and I nodded to him as I strode past.

Although I knew Adela would be worried about my safety, I did not go straight home, but treated myself to a beaker of ale at the Green Lattis, where I found a secluded corner and sat, going over my meeting with Elizabeth Alefounder in my mind. Her unguarded remark that there were other contenders for the English throne had made a deeper impression on me than anything else she had said. Something was afoot; something that had brought Timothy Plummer hotfoot from London to Bristol.

But why Bristol? There were many other ports far better situated for any matters concerning the Tudor court – if one could dignify it by that name – in Brittany. Bristol looked towards Ireland, and much of its commerce, good or bad, was then, as now and as it forever had been, with the inhabitants of that island. But Ireland had always been a hotbed of intrigue, of seething unrest and a desire to put a spoke in England's wheel whenever and wherever possible. Furthermore, Eamonn Malahide had been Irish.

Someone sat down on the stool beside mine. He looked dreadful and smelled worse. I choked into my ale.

'You shouldn't take on these undercover duties, Master Plummer,' I advised. 'It's over and above the call of duty. Go back to serving Duke Richard. He's not a man for disguises and skulking around back alleys. He accords his servants dignity and comfort.'

'You recognized me.' Timothy was disappointed.

'I'm afraid so. But then, I know you so well.'

'Then if you know me well, you also know that I mean what I say,' he rasped. 'You've been to visit Mistress Alefounder. I thought I told you to keep your long nose out of this business.'

'I couldn't help it,' I protested. 'She sent for me.'

'What did she want?'

'To offer me a bribe.' Briefly, I gave him details of my conversation with Elizabeth Alefounder, including her unguarded remarks on the subject of Henry Tudor and his not being the only contender for the English crown. 'What's going on, Timothy?'

'Nothing you need worry about,' he answered shortly.

'Oh, I know that,' I agreed humbly. 'Not while you're in charge of things, at any rate.'

He eyed me severely, uncertain if I were joking or not. He decided I probably was and rose with as much dignity as his smelly rags permitted.

'I'm telling you for the last time, keep your long nose out this, Roger!'

He disappeared as abruptly as he had appeared, melting into the crowd in the Green Lattis taproom. This was now filling up fast with people getting into the holiday spirit as they looked forward to the next few days of midsummer jollification. I remembered that I had to be up before dawn the following morning, and set out on my belated way home.

As I approached Saint Giles's Church, I noticed a woman entering by the Bell Lane door. I was unable to see her face because of an all-concealing hood. But then the skirt of her cloak was blown aside by the breeze, revealing a blue brocade gown.

Eleven

I called out, 'Mistress Hollyns!' and quickened my stride. I thought, from the slight movement of her head, that she had heard me and would wait for me to catch her up. But then she pushed open the church door and disappeared inside.

Bell Lane was quiet at that time of the evening. It couldn't have taken me more than a minute to cover the ground between myself and Saint Giles's, but when I entered, the nave was empty.

'Mistress Hollyns!' I called again. There was still no answer.

I descended to the crypt. There was no one there either, and I searched the next two chambers, but to no avail. I recalled Luke Prettywood telling me that the old synagogue cellars stretched the length of Bell Lane as far as Saint John's-on-the-Arch, but the distance seemed twice that length as I cautiously edged my way forward, every nerve tensed in expectation of sudden confrontation. But it soon became apparent that wherever Rowena Hollyns had gone, she was not in the church. She must have walked straight out of the opposite door into Jewry Lane. A short cut to the quayside perhaps? Or had the sound of my voice and the possibility of an encounter with me frightened her away? And if so, why?

I did not linger. The place filled me with the same sense of unhappiness and suffering that I had experienced once before. Grief and despair seemed embedded in the very stones. I shivered and made my way back outside, where the warmth and sunlight were like a benediction.

I went home.

*   *   *

The following morning, we were all up and dressed while it was still dark. Adela saw to that.

The two older children, robbed of their sleep, were fractious, while Adam, in no mood to be trifled with, was vociferous in his disapproval of being awakened so early. And long before we had finished a hasty breakfast, I was feeling positively liverish. Adela, however, with admirable fixity of purpose, ignored our collective bad temper, assembled warm cloaks and sensible shoes for each of us and put slices of honey cake, wrapped in dock leaves, into a basket to sustain us later on. The basket would also hold the necessary herbs.

'Now,' she said, 'you know what we're looking for. Saint John's wort, mugwort, plantain, corn marigold, elder, yarrow, ivy and vervain. They'll all be woven into the garland which I shall hang on the street door tonight to ward off the witches and other evil spirits of the air. And after dark, when the bonfires are lit on the high ground above the city, you may stay up late to see them. If you are good.'

'Does that include me?' I enquired caustically.

My wife gave me a look, but made no reply.

We joined the general exodus from the Redcliffe Gate to the meadows beyond, calling for Margaret Walker on our way. She was another staunch believer in propitiating the ancient gods, and together with the toothless Maria Watkins, who had also joined our party, kept up a constant refrain about the good old days and how nothing was the same today. Hercules and Margaret's dog, a small black and white mongrel to whom she had given a home the previous year after its mistress had deserted it, cavorted at our heels, intoxicated by all the fresh air and the prospect of innocent little rabbits to chase.

By the time we reached the fields beyond the church of Saint Mary Redcliffe, the darkness was lifting to unveil a misty sun. The early morning distances were here fretted with gold, there flooded with shadow. Campion, foxglove and the foaming heads of cow parsley starred the meadows, and the scent of crushed wild thyme, thick as incense, rose from beneath our feet.

I looked for, but failed to find, anyone from the Avenel

119

household except for Marianne, walking sedately beside Luke Prettywood. Her dancing eyes and sudden spurts of infectious laughter belied this decorous behaviour, and I was not surprised, a little later on, to discover that the pair of them seemed to have vanished. However, the crowds were so great by then that I was forced to give them the benefit of the doubt and assume that they had simply moved beyond my range of vision.

Most of the children ran riot, rolling in the dew-wet grass and being of little help to anyone. Our three were as bad as the rest, and twice we lost Adam, only to have him returned by neighbours who had recognized his indignant roar. (Once heard, never forgotten.) But, eventually, everyone had collected all the herbs and plants they needed, by which time the larks were shrilling overhead in a hot blue sky and the fields, cleared of mist, spread green and gold all around us. We could see the hedgerows bright with white and pink wild roses.

'Aren't you going to pick one for me?' Adela asked as we made our way back to the Redcliffe Gate.

I shook my head. 'This year I'm buying you a rose from one of the street vendors,' I announced, enjoying her look of astonishment. 'You can pull it apart at this evening's feast and surprise us both.'

'Does this mean that you, also, need to find out if you still love me?'

She had put an entirely different interpretation on my action to the one I had intended, so I thought it wisest not to answer; in any case, my attention had been distracted. As we passed William Canynges's great church, I saw Marianne Avenel and Luke Prettywood loitering in its shadow, his head bent to hers, her flower-like face upturned in adoration, the pair of them so close together that, at first glance, they appeared to be a single person. He was talking earnestly to her, and at one point I saw her laugh. Then I was swept along by the crowd and they were once more lost from sight.

The rest of the day was spent in a little desultory peddling around the town, before abandoning all pretence of work and lending assistance to my fellow citizens, who were setting up trestle tables in the streets ready for the Midsummer Eve's feast. Adela and I, uneasily conscious of the animosity of some of our Small Street neighbours, had agreed to walk as far as Redcliffe and take our supper with Margaret Walker and her friends. And although this almost certainly meant encountering the ill will of my own erstwhile friend, Burl Hodge, in general the inhabitants of the Redcliffe Ward cared little for my new-found status as a householder.

Consequently, four o'clock found Adela, the children and myself on the other side of the Avon, seated at one of the long tables set up in Redcliffe Street. We sat next to her cousin and opposite Margaret's closest companions, Bess Simnel and Maria Watkins. Neither dame resented my stroke of luck, and treated me with the same good-natured contempt that they had always shown towards me. Jack Nym and his wife waved to us all as they took their places further along the laden board, while Nick Brimble, Goody Watkins's nephew, slapped me on the back as he passed. I also recognized two old friends in Ned Stoner and Rob Short, both of whom now worked for Redcliffe masters; but either they failed to hear me when I shouted to them, or, having become aware of my presence, they deliberately refused to glance my way.

Not so Jenny Hodge, who left her seat at a neighbouring trestle to speak to both Adela and myself, displaying all her usual gentleness and good humour.

'Take no notice of Burl,' she said on parting. 'He'll get the better of his envious feelings given time.'

Looking at her husband's scowling face, I hoped she was right. I missed his friendship, and also that of his two happy-go-lucky sons, Jack and Dick.

The feast was provided by the master cooks, bakers and butchers of the city and served by their long-suffering apprentices, many of whom muttered mutinously to themselves and to one another as they struggled with the heavy trays of food and beakers of ale in the late-afternoon heat. The Midsummer Eve's feast had not always been blessed with good weather, but that year the atmosphere was stifling. I saw Luke Prettywood overseeing a couple of brewer's lads and occasionally lending them a hand, the sweat pouring down his face and nearly blinding him.

'What are you doing over here?' I asked him as he refilled my beaker.

'I live in Redcliffe.' He wiped his forehead on his sleeve. 'I might ask you the same question, with better cause.'

'Oh, I'm a guest of Mistress Walker,' was my prompt reply. 'My daughter is her granddaughter.'

I glanced at Elizabeth as I spoke, but she was too busy even to talk to her stepbrother, let alone to notice me. She was trying to cram a whole raston into her mouth at once, the crumbs, butter and honey from its scooped-out interior dribbling down her chin and rendering her speechless. Nicholas himself was little better. He was just reaching for another piece of curd tart, the state of his mouth and fingers betraying the fact that he had disposed of several slices already. As for Adam, he was awash with cream syllabub and junket, which he had managed to get all down his little tunic, up his nose and around his eyes. I shuddered and looked away. He was not a pretty sight.

The feasting over at last – which only happened when we could barely move, even to go and relieve ourselves behind a convenient wall – the dirty dishes were cleared away by the exhausted apprentices and it was time for the games to begin.

The first ceremony was that of the Midsummer Rose itself. Each husband or sweetheart presented his lady-love with the rose he had either bought or picked for her and waited anxiously while she tore it to pieces, petal by petal.

'He loves me! He loves me not!'

I gave Adela the overblown monstrosity I had purchased from a seller in High Street and watched, with bated breath, as she went through the ritual. I suddenly found that I really cared about the outcome, praying for the correct conclusion as some sort of proof to me, as well as to her, that our marriage was as strong as ever. Margaret Walker, Maria Watkins and Bess Simnel also took a gloating interest in the proceedings, ready to cackle with laughter and overwhelm me with mock reproaches if things failed to work out.

The rose was almost denuded. 'He loves me . . . He loves me not . . . He loves me!' Adela turned with a triumphant smile and invited my kiss. The three goodies made no effort to hide their disappointment. Further along the board and at neighbouring trestles, other swains and spouses were feebly protesting their devotion and swearing that the Midsummer Rose had lied. There was a lot of laughter, a few tears and some dissension before the head man of each table called for order and we passed on to the next ritual.

Great pans of water were placed on each table by the sweating and hard-working apprentices, and each citizen was handed a paper boat holding a stump of lighted candle. These were floated on the water to the chant: 'Green is gold, fire is wet, fortune's told, dragon's met.' Good fortune was yours if the boat floated to the opposite side of the pan before sinking and extinguishing its flame.

Both Adela's boat and mine sank within seconds of each other, but Margaret Walker, by dint of some judicious cheating, kept all three children's candles afloat long enough to ensure their good luck for the rest of the year.

Finally, a huge pastry subtlety, in the shape of a dragon, was set in the middle of every trestle and, at a given signal, a 'Saint George' leaped on to each table and 'killed' it. Our table's Saint George was Luke Prettywood, and a fine, dramatic job he made of it, ripping the pastry beast apart with his sword – well, his knife, more accurately speaking – until a shower of coins spilled out across the board. There was an undignified scramble for this gift of money from the Mayor and aldermen of the city, most of it ending up, as usual, in the purses and pockets of the elderly, who were utterly unscrupulous in the methods they employed to obtain more than their fair share of booty. The younger folk nursed bruised ribs, cracked knuckles and scratched hands for many a day afterwards.

By now, it was beginning to grow dusk, and the first of the bonfires had been lit on the heights above Bristol – those 'bone-fires' on which our pagan forefathers, the Druids, had burned the bones of animals in honour of their great god Bel. One by one, they pricked the gathering darkness, and the acrid smell of burning was carried on a cloud of sparks down to the ancient city below, cradled in its marshy bed.

Bonfires were also lit in the streets, and it was time to form the midsummer processions. As I helped Adela to rise from the bench on which we had been sitting, I saw something flutter to the ground, something she had been concealing in the palm of one hand and accidentally released as she reached for mine. I stooped to pick it up – and found myself looking at a crimson rose petal, as soft as velvet.

'He loves me not.'

The revels were nearly over and people were reluctantly beginning to disperse. But movement was necessarily slow as neighbours stopped to laugh and exchange titbits of gossip. Adela, with Adam asleep on her shoulder, had joined the group of women gathered around Margaret Walker. Nicholas and Elizabeth, together with several other children, were chasing in and out amongst those tables that had not yet been dismantled and carried away. I allowed my attention to wander.

A man, coming from the direction of Bristol Bridge, was weaving his way swiftly through the crowds, making himself as unobtrusive as possible by hugging the walls of the houses bordering the quay, head well down, hat pulled forward over his eyes, a cloak enveloping him from neck to ankles. Now and then he collided with a passer-by, but for the most part people were too busy about their own concerns to take much interest in him.

He interested me, however. Robin Avenel had evidently left the feasting and merrymaking on the other side of the Avon to cross into Redcliffe, where, judging by his purposeful gait, he was on his way to some rendezvous. Abruptly, he turned down one of the many alleyways that led on to Redcliffe Back.

I touched Adela's arm. 'Go home with Margaret and wait for me there. I've just seen somebody I know. I shan't be long.' And I took my departure as quickly as I could, deaf to her questions and protests.

Redcliffe Back had obviously been the scene of as much revelling and feasting as the inner streets. More, perhaps, as residents there had been joined by many of the foreign sailors whose ships were berthed at the wharfside. Scraps of food, rose petals, paper boats and stumps of candle littered the cobbles so thickly that my boots squelched on the debris with every step I took. Some tables had been overturned, a noisy crowd was still roistering around the bonfire in the middle of the quay, while others were heaving up the contents of their stomachs into the Avon. The river itself seemed to be a sheet of flame, reflecting the light from the many fires on Saint Brendan's Hill and the heights leading to Durham and Clifton.

A disturbance had broken out – a drunken brawl, by the sound of things – but for the moment, there seemed to be no cause for concern. Wall torches and cressets had now been lit, adding their smoky glow to that of the bonfires.

I paused in the mouth of the alleyway before locating Robin Avenel almost straight ahead of me. He was talking to a man who stood, listening impatiently, one foot on the quayside, the other on the gangplank of a ship. This, together with his mode of dress, told me he was a sailor, and a foreign one at that. Irish? French? Breton? I was too far away and there was too much noise to hear anything that might have given me a clue. But I could see that Robin was importuning the other for a favour, which the sailor appeared loath to grant. There was urgency in every line of Robin's body and in the general earnestness of his demeanour, but his companion shook his head and would have continued mounting the gangplank if Robin had not tightened his grip on the other man's wrist.

I edged a little nearer, my quarry seemingly unaware of anything going on around him. The commotion further along the quay was beginning to escalate and to attract general attention: no one would be interested in my movements. But I had left it too late. Even as I took a step forward, someone shot past me through the alleyway, seized Robin Avenel by the scruff of his neck and whirled him round.

'What do you mean, you revolting piece of frippery, by

telling my Jenny to keep away from your wife?' roared Burl Hodge's unmistakable tones. When Burl was angry, everyone knew it.

It took Robin Avenel several seconds to realize what was happening. The sailor, seizing his chance, hastened up the gangplank to the refuge of his ship.

I could hear Robin's furious bleats of protest at this rough handling, and hurried forward myself, not so much to save his skin, as to prevent Burl doing something he would later regret.

'My wife,' Burl was yelling at the top of his voice, 'is every bit as good as that empty-headed little whore that you married! And if you're ever rude to my Jenny again –' he began punching Robin in the chest with a vigour that made me wince – 'I won't be responsible for the consequences. Do . . .' (thump) 'you . . .' (thump) 'understand me?' (Yet another thump.)

'Leave him, Burl!' I seized the tenter's wrists. 'He isn't worth it.'

'What? What the . . .?' Burl turned to see who had so rudely interrupted his sport, and in the glow from the fires I could see his eyes darken with anger. 'Oh, it's you, is it? I might have guessed. You never can keep that great nose of yours out of other people's business. It's high time someone taught you a lesson, chapman, and I'm in just the mood to do it.'

'Don't be a bloody fool,' I told him, indicating with a jerk of my head to Robin that he should go while the going was good.

He didn't need a second bidding and sloped off into the night, but not before he had given Burl a vicious kick on the shins. And that about summed up the man: valiant only so long as there was no risk to himself.

Burl, robbed of his prey, was beside himself with fury. As soon as I released his wrists, he took a wild swing at my jaw but missed me by miles. I made the mistake of laughing. He came for me then, throwing all his weight against me and bearing me to the ground, where we rolled over and over in the dirt, writhing and kicking and hitting each other like

126

two gutter urchins. How long this undignified spectacle might have continued is difficult to say, but the sudden yells of 'Riot! Ware riot! Apprentices! Apprentices!' made us leave off and scramble hurriedly to our feet.

It was a year or more since there had last been an apprentices' riot in the city, but the long, hot, toilsome day and evening, waiting on others, followed by the release from labour and some heavy drinking, had fuelled tempers and made them ripe for mischief. Suddenly boys were everywhere like a pack of bloodthirsty hounds in full cry, hallooing and hollering to their fellows to join in the hunt. I had seen a few apprentice riots in my time, but this bade fair to be one of the worst. Anyone who stood in their path was knocked down and mauled.

Within ten minutes or so, the whole of Redcliffe was a seething mass of violent, drunken apprentices, and the riot was spreading across Bristol Bridge and into the main part of the city. Someone had ordered the alarm bell to be rung, and its deep notes tolled out, warning all respectable citizens to seek the safety and shelter of their own homes. But even these citadels were not necessarily safe, as pot-valiant youths hammered on windows and shutters and mouthed obscenities through keyholes.

Wishing to heaven that I had brought my cudgel with me, and wondering how long it would take the Watch and the City Militia to arrive and quell the riot, I fought my way through the melee by the simple expedient of knocking heads together and generally making use of my superior height and strength until I reached Margaret Walker's cottage. There, I discovered a handful of youths banging on the door and laughing uproariously at the sound of my children's frightened wailing on the other side. But I made short work of them. Furious, I booted one up his backside so hard that I reckoned he wouldn't be able to sit down for a week; I hit another with such force that I heard his jawbone crack, and I drove a third one's head against the wall so violently that he slid to the ground unconscious. The fourth didn't stop to find out what I had in store for him, but took to his heels, vanishing into the flame-reddened night.

'It's me!' I shouted. 'Adela! Margaret! Let me in!'

The cottage door creaked open an inch or two, just wide enough to admit me without doing permanent damage to my limbs and other vital parts. I squeezed inside, but if I had expected to be the hero of the moment after my admirable display of Herculean prowess outside, I was destined to be disappointed.

'Roger! Where have you been?' my wife demanded reproachfully.

Margaret Walker was more forthright. 'Just like a man to go sloping off somewhere when he's needed. Your women-folk and children could all have been murdered where they stood.'

I was irritated and showed it. 'A gross exaggeration, Mother-in-law, and you well know it. No one gets murdered during an apprentices' riot. Oh, I grant you there'll be a fair lot of damage to property, broken noses, black eyes, bruised shins, that sort of thing, but nobody will be dead. It's mostly high spirits and mischief exacerbated by drink. They don't mean any real harm.'

'Harm!' screeched Goody Watkins, and for the first time I became aware of her and Bess Simnel's presence in the cottage. 'Harm! The varmints have broken one of my shutters and Bess here has had her door kicked in! If I catch one of 'em what did it, I'll cut off his balls with my carving knife!' With which bloodthirsty utterance she burst into tears.

Margaret tried to comfort her, glaring at me as she did so. 'Now see what you've done!'

'Listen!' I held up my hand for silence.

The quality of the noise outside had altered. The triumphant yells of the apprentices had changed to cries of dismay. There were sounds of horses' hooves, the rattling of swords, the upraised voices of Authority. The Watch, the Petty Constable and the City Militia had arrived at last, followed eventually by the Mayor, who climbed on to one of the remaining tables and read the Riot Act. Some youths were rounded up and marched off, under escort, to the bridewell. The rest were claimed by masters whose wrath would only

128

be appeased by beatings and floggings that would continue for many days to come.

At last, we were free to go home.

Twelve

It was a disturbed night. Adela, myself and the three children, not to mention Hercules, were awakened in the small hours of the morning by the thunderstorm that had been threatening the previous day. I went downstairs to calm the dog, and returned to find my place usurped by Adam, who refused point-blank to return to his attic room.

By this time, I was in one of my foulest moods, the bruises and cuts I had received during my fight with Burl Hodge beginning to make themselves felt. I shunted my son to the middle of the mattress, fell in beside him and tried to sleep.

But the events of the previous evening kept going around and around in my head while I tossed and turned and tried to get comfortable. It must have been nearly dawn when I finally drifted into an uneasy doze, from which I was aroused all too soon by the sound of someone banging loudly on our outer door. Groaning and cursing, I heaved myself up, searching for shoes and a cloak with which to cover my nakedness.

Adela was already out of bed, shrugging on a long, loose gown over her nightrail and twisting her two thick braids of dark hair up around her head.

'Whoever can that be?' she asked, perturbed. 'I hope Margaret hasn't been taken ill!'

I ran downstairs, careless of my state of undress, and unbolted and unlocked the street door, expecting to see either Maria Watkins or a distraught Bess Simnel standing outside. Instead, it was one of our neighbours from across the street, a widow who, so far, had steadfastly refused to acknowledge our existence. But now, she was even moved to seize my hand.

'Have you heard?' she gasped. But before I had time to shake my head, she continued. 'Robin Avenel was found murdered late last night in Jewry Lane.' She shuddered dramatically. 'Stabbed through the heart, they say. Left to welter in a pool of blood!'

It was Midsummer's Day, the Feast of the Nativity of Saint John the Baptist, and we were all going to church at Saint Lawrence's.

Dressing was a difficult business: it was impossible to concentrate with a mind in turmoil. I cut myself twice while shaving because I had forgotten to sharpen my knife, and because I wouldn't wait for the water Adela was heating over the fire, but used cold from the pump instead. My fingers were all thumbs, and in trying to fasten my shirt to my breeches I tangled the laces and had to stand impatiently while Adela unknotted them.

'For goodness' sake, you're worse than a child,' she admonished me in a very wifely fashion. 'This doesn't concern you, Roger. It's not your business. What needs to be done will already have been taken care of by the Sheriff's Officers and members of the Watch. Now, sit down quietly and eat some breakfast before I lose my temper. You look terrible. Your face is covered in scratches, your eyes have black rings under them from lack of sleep and you're wearing a dirty shirt that I had put aside to be washed. In addition,' she went on severely, 'you've been warned by Timothy Plummer to steer clear of any matter concerning Robin Avenel.'

'Bad man!' Adam shouted at me, banging his spoon on the kitchen table to indicate that his bowl was empty.

He was learning to speak fast, and I wasn't sure I cared for this latest addition to his vocabulary, especially as it afforded such amusement to his half-brother and sister. But Adela was right. There was nothing I could usefully do besides ascertain the facts. I had been warned to keep my nose clean or face unpleasant consequences for myself and my family.

But fate was busy taking a hand. I was about to become embroiled whether I wanted to or not.

I was just wiping the grease from my chin after consuming

a second bacon collop – all the sweeter because we usually fasted before going to Mass, but Adela had decided this morning that I was in need of nourishment – when there was another knock on the street door; a loud, purposeful banging that, to my ears at least, clearly betokened Authority.

'Now, who can that be?' Adela asked of no one in particular. She tidied away a few strands of loose hair beneath her linen cap, smoothed down her apron and went to answer the summons. The children, uninterested, continued eating voraciously, not even glancing up from their bowls when she returned.

'It's Richard,' Adela announced, a tinge of uneasiness colouring her tone.

She stood aside to allow Sergeant Richard Manifold into the kitchen, an unwelcome guest who was followed by his two equally unwelcome henchmen, Jack Gload and Peter Littleman. Meanly, I was secretly delighted to note that the former's weaselly little face was disfigured by a very swollen nose and a black right eye. Someone had set about him with a will. I silently cheered that someone.

'What a nice surprise,' I said. Hercules began attacking Peter Littleman's ankles, but unfortunately made no impression on his thick leather boots. Still, I didn't discourage the animal; he was only doing his duty as a guard dog, after all. 'I don't recall inviting you three to breakfast.'

'Roger!' Adela said warningly. She satisfied herself that the children had finished eating, then sent them off to play in the buttery. 'Please, sit down,' she invited our intrepid law officers politely. 'Would you like some ale?'

I frowned, but happily Richard Manifold overruled the eager nods of Jack and Pete with a shake of his head. 'We're on official duty,' he said.

'What sort of official duty?' Adela sounded anxious, no doubt recalling the time her former admirer had arrived at our cottage in Lewin's Mead to arrest me for murder.

The sergeant smiled thinly, obviously reading her thoughts.

'It's all right, my dear.' Who asked him to call my wife his *dear*? My hackles rose. 'On this occasion Roger is a

witness, not a suspect.' A witness? To what? I was mysti-
fied. Richard continued. 'You've no doubt heard the news?'
'About Robin Avenel's murder, you mean?' I leaned
forward, suddenly all attention. 'A neighbour told us earlier
this morning. Stabbed to death in Jewry Lane, I understand.
Do you have any idea when it happened?'

Richard looked annoyed at this turning of the tables on
what, after all, was his interrogation.

'It has to be some time between nine o'clock and midnight,'
he answered grudgingly. 'Members of the Watch passed along
Jewry Lane on their way to help quell the prentices' riot.
The body wasn't there then. And Edgar Capgrave says he
saw nothing after he'd locked the Frome Gate at curfew,
when he walked along Jewry Lane to his home in Fish Lane.
But at midnight, when the Watch were back on normal patrol,
they found Master Avenel's body sprawled outside Saint
Giles's Church.'

'So how can I help you?' I asked. 'To what am I supposed
to have been a witness?'

'Not *supposed* to have been,' was the retort. 'According
to my information, you *were*.' Richard Manifold's chest
swelled importantly. 'We think we already know the murderer.
Burl Hodge.'

'Burl Hodge?' I was scathing. 'You must be joking! Burl
wouldn't murder anyone. Oh, he has a hot temper, I grant
you that, but he'd never kill someone. Why in the name of
Hades do you think it's Burl?'

'He deliberately picked a fight with Robin Avenel last
night. Accused him of insulting his wife, or some such thing.
You can't deny it, Roger. He would have assaulted Master
Avenel even more violently if you hadn't arrived to prevent
him. Then he turned on you. But during your little scuffle,
his intended victim escaped. Burl must have sought him out
later and finished what he'd started.'

'How do you know all this?' I demanded. 'Who's been
spying on me?'

'No one's been spying on you.' Richard snorted contemp-
tuously at the very idea of such a waste of his and his men's
precious time. 'You were seen. There was another witness

133

who saw everything. An old beggar who's been hanging around the town for a week or two now. Comes and goes, but I've noticed him about on several occasions.'

Timothy Plummer! Perhaps his disguise was better than I'd thought. Richard apparently hadn't recognized him, in spite of having encountered Timothy the previous summer in the latter's official capacity as the King's Spymaster General.

Where had he been yesterday evening? Standing somewhere behind me in the alleyway leading to Redcliffe Back. I hadn't been aware of him and I offered him a silent apology: he was obviously better at his job than I'd given him credit for. But what underhand game was he playing? It was plain to me that Timothy was the person subtly directing the sergeant's attention towards Burl Hodge. He had observed Burl's attack on Robin Avenel and his subsequent tussle with me, and was using both incidents for his own nefarious ends.

Which were? I was unable to say for certain, but I suspected it was a diversion of some sort to distract attention from the Avenels' other, more treasonable activities. Would Timothy care if a man were hanged for a murder he didn't commit? I reached the reluctant conclusion that he probably wouldn't.

'So, where does Burl say he was last night?' I enquired.

Richard shrugged. 'Where you'd expect. Says he was at home in bed with his wife. Says they both headed for their cottage as soon as the riot became serious, and stayed there.'

'That sounds like good sense. Jenny confirms this?'

'Naturally. But it's just what she would say, isn't it? In these circumstances, her testimony is useless.'

I curled my lip. 'You know Jenny Hodge as well as I do, Sergeant. Probably better. Do you really think her a woman who would lie to save a murderer? Even her own husband?'

Richard Manifold shifted uncomfortably on his stool and made no answer. I guessed that the Sheriff and other civic eminences had pressed for an early arrest. An important and wealthy citizen had been done to death, and such a killing called for swift, if not immediate, retribution.

'Where is Burl?' Adela asked, speaking for the first time. I could hear the anger trembling in her voice.

Richard cleared his throat, a little too noisily. 'He's in the bridewell.'

'And you've pursued no other lines of enquiry?' I didn't bother to hide my disgust.

Richard flushed angrily. 'We don't believe in wasting public time and money. There are no other suspects. With the beggarman's testimony and yours, why should we search any further?'

I sprang to my feet. I wasn't aware of how I looked, but Adela later described my expression as murderous. I advanced my face to within about two inches of Richard's.

'What you mean is that our precious Mayor and Corporation want this murder solved in double-quick time and with no awkward questions asked. The Sheriff, at least, must know that there are suspicions of treasonable activity in connection with Robin Avenel. That I, myself, have implicated him in what happened to me at Rownham Passage. That I am still willing to swear that Elizabeth Alefounder and her maid were present, that they assaulted me, and that one of them killed the Irish sea captain, whose body was dragged out of the Avon twelve days ago. But Robin Avenel was a respected citizen of this fair city –' I sneered openly – 'and his father, the soapmaker –' I managed to make it sound like an insult – 'has a bottomless purse that is always at the disposal of the City Fathers. And we don't want to sacrifice a good Bristol citizen and sully his name with accusations of treason, do we? Especially not when Providence has so thoughtfully provided us with our very own ram in the thicket. Well, I'm not going to let it rest there!'

Richard Manifold had the grace to blush, but he answered steadily. 'Then you're an even bigger fool than I take you for. Remember, you're a family man now. You can no longer afford to take the law into your own hands.'

'And if I refuse to testify against Burl?'

'You'll find yourself in the bridewell on a charge of obstructing justice. You may also find yourself accused of being an accessory to murder. Don't forget we have the beggar's testimony.' He appealed to Adela. 'Make him see sense, my dear.'

'Roger . . .' she began, but I interrupted with a roar.

'Who asked you to keep calling my wife your dear? Get out of my house before I lose control and give you the same treatment that your red-nosed friend here has suffered at some other hero's hands. Whoever it was, he has my undying admiration.'

'It was Luke Prettywood,' Jack Gload snuffled, fingering the swollen member tenderly. 'Well, he's got his comeuppance.' He tried to grin, but I was happy to note that it hurt his face, so he desisted.

Richard got to his feet with more dignity than I think I could have mustered in the circumstances. He nodded to Adela, then turned to look at me.

'I shall expect you this afternoon, Roger, at the Councillors' Meeting Hall to make your deposition. Don't let me wait in vain.'

And on this warning note, he left, Peter Littleman and Jack Gload trailing in his wake.

I have been inattentive in God's house many times in my life, but that Midsummer morning I don't believe that I was aware of a single thing that went on around me. In my own defence, I have to say that I was not the only person paying scant attention. There was an undercurrent of unease, of feverish excitement, and a constant sibilance that suggested much whispering behind hands and an even greater disregard of the priest than usual. And, once released from our devotions, the babel of voices was worthy of the great tower itself. The names of Burl Hodge and Robin Avenel were on everybody's lips.

There was no sign of any member of the Avenel household present, but that was hardly surprising. They must still be coming to terms with their recent bereavement. But I couldn't help wondering how the smart young widow was bearing her loss. And what of Luke Prettywood? How was he taking the news? Where had he been when Robin Avenel was murdered?

The tidings that I was to be one of the Crown's two chief witnesses against Burl Hodge had not yet reached a wider

136

public. So Adela, the children and I were allowed to escape the crowds still milling around Saint Lawrence's Church, not yet sated with gossip, and make our way home to Small Street unmolested. But we breathed a sigh of relief too soon. Dreams of a quiet family dinner while we took stock of the situation were shattered as soon as we saw Margaret Walker standing outside the house, impatiently awaiting our return.

'Roger!' She wasted no time on any other greeting. 'Have you heard about Burl?' When I nodded, she went on urgently, 'You must come back with me to Redcliffe and speak to Jenny. She's beside herself with anxiety. She thinks you might be able to prove Burl's innocence. Don't shake your head like that. You've solved other mysteries. You helped me and Lillis. Don't worry about your dinner. I'll feed you all. Just come!' As I hesitated, she lost her temper. 'Oh, by the Blessed Virgin! You're not so petty as to hold Burl's recent animosity against him, are you? Think of Jenny! Think of the boys! Adela! Persuade him!'

'It's all right, Mother-in-law,' I said quietly. 'Adela doesn't need to persuade me. I'll just fetch Hercules. I can't let him remain mewed up all day on his own. You and Adela and the children go ahead. I'll catch you up.'

Once indoors, I dealt with Hercules's effusive welcome – he always greeted me as though I'd just returned from a three year voyage to the realms of Prester John – found his rope halter and leading string, then sat down at the kitchen table for a moment or two, savouring the tranquillity of the empty house and marshalling my thoughts.

Somehow or other, I had to find Timothy Plummer and discover what exactly he was up to. I entertained a faint hope that I might be able to convince him to disappear for a while without giving further evidence to the magistrates, forcing them to rely on my word alone. Then if I denied what had happened . . .

But that would do no good. There must have been other witnesses to Burl's attack on Robin Avenel. There was the ship's master to whom Robin had been talking for a start. But he was a foreigner. Maybe he spoke little English. I must try to see him as soon as possible . . . There was a lot to be

137

done, and I recollected with a sigh that I also had to report to Richard Manifold at the Councillors' Hall sometime that afternoon.

I glanced down at Hercules who, once in his harness, was anxious to be off and chafing at the delay. I cast a regretful eye over Adela's preparations for dinner, which appeared to be one of her succulent rabbit pies, followed by junkets and stewed pippins. A Midsummer's Day feast to remember. Ah well!

I wanted to visit Jewry Lane to see for myself the place where Robin Avenel's body had been found. But I guessed that, by now, Adela and Margaret would be wondering why I hadn't caught them up, so Hercules and I set off up Small Street without more ado.

At the top, we turned left into Corn Street and made for the High Cross. Immediately ahead of us was Wine Street, where I could see a small, angry crowd surrounding the pillory. Investigation revealed that two of the ringleaders of last night's apprentices' riot had been placed there and were being pelted with refuse from the central drain. I threw a few handfuls of rotting vegetables myself, just to let them know how I felt about my wife and children having been frightened by their antics, then walked down High Street to Bristol Bridge, where I eventually overtook my family.

By now, my stomach was rumbling and I was in urgent need of sustenance, so I was not best pleased to discover that we were going straight to the Hodges' cottage to see Jenny. But in Temple Street I found a repetition of the scene I had left behind on the other side of the Avon. Set in the Redcliffe pillory, near Temple Church, were two more ring-leaders of the riot and one who had been arrested for assault. Luke Prettywood!

He was being pelted with filth by a crowd of street urchins who were promptly shooed away by Margaret Walker. Luke, as he had informed me the night before, was a Redcliffe man, and Redcliffe people look after their own, no matter what they've done. Moreover, this was the hero who had set about Jack Gload. I patted his matted hair. He gave me a sheepish grin.

'How long?' I asked.

He knew what I meant. 'Until curfew,' he croaked, his neck restricted by the confining headboards. He looked awful, with an unshaven chin and bloodshot eyes, muck and ordure streaking his face. 'Hit Jack Gload. Shouldn't have done it. Too much cuckoo-foot ale. Y'know what that stuff's like.'

I did indeed, but Adela always kept a careful eye on the amount that I consumed. Spiced with ginger, basil and dill, it was a refreshing drink for a hot night that seduced you into thinking it harmless until you swallowed one draught too many. Then it kicked like a mule, and within minutes you were ready to fight the rest of the world. And, as in Luke's case, you probably did.

'Cheer up,' I said. 'At least you have the consolation of having picked the right target. Jack Gload has a marvellously swollen nose and black eye.'

Luke gave a strangled gurgle that might have been an attempt at laughter, then groaned. 'My head's bursting.'

'Roger!' Margaret's voice rang out peremptorily. 'Jenny's waiting for us.'

I grimaced at Luke and moved away. Then, realizing that he might not yet have heard the news, turned back.

'Robin Avenel's dead,' I said. 'Murdered. That idiot Richard Manifold has arrested Burl Hodge.'

I hadn't thought it possible for Luke's face to get any whiter than it already was, but I was wrong. Every last trace of blood seemed to disappear, leaving his skin, beneath the dirt, the colour of old parchment. He struggled for words and finally whispered, 'Marianne . . . How's Mistress Avenel?'

'I don't know,' I answered, my sympathy for him evaporating. 'My concern's with Jenny Hodge. I'm sure Mistress Avenel won't prove inconsolable.' Then my conscience got the better of me. I patted one of his hands, where it hung limply through the boards. 'I'll let you know if I get any news of her.'

As I moved out of range, another mob of children arrived to pelt Luke and the unfortunate apprentices with handfuls of dung which they had stolen from a cart further along the street. But by this time, Margaret Walker, together with Adela and the children, had walked on to the Hodges' cottage, so there was no one to reprimand them.

The one-roomed dwelling was overflowing with people – concerned neighbours who had been told of Burl's arrest and had come to express their outrage. There were a few faces I failed to recognize: strangers from without the city walls. I knew that Jenny and Burl were Lollard sympathizers, although the fact was never mentioned aloud.

'Roger!' As soon as Jenny caught sight of me, she leaped up from her stool, pushing aside her many well-wishers, and came towards me, hands outstretched. She had been crying; her face was puffy and tear-stained, and when I took her in my arms, I could feel her trembling violently. Jack and Dick were right behind her, her protectors; two boys who had been forced to grow up overnight and learn to act and think like men.

'It's all right,' I soothed, awkwardly patting her back. 'It's all right.'

But of course it wasn't all right: everyone knew that. Nevertheless, they all looked hopeful, as if they were expecting me to perform an instant miracle and tell them who had really killed Robin Avenel. I glanced despairingly at Adela, but she was busy soothing Adam, who was not only hungry, but highly annoyed at finding himself in a crowd of people to whom he had taken immediate exception. Margaret had her hands similarly full with our two elder children and the dog.

Something had to be done. I raised my voice. 'I should like to speak to Mistress Hodge and her sons alone, and I'd be grateful if you would all go home. Margaret, take Adela and the children back with you and feed them. Hercules, as well. It's past their dinnertime. I'll join you later.'

There was a good deal of muttering and indignant sniffing, but eventually, urged more diplomatically by Jenny and her boys, the neighbours dispersed one by one until I was left alone with her and Jack and Dick. Adela pressed my arm lovingly as she went, her way of wishing me good luck.

I sighed. I was going to need it.

Thirteen

I knew Jenny's story would be the same one she had already told to Richard Manifold, but I wanted to assess her truthfulness for myself. In spite of my remarks concerning her honesty, I thought it possible that she might lie to save her husband.

'Burl came to find me shortly after the fighting started,' she said, drawing me forward to sit at the table. 'We both of us knew that apprentices' riots can turn violent. It was obvious Burl had been brawling, but I didn't realize then it was with you. We looked for the boys to make sure they weren't involved.'

'Got more sense,' grunted Jack.

'More sense,' agreed Dick, and I remembered how, when they were children, he had always echoed his elder brother.

'We never touch cuckoo-foot ale,' Jack went on. 'We've seen what it leads to. Seen what it leads to with Father.'

'With Father.'

Jenny flushed painfully. 'That's one of Burl's failings, Roger, as you know. He can't hold his drink. Anyway,' she continued, 'we found the boys, came home and waited for the Deputy Sheriff and his men to arrive. Once they did, the riot fizzled out, as we'd known it would. Then we went to bed.'

'You two, as well?' I glanced across the table at the boys, who nodded. 'And did you sleep soundly? You didn't wake up?'

This time they shook their heads, although I thought Jack hesitated a second or two before doing so.

I looked back at Jenny. 'And you and Burl? You slept the night through as well?'

She returned my look defiantly. 'Yes. Both of us.' Her expression softened and she appeared to be on the verge of tears. 'Oh, Roger! I've shared the same bed with Burl for over sixteen years. His slightest movement wakes me. I think I'm conscious of his body next to mine even when I'm asleep. I should know if he got out of bed, let alone if he left the cottage.'

I believed her. She and Burl had their disagreements, but there was a closeness between them that I had often envied. I leaned forward, resting my folded arms on the table.

'Jenny, forgive me, but I have to ask you this. Even if you suspected Burl of being Robin Avenel's murderer, wouldn't you still protest his innocence? Wouldn't you protect him?'

Jack jumped to his feet. 'If that's all you have to say, chapman, get out now!'

'Get out now!' came the faithful echo.

'Sit down, the pair of you!' Jenny ordered fiercely. 'And mind your manners. Roger's here to help us. He can't do that if he doesn't get at the truth.' The boys subsided reluctantly and she turned to me. 'Yes, I would. Of course I would. I'd even endanger my immortal soul and commit perjury for Burl if I thought it necessary. But it's not necessary. I swear to you, Roger, as I trust in the Lord Jesus Christ and hope for eternal salvation, Burl did not stir from my side all night.'

I laid a hand over one of hers. 'Your word's good enough for me, Jenny, but we'll need more evidence than that to convince Sergeant Manifold that he has the wrong man. What was Burl's quarrel with Master Avenel?'

I knew, of course, but I wanted her version of events.

'It was so foolish. When I was a girl, I worked for Gregory Alefounder and his family. Marianne Alefounder, as she was then, was a pretty, lively little soul, very spoilt and allowed to run a bit wild. She spent more time in the kitchens than she did at her lessons. I was the youngest of the maids and she took a fancy to me. I taught her how to cook, and in spite of the difference in our ages, we became friends. And we stayed friends, even after I got married and she grew up.

142

Her father made no objection. But when she married Robin Avenel, it was a different story. He found out that she still came to visit me and was furious. He told me to my face that no wife of his was going to consort with a low-born wench who'd worked in his father-in-law's kitchen and was married to a tenter. I didn't take any notice. Nor did Marianne; she just went on coming to see me. But when Burl found out what had happened, he was angrier than I've ever known him. I begged him to let the matter drop, but he swore he was going to get even with Master Avenel. I know that sounds bad, but it didn't mean he wanted to murder Robin. The truth is, he's never liked him. All those airs and affectations . . .' Jenny's voice faltered, then died altogether.

I glanced at Jack. 'Did either of you two know about this?'

Jack shook his head. 'If we had,' he said grimly, 'we'd probably have beaten Robin Avenel senseless ourselves.'

'Ourselves,' agreed Dick.

'Nonsense,' declared their mother stoutly. 'You wouldn't have been so foolish. Indeed,' she added, 'I was certain Burl himself had thought better of tackling Master Avenel. It was just unfortunate that Robin decided, for some reason or another, to come into Redcliffe last night, when Burl had had too much cuckoo-foot ale to drink. But to suggest Burl murdered him is ridiculous. You know him, Roger. He really wouldn't hurt a fly.'

I grunted non-committally, remembering Burl's face, reflected in the glow from the bonfires, as he attacked the man who had insulted his wife. All the same, in one way Jenny was right. Burl could well have killed Robin by accident, in a rage – and I'd thought at one moment he was going to – but he would never deliberately seek out a man and stab him to death in cold blood.

'You will help us, Roger, won't you?' Jenny asked, seemingly worried by my silence.

'Yes, of course.' I gave her hand a final squeeze and released it. 'But, Jenny, you mustn't expect too much of me.'

I couldn't tell her that there were other forces at work here; that I didn't think Burl's arrest just a simple miscarriage of justice. For one thing, I had no proof to substantiate this claim. For another, it would have meant too long and too complicated an explanation. Nor could I admit that I was one of the chief witnesses against her husband. She would discover that soon enough. I got to my feet. My stomach rumbled again: I was in need of my dinner.

'I'll do what I can, Jenny. I promise you that.'

She thanked me with tears in her eyes and gave me a grateful hug. I felt like Judas.

To my surprise, Jack followed me into the street. 'I'll walk with you as far as Mistress Walker's cottage,' he offered. 'The weaving sheds are closed today, in honour of the Baptist, so my time's my own. I could do with stretching my legs.'

'Does Master Adelard know Burl's been arrested on suspicion of murder?' I asked. 'Will he penalize you for it?'

Jack laughed shortly. 'Thomas Adelard's interested in two things only: weaving and making money. He knows I'm good at my job, and for that reason alone he'd never terminate my apprenticeship.' He went on uncomfortably, 'I didn't quite tell you the truth back there. I *was* awake during the night. That's how I knew Father was there, too, in the cottage.'

'You saw him?'

'N–no. I heard him . . . him and Mother doing . . . well, you know! Doing what married people do.' He coloured slightly.

'Ah! Do you have any idea what time that would have been?'

Jack puckered his lips. 'I don't think I'd been asleep long. Dick was snoring and he always snores just after he dozes off. But what I'm saying is . . .' He paused, unsure how to continue.

I finished for him. 'You don't think a man would make love to his wife and then go out and murder someone. Is that it?'

'Well, certainly not Father. Although I don't believe he'd kill anyone at any time, except by accident. But I can't admit I heard them. It would embarrass Mother.'

'It wouldn't make any difference if you did,' I assured him. 'Your testimony, like Jenny's, would be suspect.'

We were in sight of the pillory and Jack exclaimed in

surprise to see Luke Prettywood standing there. 'But why?' he demanded. 'He's no longer an apprentice.' I explained what had happened and Jack shook his head. 'More fool he! He should know better than to be drawn into an apprentices' quarrel, let alone assault a law officer. Another victim of cuckoo-foot ale, I suppose.'

We had reached Margaret Walker's cottage, but as I was about to take my leave of him, I decided to make a clean breast of things and confessed that I had been summoned to bear witness against his father.

Jack flushed angrily. 'You volunteered this information to Sergeant Manifold? I thought better of you, chapman. Just because Father's been a bit hostile towards you lately, it's surely no reason . . .'

I flung up a hand. 'You're jumping to conclusions. I have no choice. There's another witness who also saw what happened, and who knows I was there. A beggarman who's been wandering around the town for a week or so now.'

Jack's attitude softened. 'The stranger, do you mean? Yes. I've seen him. He's not a Bristol beggar. In fact, I understand our own men have been pretty rough with him; they don't like foreigners trying to steal their trade. I know for a fact he's been chased out of the city on at least two occasions, and I heard he'd been given a good kicking by Long Tom and his gang.' I could hardly conceal my glee. Jack continued. 'It's odd that you should mention him, though. I've seen him once or twice drinking in the Green Lattis and thought him a whingeing, cringing, whining sort of a fellow. Not one of your brazen kind who'll threaten violence if you don't put a coin in his little tin cup. But yesterday morning, I saw him in the Full Moon. I'd been sent over to Saint James's Priory on an errand for Master Adelard. It was very hot and I was feeling thirsty, so I slipped into the Full Moon for a pot of ale.'

'And?' I urged as he paused.

Jack rubbed his chin, fingering a small patch of stubble which he had missed while shaving that morning. He was still young enough to be a novice at the art.

'The stranger was there. I didn't notice him to begin with.

145

As I said, I was very hot, and I went to sit in the darkest, coolest corner I could find. It was early, and a fairly quiet time of day. I kept my head down, so it was a few minutes before I noticed the beggar and his companion.'

'Companion? You mean another beggar?'

'No. That's the funny thing. This other man was quite well dressed. And an even funnier thing is that the beggar himself seemed to be conversing with him on equal terms. In fact, he appeared to be doing most of the talking. The second man just listened and nodded.'

'You didn't happen to overhear any of their conversation?'

'I was too far away. But as I passed them when I left, I did catch one phrase. The beggar murmured something that sounded like "the Midsummer Rose" and he laughed as he said it, as if it were some sort of joke.'

'The Midsummer Rose? Are you certain?'

'Not certain, no. But that's what it sounded like. I couldn't linger. I didn't want to attract attention to myself. All the same,' Jack went on, worrying at his chin again, 'it was odd. The beggarman was like a different person. Someone with authority . . . What do you know about him, Roger? I can tell by the look on your face that you're not surprised by what I've told you . . . Has this anything to do with my father?'

'No, no!' I said quickly, which could have been the truth. Whatever Timothy was playing at, he had nothing personal against Burl Hodge. The tenter was no more than a pawn in his particular game of chess. 'Jack, please don't ask me any further questions. There's a lot I'm not sure of myself as yet. You and Dick and your mother will simply have to trust me. I'll do the very best I can to prove Burl's innocence.'

'All right,' he agreed reluctantly. 'But try not to take too long. I'd rather Father wasn't brought to trial if we can help it. The suspense will make Mother ill.'

I gave him my hand. 'Tell Jenny I'm a witness and why. But keep everything else to yourself.'

He nodded, returned my handshake, then went on his way.

*   *   *

146

Adela and Margaret had finished their dinner, but my place was still laid. A good thick trencher of stale bread sat next to a horn spoon, placed face downwards to prevent the devil from sitting in its bowl. The two elder children, fed and contented, were playing a game of Three Men's Morris, with pebbles for counters on a board scratched on the cottage floor. Adam was doing his best to ruin it for them by running off with the pebbles, while even Hercules ignored my arrival, being preoccupied with outfacing Margaret's black-and-white mongrel.

'How's Jenny?' Adela looked anxious.

'I hope you told her you'd be doing something about this ridiculous arrest,' my former mother-in-law cut in severely, as she ladled pottage into a bowl and lifted a bacon collop from the skillet. I like bacon collops, but I'd already had two for breakfast. I thought longingly of Adela's rabbit pie.

'Jenny's upset, naturally.' I answered Adela first. 'Scared, too. And yes, I have assured her that I'll do my best to prove Burl innocent. I can't do more.'

'You're a witness against him,' Margaret accused. 'So Adela tells me.'

'And I explained why,' my wife protested.

Her cousin snorted. 'I've seen that strange beggar around here once or twice,' she said. 'If I see him again, I'll have him chased out of town so fast, his feet won't touch the ground.'

I caught Adela's eye. She knew who the beggarman was, but would say nothing unless I gave her permission.

'You don't have to be at the Councillors' Meeting Hall until this afternoon,' she chided me. 'There's no reason to bolt your food like that. You'll give yourself indigestion.'

Nicholas and Elizabeth, whose ears were always attuned to the adults' conversation however much it might appear to the contrary, both made a noise like an enormous fart, then rolled around the floor giggling helplessly. Adam, entranced by their atrocious behaviour, tried making similar noises, but only succeeded in blowing a froth of bubbles, which had the other two doubled up and choking with laughter. Even Margaret's and Adela's lips twitched.

I swallowed the last mouthful of bacon and pottage, washed it down with ale and stood up. I whistled to Hercules, put on his rope harness and thanked Margaret politely for my dinner. I had had enough of being the butt of my family's derision.

'And where do you think you're going?' she demanded irritably. 'Adela and I want to discuss Robin Avenel's murder with you.'

'We want to know what you think,' added my wife.

'You also want me to prove Burl's innocence,' I pointed out. 'Therefore, I have things to do.' I kissed Adela. 'Take the children home when you're ready. I'll follow later.'

It was still not midday, although the sun had almost reached its zenith. I pushed my way through the throng of people on Bristol Bridge, up High Street, down Broad Street, under the Frome Gate, across the Frome Bridge, Lewin's Mead, Saint James's Barton, past the Priory . . . I was sweating so much by now that my feet were swollen and my boots inflicting a blister on every toe. Hercules was winded and panting and showing a marked tendency to drag on his rope. He thought we'd gone far enough.

'Not much further, boy,' I encouraged him, and indeed, the Full Moon was at last in sight.

Of course, just my luck, it was busy. A large party of pilgrims, on their way to the shrine of Saint Mary Bellhouse in Saint Peter's Church, had paused for refreshment and to stable their horses. Regulars from Lewin's Mead were lingering over after-dinner ale and postponing the inevitable return to work. I was hard-pressed to find a seat, let alone catch the landlord's eye, but eventually I managed to grab the tunic of a passing pot-boy. While I was waiting for him to bring my drink, I scanned the faces of the customers in the faint hope that Timothy Plummer might be among them, but there was no sign of him. Hercules took advantage of my inattention to make advances to a large, black bitch, who, as females will, suddenly decided she'd had enough and turned on him, trying to gouge out his eye. He retired beneath my stool, whimpering pitifully.

'That'll teach you,' I told him callously. 'Never trust a woman.'

The pot-boy finally remembered me and arrived with my cup of ale. I grabbed him by the tunic for a second time.

'I want to speak to the landlord,' I said. 'Privately.'

He was inclined to scoff until I offered him a groat. 'I'll see what I can do,' he promised.

But it was another half an hour before the landlord presented himself, sweating profusely and with a face like a thundercloud.

'What do you want, chapman? Can't you see how busy we are? You're not even one of my regulars.'

'I'm making enquiries on behalf of Jenny Hodge,' I told him. 'Burl's been arrested on suspicion of murdering Robin Avenel.'

'What's that to do with me?' But then the landlord gave a resigned sigh and wiped his wet hands down the front of his leather apron. 'All right. Step out to the back yard. To tell the truth, I shall be glad of a moment or two's peace and quiet.'

I rose and followed him, dragging Hercules with me, to a door at the rear of the alehouse that gave on to a small, paved yard, at present crowded with empty beer barrels. The landlord regarded them with a certain amount of indignation.

'I've been hoping that Luke Prettywood and a couple of Gregory Alefounder's apprentices would turn up this morning to cart this lot away. But I suppose they're having a Midsummer holiday.'

'A Midsummer hangover, more like. Especially Luke,' I said, and told him what had happened.

'Bloody fool,' the landlord remarked dispassionately. 'Picking on a law officer is never a clever idea. You can't win. But these hot-headed young fellows won't learn. Cuckoo-foot ale, was it? Usually is at these Midsummer feasts. Now, what can I do for you, chapman? I'll have to get back inside soon. I can't leave it all to the boys. It would be chaos if I did.'

He seated himself on an empty barrel and indicated that I should do the same. Hercules sat disconsolately at my feet,

149

dreaming, presumably, of a lost opportunity to display his sexual prowess.

'Yesterday,' I began, 'a beggarman came in here. A stranger. He's been hanging around the city for weeks.'

I had no need to proceed any further. 'Oh, him!' the landlord exclaimed knowingly. 'He's been in here a couple of times, and if there's one thing I'm sure of, it's that he's no beggar.'

I didn't enlighten him. 'What about the man he met?'

'Huh! Shan't forget him in a hurry, because I had the Devil's own work to understand what he was saying. Got the hang of it in the end if he spoke very slowly and distinctly. He was a Scot.'

'A Scot?' I echoed in disbelief.

But if that were true, Jack Hodge would have been none the wiser, even had he been able to overhear the man's conversation with Timothy Plummer. For the speech, not only of Scotsmen, but also of our own countrymen from the wild wastes in the north of England, is as incomprehensible to a Wessex man's ears as our way of talking is to them. Bristolians are attuned to the way Irishmen, Frenchmen, Bretons, Castilians, Aragonese, Portuguese and any other nationality whose ships tie up daily at our wharves mangle our tongue. But Scotsmen are a mystery, their country as remote as the moon. Presumably Timothy had been able to understand this man; but then, Timothy was a part of the court, which was constantly on the move, travelling the length and breadth of the country and in communication with all sorts and conditions of people.

But what on earth was a Scot doing in Bristol?

Without realizing it, I must have voiced the question aloud, because the landlord of the Full Moon shrugged and said, 'All I know is there's been some sort of trouble between the Scottish king and his brothers. Pretty much like our lot when you come to think about it.'

I raised my eyebrows at him. 'How do you know?'

He eased himself further back on his barrel, so that its raised rim cut into his ample thighs at a different angle.

'Some weeks back, a Dominican friar stopped here on his

150

way to the friary in the Broad Meadows. He'd come from way up north – Durham or some such godforsaken place.' We're nothing if not biased down here in the west. 'They're nearly as close to the Scots there as we are here to the southern Welsh. Apparently, the rumours from across the border are that King James has accused both his brothers of treason and the younger one, the Earl of Mar, has been found dead in suspicious circumstances. The older one, the Duke of Albany, has vanished. Wise fellow! No one knows where he is, but the odds are on him having fled to England with a view to making his way across the Channel to France.' That made sense. The French and the Scots have always been as thick as thieves. The landlord heaved himself off his barrel. 'Now, I must be getting back,' he went on. 'I'm sorry not to have been of more help. When you next see Jenny Hodge, tell her I think Richard Manifold's a fool, if that's of any comfort to her.'

I nodded. 'Do you mind if I stay out here for a while? Just to give myself time to think.'

'By all means.' The landlord spread his hands. 'You're not disturbing anyone. I'll send a lad out with a mazer of ale.'

I thanked him and he vanished indoors, where I soon heard his voice raised in anger at one of the pot-boys. I stared ahead of me, deep in thought, impervious to Hercules' tugs on his lead. The dog gave one final disgruntled yap before settling down, but he let me know he wasn't pleased by cocking his leg and peeing all over my ankle. But even that didn't bother me; at least, not for the moment. I was too deep in thought. Later, I might find time to get annoyed.

Trouble in the Scots royal family was probably as commonplace as it was in our own, and recalcitrant brothers were no novelty for any ruler. All the same, if the Dominican friar were to be believed, this sounded a little more serious than most fraternal disagreements. Accusations of treason were being levelled by King James, and one of his brothers, the Earl of Mar, had already been found dead in dubious circumstances. The Duke of Albany was probably in hiding somewhere in this country, trying to find a ship to carry him to France.

151

So, who would be looking for him? King James' agents for a start, hoping to drag him back to Scotland to face almost certain death. Secondly, our own king's spies would be scouring the country, needing to discover him before the Scots did if King Edward were to gain a valuable hostage and a pawn in the bargaining game. Or they might be working together.

And where would these gentlemen be searching for their quarry? Common sense suggested the harbour towns and ports of south-east and southern England as the likeliest places. Dover. Rye. Sandwich. Portsmouth. Plymouth.

So why were Timothy Plummer and a mysterious Scotsman meeting secretly in a Bristol alehouse?

Fourteen

'You're late,' Richard Manifold said as I presented myself in the Councillors' Hall beside Saint Ewen's Church.

'How can I be late?' I countered. 'You set no specific time. Afternoon, you said. It's afternoon.'

'Don't be obstructive.' He beckoned forward his clerk, a sour-faced man with a scrawny throat and a sharp little nose that quivered in constant anticipation of trouble. 'Master Peters will take down your statement.'

I looked around me, pointedly ignoring the clerk's raised quill as it hovered above the inkwell.

'Where's the beggarman?' I asked. 'Or has he been and gone? If so, I'd like to hear exactly what he had to say.'

I noted the flicker of a glance between sergeant and clerk before Richard said firmly, 'You're here to give *your* statement. Nothing else need concern you.'

'He hasn't made one, has he?' I asked, hazarding a guess.

But it didn't need second sight to work out that Timothy had never intended to present his evidence formally. Having directed Richard's attention towards Burl Hodge and away from the Avenel family and their activities, he would make himself scarce. If he did reappear in his beggarman's disguise, which I somehow doubted, he would steer clear of the law as much as possible.

'I know where to put my hand on our friend when I want him,' Richard boasted, but I could see by the shifty gleam in his eyes that he was lying. 'You just give me your version of Burl Hodge's attack on Robin Avenel yesterday evening. I've told you: that's all you need worry about.'

I thought of refusing, but there had to be other witnesses beside Timothy and myself who had observed the quarrel.

153

What was to be gained by landing myself in the bridewell?

So I told the clerk what he needed to know, mitigating Burl's part in events as far as possible, but without much success. On Richard's command, whole sentences were struck from the record as being irrelevant. At last, however, I was free to go; which was just as well because by this time I was in a towering temper. I untied Hercules' string and dragged him downstairs and out into Corn Street, where I crossed to the Green Lattis. A cup of ale would speed my recovery. I wanted to think.

I had proceeded to the Councillors' Hall directly from the Full Moon, having decided to get the unpleasant business of the afternoon over and done with before considering the fresh knowledge with which the Full Moon landlord had presented me. But while walking across the Frome Bridge, I had recalled the man I'd heard in the 'murder' house at Rownham Passage; remembered the accent I had been unable to place. Could its owner have been a Scot? Yet his words had been clear enough. 'What are we going to do with him? Toss him in the river?' And then, 'I'll use my knife. Finish him off.'

I sipped my ale thoughtfully. So . . . A Scot whose way of talking was not totally incomprehensible to my Saxon ears. An educated man, therefore; one who was accustomed to mingling with Englishmen and to modifying the thickness of his speech for their understanding. I recollected the ring I had found embedded in the mattress and which now reposed in my secret hiding place at home; the rich chasing of the gold band and the two letter As carved into the roundel. A for Albany, perhaps? But if that were so, it brought me full circle to my original question. What would the king of Scotland's fugitive brother be doing in Bristol? And what possible connection could he have with Robin Avenel and his sister? There was no explanation that made any sense.

I abandoned the riddle, for the time being at least, and started looking about me in the vain hope of spotting Timothy, but to no avail. I therefore finished my drink and considered what to do next.

After some reflection, I decided to call at the Avenel house in Broad Street and offer my condolences, but second thoughts told me I was unlikely to be a welcome visitor. However, I had never found this an insurmountable difficulty in the past: I simply took my pack and went to the kitchen door instead of to the front. And servants were very often a more valuable source of information than their masters. I doubted if Robin Avenel's servants would be mourning his death with any great sense of loss; at any rate, nothing that the prospect of a yard or two of ribbon or a cheap pair of laces wouldn't cure. He had never really been popular with any of them.

I stepped out of the cool shadows of the Green Lattis into the blazing heat of the busy street, dragging a reluctant Hercules behind me. For many people the Feast of Saint John the Baptist was a holiday; but as happens so often on these occasions, some are forced to work, some choose to work, and others, like myself, who ought to work because they need the money, use it as an excuse to loaf around and do nothing. So Adela, who had returned home from Redcliffe with the children some time before, was pleasantly surprised by my sudden appearance and my declared intention of collecting my pack.

'But what about Burl?' she demurred.

I could tell, however, that her enquiry was half-hearted. I muttered something indistinguishable, adding, 'I'll leave Hercules with you,' and slipped quickly out of the street door in case she should protest. I poked my head back in just long enough to shout a request that we had the rabbit pie for supper, then was gone before there could be any argument on the subject.

I retraced my steps to Corn Street and turned into the narrow lane that runs along the backs of the Broad Street houses, unlatching the gate of the Avenels' walled garden and letting myself in. Here, at least, very little had changed since Alderman Weaver's day. The pear and the apple trees still flourished, as did the bed of herbs and simples, although the border of flowers had disappeared. The lean-to privy looked somewhat more dilapidated than I remembered it, but that was only to be expected with the passing of the years.

155

My knock on the back door was answered by one of the kitchen maids, whose eyes brightened when she saw me.

'It's the pedlar,' she hissed over her shoulder. 'Shall I let him in?'

Three more girls crowded round, giggling. 'We ought not,' said a freckle-faced beauty with sapphire-blue eyes. 'Haven't you heard, chapman? Master Avenel's dead. Murdered.'

'That's why I thought you might need cheering up,' I lied.

After a whispered consultation, they decided that perhaps they had better not let me in. The housekeeper, who it seemed was at present closeted with Mistress Alefounder, was a dragon who would probably dismiss them on the spot if they did. But they showed no signs of wanting me to leave, and three of them jostled for position in the open doorway, having detailed the smallest and youngest girl to keep watch for the dragon's return. I crouched down and spread my open pack on the ground, although I guessed they had little money to spend.

'How is Mistress Avenel bearing up in these fearful and tragic circumstances?' I enquired. 'It must be a terrible day both for her and for Mistress Alefounder.'

The freckle-faced girl sniffed. 'Well, I suppose it was a shock for them both when Sergeant Manifold called round this morning to break the news. It was a shock for all of us if it comes to that. Dame Dorothy couldn't speak for a full ten minutes. Longest any of us can remember her holding her tongue.'

Her two companions sniggered. The snub-nosed girl with a cast in one eye remarked nastily, 'The old dragon fancied 'im, you know – the master, I mean, though 'eaven knows why. It's more 'n the mistress did.' There was another explosion of laughter, hastily suppressed.

'Not a happy marriage, then?' I suggested.

The tallest of the maids, a plain, dour girl with a small, set face, who smelled faintly and pleasantly of lavender, snorted her agreement. She had a brighter, more intelligent look than her companions, and giggled less.

'According to my mother, it was a marriage arranged by

156

their fathers,' she said. 'But Ma always reckoned it was never going to work. She says Master Robin could never put up with a wife who's prettier than himself . . . Who *was* prettier . . .' she amended, her voice suddenly tailing off.

Her companions laughed, then sucked in their breath as the realization of their master's death began to sink in. But the pause was only momentary. The next minute, they were rummaging in my pack, searching for something they could afford to buy. I let them get on with it and addressed myself to the tall girl.

'Mistress Avenel isn't as upset as she might be, then, about her husband's murder?'

'I didn't say that,' she whipped back at me. 'Murder's a shocking thing, when all's said and done.'

'Very true . . . So how has Mistress Alefounder borne the news?'

The girl looked uncomfortable, plainly wondering if she should even be discussing the matter, let alone advancing an opinion. She cast another glance across her shoulder, but the little kitchen maid called Bet indicated that there was as yet no sign of the housekeeper's return. Reassured, Jess made the decision to take me into her confidence.

'Mistress Alefounder's upset, all right, though she ain't the sort to do a lot of wailing and gnashing of teeth. She don't put on a show for other people's benefit, nor does she give them what they expect to see. There's been visitors a-knockin' at the door all morning, but she's the one who's received 'em. Mistress Avenel's been laid down on her bed, the chamber shutters closed, pretending she's too afflicted even to accept condolences.'

The other two girls, their attention caught, sat back on their heels to listen. The freckle-faced one laughed.

'Miaow! Miaow! You always did fancy that Luke Prettywood yourself, didn't you, Jess?'

Jess coloured up to the border of her linen cap, but, to her credit, ignored the jibe.

'You were saying? About Mistress Alefounder?' I prompted her.

She rubbed her nose reflectively. 'Like I told you, she's

upset all right. But . . . Well . . . I'd say she's as much angry as tearful. Old Master Avenel come round this morning. Now he *was* in a state, and no mistake. But it didn't stop Mistress Alefounder shouting at him. We all heard her. Couldn't help ourselves. "The fool," she was saying. "Picking a quarrel with that Burl Hodge! Thinking himself better than other people. I warned him no good would come of it."'

I bit my lip. 'You're sure that's what she said?'

'Oh yes,' the snub-nosed girl confirmed. 'The kitchen door was open and she and old Peter Avenel were stood in the hall.'

This was bad news as far as Burl was concerned. If this were to be cited in evidence – and there was no doubt that Richard Manifold, in his slow but thorough way, would get around to questioning members of the Avenel household when he considered the time was right – it would make the case against him appear even blacker.

'I'll tell you something odd, though,' Jess remarked suddenly.

I rose, rubbing my aching thighs. 'What?' I asked hopefully.

'She's coming,' squeaked our lookout as she scuttled back to the kitchen table to resume her pastry-making.

Snub-nose and Freckle-face joined her, the first to chop herbs, the second to pound strips of meat into submission with a wooden mallet. But Jess, my informant, was made of sterner stuff.

'Tell her I'm in the jakes,' she hissed, pushing me backwards and resolutely shutting the kitchen door behind us.

She helped me bundle my goods into my pack, then led me round to the other side of the privy, out of sight of the kitchen.

'What did you want to tell me?' I urged again, as she once more appeared to hesitate.

'Well . . . it's nothing much, really. It's just that I was the one who opened the door to Sergeant Manifold this morning. It was very early, not long past cockcrow. He told me to wake the mistress and the master's sister and fetch 'em downstairs as he had some very bad news to tell them. Which of course I did . . . But then I hung about trying to hear what it was he had to say.' Jess blinked guiltily.

'A very natural thing to do,' I consoled her.

'Yes . . . well . . . that's as maybe.' She was nobody's fool, this girl. 'I followed Mistress Avenel and Mistress Alefounder downstairs and then just stood there instead of going back to the kitchen. They forgot about me, you see, but I had a clear view of both of them as the sergeant broke the news of the master's murder . . .' Jess drew a deep breath. 'Look,' she said, 'I know Burl Hodge has been arrested, and I know your reputation in this town. I know, if the others don't, why you've come snooping around here this afternoon, pretending to peddle your goods. I know what you're up to.' She knew altogether too much, this one. 'So you must understand that what I'm going to say is only a feeling on my part. Nothing more.'

'I accept that,' I said gently. 'But tell me all the same.'

She nodded. 'It's just . . . Well, I just had the impression that the news wasn't as great a shock to either of them as they tried to make out. Oh, they put on a brave show,' she added with a cynical little smile, 'and it fooled the sergeant and Dame Dorothy, Mistress Hollyns and the rest of the servants, who all came running to see what the noise was about. Mistress was shrieking fit to waken the dead and Mistress Alefounder was white as a ghost, but . . .' Jess broke off, shrugging.

'But it didn't fool you. Why not?'

She chewed her bottom lip, struggling to frame an answer.

'They . . . They accepted what they'd been told too readily. There was . . . What can I say? There was no *disbelief*. Does that sound silly?' I shook my head. She continued, 'If someone told me something like that, they'd have to tell me two or three times before I could take it in. And there was another thing. One of them – but I can't be certain now which of them it was – said something about blood. But I'd swear no one had mentioned then that the master had been stabbed. "Murdered", was all the sergeant had said. But . . . Well . . . I could be wrong. He didn't seem

159

to pick it up. Or if he did, he didn't seem to think it of any importance.'

No, he wouldn't, I thought meanly. I'd never had a high opinion of Richard Manifold's quickness of mind. (But Adela would tell me that I was prejudiced.)

Someone opened the back door and a stern voice called, 'Jess Morgan! Get back in here this minute! I know what you're up to! Sitting on that jakes, wasting time! You can't fool me, my girl!'

'Coming, Dame Dorothy!' Jess put a hand over her mouth to muffle the sound as though she were inside the privy. A resourceful girl, I decided, who, if there was any justice in the world, should go far. Unfortunately, justice is all too often in short supply. At least, that's been my experience.

'Here!' I whispered, laying a detaining hand on her arm. I delved into my pack and brought out four lengths of silk ribbon. 'Share these with your friends.'

'Thank you,' she answered gruffly and turned to go, but once again I stopped her.

'What about Mistress Hollyns?' I asked. 'You haven't said anything about her. Was she upset?'

Jess laughed shortly; a small, snorting sound. 'Not so's you'd notice, but she's a deep one, she is. The master took a fancy to her, I feel sure o' that. He had a roving eye – and roving hands to match,' she added viciously. So viciously, in fact, that I began to suspect Robin Avenel had passed Jess over for her prettier, more nubile kitchen companions.

'Why do you believe Master Avenel fancied Mistress Hollyns?'

Jess shrugged. 'I overheard him discussing her once with Mistress Alefounder. He referred to her as a midsummer rose. Well, there ain't no one else in the house who'd answer that description except the mistress, and I'm sure he wasn't talking about her, or he wouldn't have been so angry when he saw me in the doorway and realized I must've overheard what he'd said. Furious, he was. I reckon he'd have turfed me out if Mistress Alefounder hadn't told him not to be such an idiot. She had a word with me afterwards and warned me not to repeat what I'd heard the master say. I told her it was

nothing to me if he fancied Mistress Hollyns, and none o'
my business. She needn't be afeared I'd go telling tales.'

The kitchen door was again flung open and a voice
screeched, 'Jess! Come out of there at once, do you hear
me? *At once!*'

'Stay out of sight until I'm indoors,' my companion advised
me, tucking the ribbons I had given her into a pocket. She
hastened round the side of the privy. 'Sorry, Dame Dorothy.
I felt a bit sick. It's the flux. I was getting some air.'

The housekeeper hissed something in reply that I couldn't
quite catch, then the kitchen door closed behind the pair of
them.

I picked up my pack and crept quietly out of the garden.

The Midsummer Rose. Those were the words Jack Hodge
thought he had overheard in the Full Moon; words uttered
by Timothy Plummer to his companion, the unknown
Scotsman – if, that was, the landlord were correct in his
assumption. And now, here was one of Robin Avenel's kitchen
maids asserting that Robin had applied the same description
to Rowena Hollyns. What was I to make of it all? Of course,
the ceremony of the Midsummer Rose had probably been in
most people's minds as the Midsummer Eve's feast
approached, so Robin's use of the term might have meant
no more than that. But I couldn't believe the same explanation held good in Timothy's case. And although I was in no
position to say for certain, I would have bet my last groat
that women played a very small and insignificant part in the
spy's life. If he needed one, he most likely crossed the Thames
and paid for one of the Bishop of Winchester's geese, as the
whores of Southwark were generally known, on account of
all the brothels in the area belonging to that reverend and
godly gentleman.

I felt even more confused. And, what was worse, I was
unable to see how any of the information I had so far obtained
would help me to prove Burl Hodge's innocence. But thoughts
of brothels and Winchester geese had put me in mind of
Silas Witherspoon. I was not that far from Gropecunt Lane.
I would pay him a visit.

'I told you! It won't be ready for a week,' was his greeting to me as I pushed open the door of his apothecary's shop and went in.

'No, no! I've not come about that,' I assured him, dropping my pack on the dusty floor and leaning one elbow on the equally dusty counter.

There was a pleasanter smell in the shop today; the chilblain remedy had evidently finished its concoction and been bottled. At the moment, he was counting out pills from an earthenware jar into a small leather box.

'Water parsnip tablets,' he informed me in that mellifluous voice of his, so at odds with his appearance. 'Just three a day will assuage the pain of hernia, disperse calculi in the body, get rid of freckles on women and scales on horses. Want to buy some?'

I shook my head. 'No, thank you. I don't have a hernia, my wife doesn't have freckles, neither of us has the stone and we're too poor to afford a horse.'

'Always as well to be prepared,' he suggested, but at my dismissive gesture, he shrugged. 'Please yourself! So what do you want? The love manual, perhaps?'

'I suppose you've heard that Robin Avenel was found murdered this morning?' I asked him.

He countered my enquiry with one of his own. 'How long have you lived in this city, chapman?'

'Six years, on and off. Why?' But I could guess what he was going to say.

'Then you should know better than to ask such a foolish question. It's what? Five, six hours now since the body was discovered? The news is probably being cried through the streets of Westbury and Keynsham by this time. Of course I know!'

'In that case,' I said, leaning a little further over the counter, 'you can tell me the truth about the house at Rownham Passage. You can't hurt Master Avenel now. Was he the person who rented it from you at the end of last month?'

Silas closed the lid of the pillbox, set the earthenware jar upright on the counter and regarded me thoughtfully. But he still seemed reluctant to speak.

'Why do you want to know?' he demanded at last.

'The information might just save an innocent man from being tried for murder,' I told him.

'Ah!' The apothecary rubbed his nose. 'Burl Hodge. Yes. I heard he'd been arrested. You think he didn't do it?'

'No. I mean yes.' I was getting confused. 'I think he's innocent of the charge that Sergeant Manifold's brought against him.'

Here, I had to wait a minute or two while Master Witherspoon attended to a couple of customers; a respectable old dame in rusty black, who I recognized as living in Wine Street, and one of the brothel keepers who kept a bawdy house further along the lane. The first wanted fleabane lozenges to burn in order to rid her cottage of fleas; the other a box of dried hare droppings to use as pessaries.

When they had departed with their purchases, Silas once more gave me his attention.

'I daresay you're close to the mark,' he said. 'About Burl Hodge being innocent, I mean. Never trust a law officer to get it right more than one time out of three, that's my motto. And a sound one! They're always too anxious for a pat on the back. Get some poor wretch dangling from a rope's end and they're happy. Never mind whether he did it or not. And Burl's a good man from what I know of him. A bit hot-headed by all accounts, but not the man to kill anyone in cold blood.'

'So?' I demanded impatiently. '*Was* Robin Avenel the person who approached you about your house at Rownham Passage?'

I really knew the answer, of course, but I wanted to hear the confirmation from the apothecary's own lips.

He thought for moment or two longer, then nodded.

'I can't see what harm it would do to tell you now. My promise was to him alive, not dead. Yes, it was Robin Avenel.'

Fifteen

Having finally admitted as much, the apothecary grew quite expansive on the subject.

'Robin called here. About the third week of May. Before his sister came to stay with him. Wanted to know if he could rent the house at Rownham Passage for a night. Beginning of June.'

'Did he say why?'

Silas leaned closer. His breath smelled powerfully of garlic.

'Two friends of his were coming from Worcester, on pilgrimage to Glastonbury. He couldn't house them because Mistress Alefounder and her maid would be lodged in Broad Street by then.'

I gave a derisive snort. 'And Bristol has no decent hostelries where they could have stayed? You didn't believe his story?'

The apothecary laughed. 'No, of course not. But that house has been like a millstone round my neck for years. I was hardly likely to turn down the chance of making a bit of money from it, now was I? And what he offered was generous, considering the state of the place. If you want to know what I really thought, it was that Robin was having a secret rendezvous with a woman. Someone he didn't want either his wife or his sister to know about. He asked if there was a bed in the house. I said yes, but nothing fit for a lady.'

'And what was his answer to that?'

'He said there was no lady, just two men. I thought he was trying to pull the wool over my eyes, but I couldn't say so.'

I digested this for a while.

'So who do you think killed Master Avenel?' Silas asked in time.

'Footpads? Pickpockets? The streets aren't safe anywhere nowadays. But of one thing I'm certain: it wasn't Burl Hodge.'

'Mmm.' Silas puckered up his mouth. 'They say Robin Avenel wasn't robbed. Still had his rings and purse on him when he was found. Leastways, that's what I was told. In which case, it doesn't sound much like thieves to me.'

I shrugged. 'Time will tell.'

The bright eyes regarded me shrewdly and Silas scratched his deformed shoulder with long, talon-like nails. 'Do you connect this murder with what happened to you at Rownham Passage?'

'Oh, you've heard the story now, have you? I didn't think, when we talked the day before yesterday, that you knew anything about it. In fact, you enquired if my interest meant that I wanted to hire the house myself.'

'Ah!' He appeared to be unnecessarily disconcerted by this remark. 'It would seem that that particular piece of gossip was slow in reaching me for some reason or another.'

'Very slow,' I agreed. 'It happened three weeks and more ago.'

'Well, there you are, then!' he exclaimed, spreading wide his beautiful hands, as if proving something.

But what he had proved I wasn't quite sure. It struck me as odd that the story had passed him by, when practically everyone else in the city had known of it from the moment I was brought home in the farmer's cart. I tried to work out why this fact might be significant, but failed.

'I must be going,' I said. 'Thank you for the information.'

'I hope it's been of some help.' His eyes twinkled roguishly. 'I shall have your order ready for you soon. A large size, I think you said?'

I suddenly felt embarrassed and made my escape. The suffocating heat of the midday streets had lessened, and between the overhanging roofs I could see a wrack of feathered cloud imprinted on the blue. I thought of Luke Prettywood and the apprentices still languishing in the pillory and was grateful on their behalf as well as my own. I paused, pondering my next move, then decided to see for myself the scene of the crime.

I made my way, therefore, to Jewry Lane. A man crossing the Frome Bridge in my direction hailed me.

'Ah! Chapman! Daydreaming as usual?' The tone was pitched somewhere between the jocular and the offensive.

I smiled. 'Master Capgrave! What a pleasure! Have you deserted your post as gatekeeper?'

He told me he was on his way home to Fish Lane, so he joined me, his rolling gait, reminiscent of a sailor's, being the only way in which his spindly legs could maintain the balance of his short, squat body. The small hazel eyes beneath their beetling brows regarded me knowingly.

'I'm not on duty today. Come to see where Master Avenel was murdered, have you?'

'I'm curious, yes. But there's more to it than that. Sergeant Manifold has arrested Burl Hodge and I'm not convinced of his guilt.'

'So you've decided to do a little sleuthing of your own, is that it? Ah well! Good luck to you. I've never thought Dick Manifold one half as clever as he thinks himself. But I can't assist you, I'm afraid.'

'You've given evidence in the case. The sergeant told me.'

'Then he must also have told you that I saw nothing. The body wasn't here when I went home yesterday evening.'

'You couldn't possibly have missed seeing it, I suppose?'

A stupid question which thoroughly deserved the scathing look he turned upon me and the note of utter contempt with which he answered.

'No! I couldn't have missed it. What sort of unobservant idiot do you take me for? There were precious few people about. They were all at the Midsummer Eve feast, stuffing their guts and getting drunk, while those poor buggers like me, who are always at the public's beck and call, were keeping the city safe. Even my wife,' he added viciously, 'had gone off with her friends.'

It was on the tip of my tongue to point out that he could have joined the feast when he came off duty, but I had

166

summed him up as one of those people who enjoy a grudge. So I merely asked, 'Did you see anyone at all?'

He shrugged. 'Only old Witherspoon, the apothecary. I don't think he cares for all this junketing, either. It's his deformity, I suppose. People laugh at him.'

'What was he doing?' I demanded.

'Doing?' The gatekeeper sneered. 'What should he be doing? He was just walking along by Saint Giles's Church and minding his own business. Going home, presumably.'

'Then he could have been to the feast and left early.'

'Could have been, aye. But I doubt it. I told you. He isn't comfortable in the presence of a crowd, especially of young people when they've had more to drink than is good for them. They pick on him. Make fun of him.' I wondered if the same applied to the gatekeeper, but kept my thoughts to myself. 'Although now I come to think of it,' Edgar continued, 'maybe he had had a drink or two. He was behaving rather oddly.'

'In what way?'

'We–ell . . . It was nothing really. Just the manner in which he was walking. He was keeping close to the wall of Saint Giles's and the other buildings, and taking very precise, evenly paced steps. I spoke to him and remarked on the increase of noise coming from the direction of the city streets, where the feast was being held. He didn't answer, although he'd heard me. He seemed to be concentrating on his feet, and it did occur to me then that he might have had a cup or two of cuckoo-foot ale. But when he reached Saint John's Arch, he turned round and called out, "Good evening to you, Master Capgrave! A growing crescendo of noise, as you say." Well, that wasn't quite what I'd said, as you can guess. A bloody great row was what I'd called it. "It sounds to me," he adds, "as if there's trouble brewing. I'm going home while the going's good, and if you've any sense you'll do the same." So I did. And he was right, as it turned out. Apprentices' riot. Haven't had one of them in Bristol for a year or two now.'

'What about your wife? Was she all right?'

'She's always all right,' he answered morosely. 'Can't get rid of her . . . And talk of the devil! I must be late for supper.'

167

A very tall, almost emaciated woman was bearing purposefully down upon us from the direction of Fish Lane.

'Mistress Capgrave,' I said before she had time to open her mouth, 'I'm afraid I'm to blame for detaining your husband.'

I smiled seductively, and for the first time that day my charm seemed to do the trick. The set, angry lines of the angular face softened slightly.

'Oh well, in that case . . .' she simpered.

'Your husband tells me you were at the feast yesterday evening. I hope you weren't harmed in the riot.'

'I can look after myself,' she retorted grimly. 'But there wouldn't have been a riot if some people hadn't deliberately stirred things up, telling the apprentices that they were put upon and overworked, while others enjoyed themselves. Encouraging them to be discontented with their lot. Easy enough to do when the silly fools are full of cuckoo-foot ale.'

'*Who* was stirring up the apprentices?' I asked.

Mistress Capgrave sniffed. 'Well, there were two of them that I could see. One was that stranger, the beggarman who's been hanging around the city this past week or so. And the other was Apothecary Witherspoon.'

'Witherspoon?' Her husband was scornful. 'He wasn't at the feast.'

'If you mean he wasn't eating and drinking and joining in the games, you're right. But he was there. My friend and I saw him. Heard him, too. We were seated at the end of a table where some butcher's apprentices were cooking meat over an open fire and sweating like the pigs they were roasting. Witherspoon was telling them how they were nothing but slaves, how their masters took advantage of them.'

'What could be his purpose in doing such a stupid thing?' the gatekeeper grumbled. 'He might have guessed what would come of it. Silly old fool! The heat's making him lose his wits.'

'And the beggarman?' I asked Mistress Capgrave. 'You said he was inciting the apprentices to riot as well.'

'Inciting is too strong a word,' she demurred. 'Sympathizing with them just enough to make them feel mutinous is nearer the mark. He was hanging around, I suppose, hoping to cadge some scraps of food and just grumbling about the world in general.'

'Do you think that Master Witherspoon and the beggar might have been in collusion?'

'Why should they have been? The apothecary, in spite of his odd appearance, is a respectable citizen and unlikely to have any truck with a beggarman. And certainly not such a strange one.'

'Then why do you think they were doing it?'

'I can't speak for the beggar,' Mistress Capgrave said. 'Apothecary Witherspoon was just being thoughtless and irresponsible, and I'm on my way to tell him so now.'

Edgar was disappointed. 'I thought you'd come to tell me my supper's ready.'

'Food! Food! It's all you think about,' his wife grumbled, and she strode on her way.

Edgar looked uncomfortable, aware that his image as a person of authority might be permanently tarnished in my eyes.

'I'll be getting home, then,' he said with what dignity he could muster. 'I've been told that Robin Avenel's body was found just over there, outside the church door. Killed with his own dagger, too. Well, good afternoon to you, chapman. Good luck.'

He rolled away along the quayside. I watched him for a moment or two, mulling over what I had been told by Mistress Capgrave and trying to work out what it might mean. As far as the apothecary was concerned, I saw no good reason why she should not be right. It had been less intentional malevolence than a stupid blunder; an attempt to sympathize with those he felt to be as much the victims of an unfair existence as himself. But Timothy Plummer was a different matter. There was nothing haphazard about any of his actions: what he did, he did with a purpose. So why would he want an apprentices' riot? There was only one answer that I could think of. He wanted a diversion for some business of his own. The murder of Robin Avenel?

169

I approached the Jewry Lane entrance to Saint Giles's Church and scrutinized the ground just outside the door and for several feet all around. But there was nothing to be seen. This was hardly surprising. The storm of the previous night would have washed away all traces of blood, and eradicated any signs of a struggle. Nevertheless, I made a thorough search just in case there was anything at all to be found, but I was out of luck. After a few moment's contemplation of the cobbles, I pushed open the door and went inside, closing it carefully behind me.

It was, as always, very cool and quiet within, the noise and bustle of the quayside penetrating the thick stone only as the distant echoes of a dream. The gold and reds, the silver and blues, the bronze and greens of walls and wood-work glowed as warmly as the precious jewels that adorned the statues of Saint Giles and Our Lady. A few candles were burning on the altar, but today's supplicants had been few in number, and the one that I took and lit was not intended as a votive offering, but to light my way downstairs.

Why I felt this sudden impulse to visit the crypt, I wasn't sure. Looking back, I feel convinced that God was taking a hand in my affairs again, but at the time, most unusually, my suspicions were not aroused.

At the bottom of the steps, I paused, raising my candle aloft, its soft golden radiance illuminating the shelves of coffins. I slipped my pack from my back, reflecting guiltily that I had sold nothing. Adela would not be pleased. She would put two and two together and realize that I had never had any intention of selling my wares, but had, in fact, been meddling in affairs that should, by rights, not concern me.

I advanced slowly into the second chamber of the old synagogue cellars. There was the familiar smell of must and damp and the sweet, stale scent of rotting wood. Some of the pieces of furniture had been stored down there so long – their existence probably now forgotten by their owners – that they were disintegrating. Experimentally, I touched the back of an old nursing chair, which promptly keeled over as one of its front legs fell off. Much of it was infested with woodworm, and a child's cradle nearby was draped in cobwebs.

I raised my candle higher and went forward into the third chamber. As always, the place gave me a sense of unease and foreboding which I found difficult to explain. The shadows curtseyed across the walls, making the very stones seem alive, the home of something dark and evil.

With an effort, I pulled myself together. I was a grown man of twenty-six, too old to be indulging in such fantasies. Yet I could feel the hairs lifting on the nape of my neck and I was suddenly convinced that someone else was in the chamber with me. I whirled around, painfully aware that I was unarmed, having foolishly left my cudgel at home.

There was, of course, no one there. Cautiously, I prowled back through the second cellar to the crypt, but both rooms were empty of any human life except my own. Then I walked back again, still unsure what it was that I was looking for.

The dark stain was in the middle of the floor in the third and final cellar, easy enough to overlook amidst the crowding shadows, but suddenly made obvious by the way in which the light was slanting from my candle. I dropped to my knees, placing the candlestick on the dusty floor, and rubbed it. The stain had dried, but I was certain it was blood, and a few dark, crusty flakes came away on my fingers. I noticed, also, that the film of dust covering the flagstones nearby was very disturbed, as if there had been some kind of a struggle. On each occasion I had been down here, there had always been footprints, but I knew that Marianne Avenel and Luke Prettywood used the cellar as a trysting place; and if them, why not other lovers?

The disturbance of the dust today, however, suggested a scuffle. Someone had recently been attacked here. And killed? Was this where Robin Avenel had *really* been murdered? But if so, who would have moved his body, and why? What would be the point of shifting it, especially if the killer had been Burl Hodge? He would have had nothing to gain . . . Unless, of course, he had been trying to make it look like a street killing. But in that case, why did he fail to remove Robin's purse and rings? Because he had no time? Because he was interrupted by the sounds of the approaching Watch? Had he panicked and run?

This was ridiculous. I was beginning to argue in favour of Burl being the murderer. I must start again.

He had gone home with his wife and their sons to take refuge from the apprentices' riot, and I believed Jenny Hodge when she said she would have known if her husband had left her side during the night. Moreover, while it was just possible that an angry man might have overtaken his quarry in the open street, it was highly unlikely that Burl would have pursued Robin Avenel into Saint Giles's and down into the crypt ... But not impossible, which would be Richard Manifold's response if I told him what I thought I now knew concerning Robin Avenel's death. *Where* he was murdered was of no importance compared with *why*. Motive was everything, and at present I could offer the sergeant no alternative to Burl's.

There was Luke Prettywood, of course, who was in love – or what passed for love – with Marianne Avenel, but he had been in the bridewell for assaulting Jack Gload. For the same reason, Marianne could be thought to have a motive, but I doubted if her affection for Luke and her discontent with Robin were sufficiently powerful emotions to turn her into a killer. Furthermore, my discovery effectively ruled her out. There was no way she could have moved her husband's body on her own, even had she wanted to. And I had no doubt that if I made enquiries, there would be enough witnesses among the members of her household to prove that she was asleep in Broad Street at the time of the murder.

All of which confirmed my original conviction that Robin's death was connected with whatever treasonable activities he and his sister were engaged in. It was equally connected with Timothy Plummer's presence in Bristol and the part he had played in throwing suspicion on an innocent man. And there was one other person I had not yet named to myself as the possible, or even probable, killer: Rowena Hollyns, the woman I had recently seen stab a man to death with as little compunction as she would step on a woodlouse. The Midsummer Rose, as Robin Avenel had called her ...

172

Words also spoken by Timothy Plummer in the Full Moon, if Jack Hodge had overheard him correctly. And it suddenly occurred to me that they must have some special significance; they were not simply an expression of Robin Avenel's lecherous admiration for his sister's maid, as Jess had assumed.

The flickering flame warned me that the candle had almost burned out. I straightened my aching legs and stood for a second or two longer staring down at the dark stain on the cellar flagstones. I decided there was nothing to be gained at present by going to Richard Manifold with my discovery: it wouldn't influence him into releasing Burl. I had to find the real murderer and trick him – or her – into admitting the fact. And first and foremost, I had to locate Timothy Plummer. I could only pray that he had not returned to London having achieved his object in Bristol by disposing of Robin Avenel.

The thought intruded again. Was Timothy the murderer? If so, I had no more hope of proving Burl innocent than I had of building a bridge between Ghyston Cliff and the heights of Ashton-Leigh. But didn't the same thing apply if Timothy had commissioned the killing from some hired assassin? Wasn't I fooling myself that, in the prevailing circumstances, I could save Burl's neck? No! I, too, had a friend at court, the most important man in the kingdom, after the King. I would appeal to the Duke of Gloucester himself, even if it meant going all the way to Yorkshire to do it. All the same, I hoped it wouldn't come to that. I would be out of my depth in the barbarian north.

I raised my guttering candle for a final look around the cellar. Had I missed something? Some telltale clue that would point immediately to the guilty person? But there was nothing, except that I was again assailed by that eerie sensation of not being alone. This time, it was a feeling of being watched, but although I examined every corner, there was nothing and nobody there. Three of the walls stared blankly back at me, the fourth beckoned with its archway, inviting me to return the way I had come.

I moved back into the second chamber among the shadowy shapes of the abandoned furniture. I remembered suddenly that, on a previous occasion, I had failed to find the bed that Jack Nym told me he had brought down here for Robin Avenel. I began to search, determined this time to locate it, but my candle suddenly sputtered and went out, plunging me into darkness. Cursing my stupidity, I barged into a pile of planks that had been stacked beside the baby's cradle, dislodged a couple, which fell with a clatter, tripped over a broken stool and measured my length on the ground. Winded and badly shaken, I lay there for a second or two recovering my breath, while the noise of the fallen timber echoed around me.

My eyes were beginning to grow accustomed to the gloom and for some reason I glanced back over my shoulder. Framed in the curve of the archway was the outline of a woman, standing perfectly still, watching me. At least, I presumed she was watching me, as she was nothing but a solid, black shape. She had been holding a candle, but its flame had been hastily snuffed out as I turned my head. I retained a vague impression of its radiance seen out of the corner of one eye.

The outline before me was neither small enough nor slender enough for Marianne Avenel, nor sufficiently tall for Elizabeth Alefounder. It therefore had to be Rowena.

I began struggling to my feet, but found that I had twisted an ankle in my fall. I swore and looked around for something to hold on to. The back of an old chair offered its support and I grabbed it thankfully before once more turning to confront the woman.

But she had gone. And, when I finally hobbled back into the third chamber, there was no sign of her anywhere.

Sixteen

I stumbled around for a minute or two, refusing to accept the evidence of my senses. The pain in my ankle receded and my eyesight improved as I slowly paced the perimeter of the chamber, half expecting the woman to materialize in front of me. But, finally, I was forced to admit there was no one there.

I rested my forehead against the cold stone of the underground chamber and took a deep breath. I was suddenly conscious of hunger and thirst, it being some hours since dinner at Margaret Walker's, and I needed sustenance. There was still much to be done, people to see, places to visit. But any further enquiries could wait until tomorrow. It had been a long, eventful and tiring day. With luck, Adela's rabbit pie awaited me.

I groped my way upstairs to the nave, made my obeisance to Saint Giles and Our Lady, genuflected to the Host, then let myself out into Bell Lane. As I did so, the first splashes of rain, harbingers of a summer shower, hit the cobbles. Hurriedly, I headed for Small Street, almost colliding with someone coming in the opposite direction; someone dressed in the black of mourning and carrying a newly dyed gown over one arm – the smell of the blackberry juice was still very potent – and keeping its skirt from trailing in the dirt with her other hand.

'M–Mistress Hollyns!' I stammered, but she brushed past me with no more acknowledgement than a fleeting glance.

I stared after her as she quickened her pace. She was running by the time she turned into Broad Street, where she vanished from sight.

Vanished from sight . . . If I hadn't seen Rowena Hollyns

in Saint Giles's crypt, then who – or what – *had* I seen? I shivered in spite of the warmth of the afternoon. Then I went home.

I had hoped to think things over in peace and quiet while I ate my rabbit pie, but I had reckoned without Adam's recent discovery that if he hammered the base of a saucepan with a wooden spoon, it made the most delightful, ear-splitting noise. In addition to this agony, the arrival of Elizabeth and Nicholas in boisterous, slightly quarrelsome mood moved me to play the tyrranical father with rather more ferocity than I usually employed on these occasions, and the meal passed in sulky silence on the part of the two elder children and in an outpouring of frustrated rage by my son. Adela let me get on with it.

'Did you sell much?' she asked during a brief lull between Adam's screams.

'Er . . . not a lot.'

She knew me sufficiently well to accept that this meant nothing at all, and lapsed into disapproving silence. But after we had finished supper and she had despatched all three children to play in the buttery, she left the dirty dishes and coaxed me into the parlour, where she sat me in the window embrasure, drew up a stool and invited me to confide in her what was wrong.

'For you looked as white as a sheet when you came in, though you seem somewhat better now. I'm afraid you haven't really got over that near-drowning in the Avon.'

I allayed her fears, assuring her that I was fighting fit, and recounted the afternoon's events, including the information I had gleaned from the Avenels' kitchen maid, my conversations with Apothecary Witherspoon and the Capgraves, and my discovery of the bloodstain on the floor of the old synagogue cellars. The only episode I omitted was the appearance and disappearance of the spectral woman, which, since my meeting with Rowena Hollyns, I was now convinced had been some sort of hallucination. I didn't want Adela fussing any more than she was doing already.

'So,' she commented, after a moment's reflection, 'you

think Robin Avenel was murdered in one of those empty chambers next to Saint Giles's crypt and his body removed later to Jewry Lane?'

'I think it possible. Indeed, I'd say it's probable.'

'But why? Why would it be necessary to move the body, I mean?'

I shook my head. 'I don't know. If I did, I might have a better idea of who the murderer is.'

Adela wrinkled her forehead. 'But where does Timothy Plummer fit into this puzzle? What's he doing in Bristol?'

I shrugged. 'At first, I thought he was just keeping an eye on Robin Avenel, but now I'm convinced there's more to his presence than that.' And I told her what I had learned from Jack Hodge and also from the landlord of the Full Moon, together with the tentative conclusions I had drawn from this information.

Adela was as incredulous as I had been.

'But why on earth would King James's brother come to Bristol?' she snorted. 'If he's trying to escape to France, surely he'd make for the eastern ports, either in his own country or in this. The west country simply doesn't make sense.'

'So I tell myself,' I answered gloomily. 'I *must* try to find Timothy Plummer. I'm certain he holds the key to this mystery. The trouble is, I've no idea where to start looking. It'll mean scouring the city from end to end. And I'll have to talk to that sea captain, the one Robin Avenel was arguing with. That's if he and his vessel are still anchored in Redcliffe Backs.' I began to fret. 'He could have sailed on the morning tide. Maybe I should go at once.'

Adela said forcefully, 'You're not going anywhere else this evening, Roger. It's raining like the Great Flood and if you get soaked to the skin you'll make yourself ill for a second time. Besides,' she added, sitting on my lap and twining her arms about my neck, 'I've bought a cabbage.'

It was so long since she was the one to make any advances, that I was momentarily taken aback.

'You hate cabbage,' was all I could think of to say.

'It's better than onion juice or bees,' she pointed out. 'But, of course, if you're not interested . . .'

I tightened my grip on her. 'Oh, I'm interested, sweetheart. It's just that I don't really believe that any of these remedies work.' A crescendo of screams and yells from the buttery made us both shudder. 'There must be a more effective way.'

'Do you know of any?'

It was on the tip of my tongue to admit the truth, but caution held me silent. It would be time enough to test Adela's reactions to the sheath once it was ready. Meanwhile, we should just have to put our faith in raw cabbage and my own ability and skill as a lover . . .

I awoke the following morning refreshed and reinvigorated, ready to face a new day, as hopeful as I could be that I had managed to avoid the conception of another child. Which was just as well, as I could already hear Adam stirring in his attic room overhead, and knew it was only a matter of minutes before our chamber door opened and he landed heavily on my chest.

Adela's insistence on eating the whole of the cabbage, in spite of my assurance that it really wasn't necessary, seemed to have done her no harm. She lay sprawled beside me, her dark hair strewn across the pillow, a sweet, satisfied smile curling her lips. The sight gave me a warm, smug glow. Abstinence hadn't made me lose my touch. I was just as good as ever I was.

Even Adam's usual breakfast-time tantrums failed to spoil our mutual feeling of love and goodwill. And although my wife suggested that I took both my pack and Hercules with me on my wanderings, she did not, in so many words, forbid me to continue with my quest to clear Burl's name, with the result that, long before the city muckrakers had finished cleaning the streets, I had crossed Bristol Bridge to Redcliffe Back and was trying to decide which of the many ships anchored there might be the one approached by Robin Avenel the night before last.

I had noticed that both the Wine Street and Redcliffe pillories were free of malefactors, and wondered how Luke Prettywood and the apprentices were feeling after their ordeal.

They would no doubt be the recipients of further punishment from their respective masters. Later on, I must seek Luke out and commiserate with him.

It was not easy to make my enquiries above the general racket of the quayside. But eventually a Portuguese sailor, who had witnessed the events of Midsummer Eve, and who spoke good English, informed me that the ship and crew I was looking for had sailed on yesterday afternoon's ebb tide.

'Do you know where the ship was from?' I asked him.

'Oh, yes. From Ireland. Gone back there now, I think.'

'Ireland? You're sure of that? Not Brittany or France?'

'No, no! Ireland. I see captain drinking with his friends in Marsh Street alehouse.'

A slaving ship, then. But why would Robin Avenel be in touch with an Irish slaver?

I thanked my Portuguese friend and walked back to Redcliffe Street, wondering what to do next. I was annoyed with myself that I had let such an obvious source of information slip through my fingers, but the tidings of Robin Avenel's murder, followed by Burl's arrest and my own summons to give evidence, had led to muddled thinking and the wrong priorities.

While I debated my next move, I heard myself hailed. 'Chapman!'

It was Luke Prettywood, looking dreadful with a black eye and a cut running the length of one cheek. Evidence of the filth and ordure thrown at him still clung in places to his shoulder-length fair hair, and his tribulations of the previous day had robbed him of all trace of cockiness. His customary satisfied smile was a travesty of its normal self.

'Luke! What are you doing in Redcliffe during working hours?' I clapped him on the shoulder and he winced.

'I was on my way home. I've been dismissed from the brewery.' He laid an urgent hand on my arm. 'Roger, have you seen Marianne? I was told you were at the Avenel house sometime yesterday.'

'But I didn't see Mistress Avenel. Nor Mistress Alefounder, either, if it comes to that. So! Brewer Alefounder has dismissed you, has he? I'm not surprised. Assaulting a law officer was

179

a stupid thing to do. So why *did* you do it, for heaven's sake? It's a few years now since you wore the apprentice's flat cap. Why get involved in the quarrels of a pack of silly, muddle-headed boys?'

Luke shrugged. 'It was something Jack Gload said. I can't even remember what it was, but it got my goat. He's such a stupid, ignorant fellow. I tell you what, chapman. Come back with me to the Green Lattis and I'll buy you a stoup of ale. I've still a few coins left in my purse.'

I knew I shouldn't oblige him – I had other, more pressing matters commanding my attention – but he looked such a sorry sight that I didn't have the heart to refuse. So I accompanied him back across the bridge to the Green Lattis, and settled with him on a couple of stools near an unshuttered window.

It was early and we had the place almost to ourselves. The pot-boy brought us two mazers of ale, Hercules curled up next to my pack and went to sleep, and I spent the next quarter of an hour listening to the sentimental maunderings of Luke Prettywood concerning his love for Marianne Avenel.

The news of Robin's murder had come not only as a terrible shock to Luke, but also as something of a release. At last he was able to speak openly about his affection for Marianne instead of always being obliged to conceal his true feelings.

'And you're quite sure she loves you in return?' I asked. 'I mean, Robin Avenel's death is bound to change things. She's now a very wealthy widow.'

'Oh, I don't know so much about that,' he said. The colour was returning to his cheeks and, with every sip of ale, he was beginning to leave the torments of the previous day behind him. 'Marianne always maintains that apart from the money he spent on clothes and his appearance, Robin was a pinchpenny. She had to economize on this, retrench on that. Although she thought that this miserliness was caused by necessity, not inclination.'

'How could that be?' I was sceptical. 'His father's a very rich man, and gossip has it that he was generous to his only son. Overgenerous, some said.'

'That's what Marianne can't understand. She reckons Peter

Avenel settled a lot of money on Robin when he got married. But where it all went, she has no idea. She did confide in me once that she was sure strangers occasionally came to the house, after she was in bed. But when she asked Robin about them, he told her she was imagining things and was so angry that she never dared raise the subject again. Could they have been debtors, or even blackmailers, do you think? She did wonder if he lent money to his sister. He and Mistress Alefounder were always close, even though they didn't seem to like one another very much. Odd that, when you think about it.'

'There are ties other than those of affection,' I suggested. 'Loyalty to a cause, perhaps. And causes, particularly lost ones, are constantly in need of money.'

Luke stared blankly at me. I changed the subject.

'So what will you do now? Become the city's chief beggar?'

'I shall soon find other work,' he bragged, his self-confidence returning. 'If it comes to that, Marianne will undoubtedly persuade her father to take me back into the brewery. She can twist the old fool around her little finger. *If* I want to work for Gregory Alefounder again, that is.' His self-conceit was very nearly restored to normal.

'That's decided then.' I grinned. 'But what about you and Mistress Avenel? You're in no position to offer for her hand.'

'Of course not.' He was at least a realist. 'She's bound to marry again sometime or other: that's only to be expected. Some choice of her father's. Rich, that goes without saying. But she won't give me up. She'll keep me as her lover.'

He sounded so confident that I didn't have the heart to prick his pretty bubble.

'You'll just go on meeting in Saint Giles's crypt, eh?' I teased him. 'Even when you're both old and grey and have to use crutches to get up and down the steps.'

'You wouldn't know anything about romantic love, now would you, chapman?' he asked me lightly. 'Not a staid old married man like yourself.'

'I wouldn't have thought the old synagogue cellars very conducive to comfortable love-making,' I smiled. 'But then,

I suppose once Mistress Avenel's got rid of her sister-in-law, she'll be able to invite you to the house.'

But he refused to be drawn, merely giving me a small, secretive smile.

'So, where was Master Avenel's body found?' he asked, after he had summoned the pot-boy and ordered two more cups of ale.

'In Jewry Lane. Outside Saint Giles's Church. He'd been stabbed, as no doubt you've heard by now.'

'I did hear some talk, yes, when I was standing in the pillory. But my mind wasn't really on what was being said, as you can well imagine.'

I could imagine. And if I needed any confirmation of his suffering, I could see it in the renewed pallor of his cheeks and his sudden, shallow breathing.

'Mind you,' I continued, in an effort to divert his thoughts, 'I don't think that's where he was killed. I believe he was murdered in the church.'

That made him laugh and he at once looked better again. 'What makes you think that? Been snooping, have you, chapman?'

'Why does everyone accuse me of snooping?' I demanded irritably. 'I don't snoop. I just try to discover the truth about things.' That made him laugh even harder. 'And as to why I think so, there's a bloodstain on the floor.'

'Really?' He was intrigued. 'Have you told Sergeant Manifold?'

I shook my head. 'Not yet. On its own, it's not evidence that would clear Burl Hodge . . . Did you know, by the way, that he's been arrested?' Luke nodded. 'Well,' I continued, 'as I say, it's not enough by itself to convince Richard Manifold that Burl is innocent. Once that man has made up his mind, he's capable of twisting every fact to fit his theory and arguing black's white and winter's summer. So, I'll wait until I have more facts.'

Luke swallowed the dregs of his second mazer. 'Do you think you'll find any?'

'I don't know. But one thing's for certain! I won't do so sitting here chatting to you.'

I rose to my feet, woke Hercules, shouldered my pack and took my departure. Luke caught me up outside the alehouse.

'Hold hard,' he begged. 'I'd like to see this bloodstain you've discovered. Could you spare the time to show it to me?'

His thin features were full of ghoulish curiosity, and I realized afresh that he was still quite young. Only those with small experience of life's cruelty can get excited by the prospect of viewing the spot where someone met a violent end. He had recovered with almost shocking rapidity from his purgatory of the previous day and I found myself envying him his ability to slough off misfortune without a second thought, safe in the conviction that it would never happen again, that the world was still a place of hope and the promise of adventure.

I knew I should waste no more time, but I was unable to resist that eager, boyish charm. Nor, if the truth be told, could I resist showing off my find to someone.

'Very well,' I agreed. 'On one condition. You mention it to no one else until I give you leave. I don't want Sergeant Manifold claiming the discovery as his own.'

Luke was scathing. 'I wouldn't talk to that piece of human excrement if he were the last man on Earth! Who do you think was responsible for having me put in the pillory?'

I laughed and we walked in companionable silence down Broad Street to the Bell Lane entrance of Saint Giles. I had chosen to avoid Small Street in case I was spotted by Adela. She could tell when I had been to the Green Lattis from behind closed doors. I was supposed to be working.

The church was, as ever, deserted. Luke advanced to the sacristy and from the shelf outside the door took down two candles which we lighted from a taper burning before the altar.

'Be careful as you descend the steps,' he advised me, for all the world as though I were his elderly uncle.

We padded through the crypt to the third chamber, holding our candles high. Silence prevailed except for our own muffled footfalls. Today, there was no phantom woman staring at me

183

from beneath the archway. My imagination was playing no tricks.

I showed Luke the stain and the scuffed-up dust by which it was surrounded. It appeared a great deal fainter than it had the previous afternoon and my companion had to crouch down to see it properly. He rubbed it just as I had done, but today no dried flakes of blood adhered to his fingers.

'That is a bloodstain,' I insisted. Luke straightened up.

'Maybe,' he said. 'In fact, I think you're right. But it could be an old one.' When I raised my eyebrows in enquiry, he went on, 'Don't you know what happened in this chamber, nearly two hundred years ago?'

I shook my head. I guessed it must have something to do with the expulsion of the Jews from England: there had been many atrocities in that year of Our Lord, 1290. Or many acts of zealous Christianity, depending on your point of view. I knew what mine was, but I pushed it down into the pool of other heretical thoughts and ideas swirling around just below the surface of my mind. When you're a married man with children you can't afford to be anything other than a coward.

'So what did happen?' I prompted.

Luke wriggled his shoulders as though they were hurting him. A day's stooping in the pillory, pinioned by neck and wrists was sufficient to give anyone backache.

'Well, according to my grandfather,' he said, 'who got it from *his* grandfather, or maybe his great-grandfather, most of the Bristol Jews fled the city early. They seemed to have foreseen what was coming and jumped before they were pushed, as the saying goes, taking ship from the Backs to France or Portugal or Spain. Apparently, the King had decreed that they should be allowed to take all money and movable goods with them – only land and property were to be forfeit to the crown – but of course this infuriated the local population everywhere. Everyone had hoped to grab a cache of the spoils for himself. The people of Bristol were no exception, and when word got round of the King's decision, they stormed the synagogue. But, as I say, most of the Jews had already gone. However, about twenty or so were trapped down here in the cellar and hacked to pieces.' Luke nodded at the floor. 'That might just be a relic of this place's grisly past.'

I understood now why I had always felt that sense of revulsion and misery in Saint Giles's crypt and its adjacent chambers. Murder, hatred and grief were a part of the very stones, not only of these cellars, but also of the church itself. I wondered if other people felt it. Maybe that was why, for most of the time, it was so deserted . . .

All the same, I thought Luke was mistaken about the stain on the floor. I raised my candle and looked more closely at it. It was too dark, too fresh, to be two hundred years old. And there was also the evidence of the dust, disturbed and scuffed as it was. There had been a struggle here, but recently.

'You're wrong,' I said. 'This is where Robin Avenel was killed, I'm sure of it.'

Luke frowned, genuinely puzzled. 'But why would his murderer bother to remove the body to Jewry Lane? Where would be the sense in that? Why not just run away? And there was the extra risk of being discovered while he was trying to lug the carcass up the steps from the crypt. As it happens, he wasn't seen, but he might have been.'

I told him what I had told Adela earlier. 'If I knew that, I'd probably have the solution to the killer's identity. Now, don't forget,' I reminded him, 'you've promised to say nothing about this to anyone.'

'Oh, you can trust me,' he assured me fervently. 'If there's anything I can do to put a spoke in Richard Manifold's wheel, you can be certain that I'll do it.'

There was no questioning his sincerity. His dislike of the sergeant made those brilliant blue eyes of his sparkle in the light from his candle.

I nodded and squeezed his arm gratefully. 'Let's go, then. Let's get out of this place.'

We mounted the steps to the nave, snuffed out our candles and were about to take leave of one another, when the Bell Lane door creaked open.

There was a flurry of black draperies and Marianne Avenel came rushing in.

Seventeen

I had a sense of having watched this scene played out before, but this time, there were differences. To begin with, there was no skirt of pale yellow sarcenet billowing about Marianne Avenel as she ran, merely the sombre swish of a gown of deepest black. And secondly, she made no effort to conceal her true relationship with Luke, throwing herself into her lover's arms regardless of my presence.

'What . . . What are we going to do?' she asked, sobbing noisily.

Luke smothered her in an all-enveloping embrace, pressing her face against his shoulder.

'Hush, hush, sweetheart. There's nothing we *can* do until the law has run its course. Richard Manifold already has a suspect under lock and key, as I'm sure you've heard by now. Master Chapman here doesn't agree with Burl Hodge's arrest, but it's up to him to prove differently, and we shall just have to wait and see who's right, him or the sergeant.' Marianne made a little mewling sound of distress, but Luke patted her back and again hushed her gently. 'Darling, believe me when I say that there is nothing either of us can do except attend upon events. For now, we must be careful. We don't want to arouse suspicions.'

I privately thought it a bit late for such a precaution – half of Bristol seemed to know of their liaison – but I didn't say so. What would have been the point? Marianne raised a tearful face from Luke's shoulder and made an effort to control her overwrought emotions.

'S–Sorry!' she gasped. 'It's just that everything's so awful!'

'It will pass,' he answered, kissing her gently between the eyes. 'Trust me. Everything will be all right.'

186

She gave a tremulous smile. 'As . . . As long as I have you,' she whispered.

And, somewhat to my surprise, I found myself agreeing with her. Luke Prettywood was behaving with a maturity that surprised me. A woman on the verge of hysterics, which was how Marianne appeared to me, can be an unnerving ordeal for a young man. She opened her mouth to say something more, but he sealed it with another kiss.

'By the way,' he said lightly, 'your father has dismissed me from the brewery because of my behaviour on Midsummer Eve. Assaulting an officer of the law is more than he's prepared to stomach. So it may be easier to avoid one another's company than we think.'

He had successfully diverted her attention away from her own woes, as no doubt he had intended.

'Dismissed you?' The vulnerable, kittenish look had vanished and the pretty, rounded features hardened with fury. '*Dismissed you?* I'll soon see about that!'

Already, as I could see, calculations were going on behind those luminous grey eyes as Marianne considered how best to persuade Gregory Alefounder to change his mind, without revealing her own intense interest in the outcome.

At this point, Hercules, who had settled down to guard my pack where I had dropped it on entering Saint Giles, ambled across and cocked a leg against one of mine, a warm, wet stream flowing down inside my left boot, while my companions, temporarily forgetting their troubles, burst out laughing.

'Does he often do that?' Luke enquired when he could catch his breath.

I sighed. 'Only when he has a grievance. At present, he's annoyed at being kept waiting while we visited the crypt.'

Marianne glanced up quickly at her swain. 'Why were you in the crypt?'

Luke hedged, plainly not wishing to upset her further just at present. 'It's . . . It's nothing important, sweeting. I'll tell you later. By the way, how did you know where to find me?'

'Oh, I was unable to stay in the house a moment longer. It's stifling in this heat, and I felt I couldn't bear Elizabeth's company for another second. She's in such a peculiar mood. More angry than grieving. Yesterday was dreadful! So I got up early and when I'd breakfasted I decided that I must go out. I went to the brewery first, but you weren't there. Of course, now I understand why. Father was horrid to me. He yelled and said I was a disgrace, wandering about the city without a maid in attendance and me a widow of only one day. I ought to be at home, keeping to my chamber. All the apprentices and carters were standing around in the yard, listening. It was so humiliating. I just burst into tears and ran away. And then I bumped into that apothecary who keeps the shop near the brothels. He was knocking on our door as I reached home. I don't know why – some remedy for Elizabeth or Dame Dorothy, I suppose – and he told me that he'd noticed you and the chapman entering Saint Giles's Church. So I came here.'

Witherspoon!

'Did you tell him you were looking for Master Prettywood?' I asked.

She shook her head. 'No, of course not. I mean, I wasn't, not exactly, but he just seemed to assume that I was. And as soon as he mentioned your name, of course I knew I *did* want to see you.' She gazed, misty-eyed, at her lover.

'Ah well,' I said, unwilling to intrude any longer upon this touching scene, 'I must be on my way before Hercules disgraces himself again.' Without thinking, I clapped Luke on the shoulder and he winced. I apologized. 'I hope your fortunes are soon on the mend, my friend. Mistress Avenel!' I gave her a little bow. These polite gestures are greatly appreciated by the gentler sex. Or so my mother always taught me. 'Please accept my deepest sympathy for your loss. Forgive me if I say that I hope soon to prove that Burl Hodge is not your husband's murderer. In which case, I might even be able to point the finger at whoever is.'

She gave me a faint, watery smile and clung even tighter to Luke. I picked up my pack, took hold of the dog's leading string and quit the church, leaving them still standing locked together in the nave.

It was nearly ten o'clock. I went home for my dinner.

*   *   *

I recounted the morning's events so far to Adela. She was unimpressed.

I could guess, by the two horn books lying on the other end of the kitchen table, that she had probably spent a couple of profitless hours trying yet again to teach Nicholas and Elizabeth their alphabet and numbers. But that pair were far more interested in inventing new games than in serious learning. As for Adam, tied into his little chair, he was quiet for once, lost in some mysterious world of his own, thumb in mouth, the brown eyes, so like his mother's, fixed dreamily on the middle distance. I wondered uneasily what mischief he was plotting.

When the meal – fish stew, as it was Friday – was over, I rose from the table and picked up my cudgel and pack. I glanced at Hercules, but he was pointedly stretched full-length beside his food and water trough, giving a good imitation of a dog exhausted by the heat.

'It seems a shame to disturb him,' I said.

'A great shame,' Adela agreed sarcastically. 'I should leave him where he is, if I were you.'

I needed no second bidding to take her at her word, however insincerely it was meant. She didn't enquire where I was going, for which I was grateful. I preferred her not to know. She would only have worried.

The noise and crowds, like the sun, had not yet reached their zenith, quite a few people being still at dinner, but it would not be long before the summer streets became unbearable. The rain of the previous evening had done little to refresh the atmosphere, and had churned the dust to a thin, gruel-like mud.

I pushed my way along Corn Street, avoiding several importunate hot-pie sellers whose trade was being ruined by the heat, succumbed to the offer of a cup of verjuice, which tasted of vinegar as it always does (I should have known better), then had to treat myself to a large honeyed fig in order to rid my tongue of the sourness. By which time, I had reached my intended destination: Marsh Street.

Marsh Street, which runs parallel with the Frome Quay and is connected to it at right angles by several noisome alleyways, ends with the Marsh Street Gate, which opens on to the great marsh itself. It also boasts one of the town's three public latrines. Not, I imagine, that this is much used by the many sailors who frequent the alehouses there: pissing against the nearest wall and seeing who can aim the highest is more their usual manner of relieving themselves.

As Jack Nym had warned me, and which I already knew, this was an alien locality for the majority of Bristol citizens, and they only ventured into the Turk's Head or the Wayfarer's Return if they had dealings with the men from Waterford. For although many foreign sailors made use of the Marsh Street alehouses, it was essentially Irish territory. You made a nuisance of yourself or asked one too many awkward questions at your peril. People had been known to disappear from Marsh Street, never to be seen or heard of again.

I walked steadily, glancing neither to right nor left, and holding my cudgel where everyone could see it, until I reached the second of the two alehouses, the Wayfarer's Return, a place I had visited some years before and whose landlord's name was known to me. Inside, it was much as I remembered it; dark, windowless, lit only by rushlight and tallow candles, whose flames could easily be extinguished should it prove necessary. Wooden trestles were placed at intervals on the beaten-earth floor and casks, three rows deep, were ranged against one wall. A back door, for a swift departure, opened on to the quayside, and a stone staircase led to an upper storey.

As soon as I made my appearance, there was a deafening silence. All heads, without exception, turned in my direction. Everyone could see the hump of my pedlar's pack, but that, after all, was no guarantee of my calling. It could have been a ruse, and no one there was so gullible as to take me at face value. I could just as easily be a Sheriff's man. The atmosphere was so charged with menace that I could have cut it with my knife.

I gripped my cudgel tighter and stayed where I was, by the door, ready to beat a hasty retreat if need be. But this proved unnecessary, thanks to the landlord, Humility Dyson, a huge bear of a man whose thick black beard was now showing the first knotted threads of grey. He came forward, rubbing his massive hands on his leather apron.

'Roger Chapman!' he exclaimed. 'And what brings you here?' He turned to his customers. 'I know this man. He's a pedlar all right. Lives in the city. He'll do you no harm.' There was a protracted, extremely wary silence, then the rumble of conversation gradually resumed. But I knew I was only there on sufferance. Danger still thrummed in the air. Make one stupid move, and I could end up with a knife in my back.

'So, what *does* bring you here?' the landlord repeated.

I plucked up courage and answered him in a ringing tone that could be heard in all four corners of the room. I figured it would be safer to be open about my business than to whisper like a conspirator and arouse greater suspicion.

'I'm enquiring about an Irish ship that was moored on Redcliffe Back until yesterday afternoon, when, or so I'm told, it sailed on the ebb tide. I don't know to a day how long since it dropped anchor, but it was certainly there on Midsummer Eve when I saw the captain talking to Master Robin Avenel.'

'You mean the man who was found murdered in Jewry Lane yesterday morning?' Humility Dyson had deliberately raised his voice to rival mine. He was making sure that all the occupants of the alehouse were aware of the circumstances of Robin's death before anyone opened his mouth to reply.

'That's right,' I added. 'A local man, a tenter, has been charged with the killing.'

The landlord threw back his head and roared with laughter.

'Don't be fooled, gentlemen!' he said, addressing the motley crew of rogues who patronized the Wayfarer's Return as if they were some noble gathering. 'If this pedlar is making it his business to ask questions, it means he thinks this tenter innocent, and is trying to pin the crime on somebody else.'

'Not on anyone here,' I assured them quickly. (Although how, they might well ask themselves, was I to know that for a certainty? They weren't fools, any of them.)

'You'd better not,' growled a man seated at the nearest table. 'Or it will be the worse for you, friend chapman.'

There was a general mutter of agreement and I prepared for trouble. But, to my astonishment, the man who had spoken made a place for me at the trestle where he was sitting by the simple expedient of shunting his two companions further along the bench.

He motioned to me to sit down and offered me a drink. 'Ale or whisky?'

I chose ale. I had heard too many hair-raising stories from men who had tried the fiery water of life so beloved by the Irish – and also the Scots by all accounts – to wish to addle my brain and lose concentration. The Irishman was disappointed, but good-naturedly ordered the landlord to bring me a beaker of 'cat's piss'.

'We've met before,' he said, 'some years back now. Briant of Dungarvon.'

I recalled him at once. I had encountered both him and his partner when I had been searching for the truth concerning the disappearance of Margaret Walker's father.

'I remember,' I said. 'You and Padraic Kinsale.'

'Padraic's dead,' he answered shortly, and from his tone I knew better than to ask for details. 'So! This man who's been arrested,' he went on, 'is he really innocent?'

'I'd stake my life on it,' I assured him fervently. 'Unhappily, our sergeant is—'

'A dolt!'

I demurred. 'Maybe I wouldn't go that far.'

'All lawmen were born with brains the size of a pea,' he said viciously. 'That's why they're lawmen.' He took a gulp of his whisky. 'So, what do you want to know about this ship that was moored in Redcliffe Back?'

I took a deep breath. 'Was she a slaving ship?'

I expected a wall of silence, possibly a request to leave. But having once decided that he could trust me, Briant of Dungarvon was seemingly prepared to be frank.

'As far as I know, the *Clontarf* was mainly a slaver, but that isn't why she was here. At least, not this time. The man you saw speaking with this Robin Avenel wasn't the captain, either. It must have been the mate. The captain disappeared after rowing himself ashore at Rownham Passage some few weeks ago. A search by his shipmates at the time proved fruitless. I think this visit must have been a second attempt to discover what might have happened to him.'

'Oh, I can tell you that,' I said, and proceeded to do so.

Briant of Dungarvon was not the only man to listen with interest to my story. I did not bother to lower my voice and it soon attracted the attention of others, not only the three men seated at our table, but also those at neighbouring trestles. When I had finished, there was a general nodding of heads, sucking of teeth and scratching of backsides, which seemed to be their way of expressing belief in what I had told them.

A big Irishman with an accent so thick I could barely understand what he was saying announced that he wasn't surprised. Hadn't he always predicted that Eamonn Malahide would come to a sticky end? (Well, that was the gist of it, anyhow, but more forcefully expressed.) Many of my other listeners vociferously agreed. I turned to Briant for enlightenment.

'I thought you slavers stuck together. *De mortuis nil nisi bonum*, etcetera.' I could have added: 'Brother outlaws, condemned by Church and State.' But I didn't.

If I had hoped to discompose him with a display of my limited learning, I was disappointed. Somewhere inside that rough exterior there was an educated man. I would have given much to know his history.

'There are rotten apples in every barrel, chapman. You may not like what we do for a living, but we do have a code of conduct. We abide by certain rules. And the first and foremost of those is, *never* take people's money and then betray them to their enemies for yet more gold. A man who does that deserves everything he gets.'

'And this is what Eamonn Malahide did?'

'In this particular instance, I cannot say, but certainly on several occasions in the past. It was only a matter of time before he himself was betrayed and he ended up as you've described, with a knife through his heart.'

193

'Who was he deceiving this time?' I asked eagerly, but the Irishman shook his head.

'I've told you, I don't know. I had as little to do with the man as possible.' He glanced at the faces around him. 'Does anyone here present know?'

But no one did. And enquiries in the further corners of the room, among those who had not listened to my tale, or not heard it properly, produced no additional information. Eamonn Malahide seemed to have been given a wide berth by his fellow slavers. But at least I now understood a little better the reason for his death. Someone had warned Elizabeth Alefounder and Rowena Hollyns that Eamonn Malahide was about to play them false. What about was still a mystery, but I hoped to find that out in due course. It explained their treatment of myself when they had mistaken me for him, and his subsequent speedy despatch at Rowena's hands.

But the women had obviously not known of his perfidy for any length of time before my arrival, or they would have left Rownham Passage and the 'murder' house without waiting to encounter their betrayer. So who had warned them?

I suddenly remembered Edgar Capgrave telling me that Robin Avenel had left on the morning in question by the Frome Gate some two hours after his sister, and had returned an hour or so before her. *He* must have carried the news. But why had the two women not come back with him? It had to be that something or someone had delayed their departure . . .

Briant of Dungarvon dug me sharply in the ribs.

'Have you finished asking questions then, chapman? Because if so, we'd like you to be on your way.' There was a vigorous nodding of heads. 'We'll pass your message on to the crew of the *Clontarf* whenever we come across them.' He added in a lower tone, 'And if I should learn anything more from them, I'll send a message to Humility Dyson. He'll call on you at home. Don't come here again. You might bring the Law trailing in your wake.'

I shook my head. 'The Law knows better than to interfere with the "Irish trade".'

'There's always one mad, zealous fool with his eye on promotion,' Briant retorted, adding with a face-splitting grin, 'And for your information, my friend, across the water we refer to it as the "Bristol trade".'

On which half-friendly, half-admonitory note, we parted. Briant called for more whisky and resumed his interrupted conversation with his companions in the lilting and, to me, totally incomprehensible Irish tongue, while I slipped quietly from the alehouse, breathing a sigh of relief that I was still alive and unharmed, and headed for the public latrine.

Having rid myself of the effects of fright and too much ale, I went back to Broad Street and, for the second time in two days, knocked on the kitchen door.

It was too much to hope that I should again be able to avoid Dame Dorothy, the dragon-like housekeeper, but my luck was in. It was the intelligent, if dour-faced Jess who answered my summons.

'Oh, not you again,' she groaned, starting to shut the door, a move which might have succeeded had I not swiftly shoved my foot into the gap. 'Go away! I nearly lost my place here yesterday after spending all that time with you in the garden.'

'Just one more question, that's all,' I pleaded. 'It won't take long, I promise.'

A face appeared over her shoulder. The freckle-faced girl hissed delightedly to her fellow kitchen maids, 'It's Jess's admirer!'

There was a chorus of giggles and several more faces joined the first, eager and bird-like, twittering with anticipation.

'Anything in your pack, chapman?' asked one with a significance of tone that caused an immediate snigger. I felt myself blushing and cursed silently.

Jess rounded on them furiously, giving the nearest girl a vicious prod in the chest and sending her and the others staggering back into the kitchen.

'Oh, get on with your work, do!' she cried. 'And if the dragon returns, tell her I'm in the jakes. Again!' She pulled me round to the back of the privy and addressed me, hands on hips. 'What is it this time? It had better be something important. And be quick about it!'

'Can you remember as far back as the beginning of the month?' I asked. 'Saint Elmo's Day, I think it was. Mistress Alefounder went out very early in the morning, just after dawn. A couple of hours later, Master Avenel went out as well. Do you have any recollection?'

Jess puckered her brows. 'That's three weeks and more ago,' she reproached me. But then, just as I would have spoken again, she held up an imperious hand and nodded. 'Wait a moment! Yes, I *do* recall the day you mean. The mistress had had belly gripe all night and I remember telling her it was sure to get better as it was Saint Elmo's Day, him being the patron saint of belly and gut disorders. But she just went on whining, especially about being disturbed by her sister-in-law, who'd gone out at the crack of dawn. "No consideration for anyone else," I remember her saying. "She knows what a light sleeper I am." Then she wanted the master. Mistress Marianne, that is. He knew she was unwell. Why hadn't he come to see her? And so on. She sent me to look for him, but he wasn't in his chamber, so I went downstairs to get the mistress a bowl of thin gruel that she fancied. That was when Dame Dorothy told me that Master Robin had also gone out. I asked why, because the mistress was sure to want an explanation. She said she didn't know why, except that someone, a man she thought, had called about half an hour previous, asking for the master most urgent, and as soon as Master Robin had spoken to him, he didn't wait even for his dinner, which was almost ready, but yelled that he had to leave right away. Which he did.'

Going, I guessed, first to the stables in Bell Lane and then on to Rownham Passage. It all fitted.

'Did Dame Dorothy happen to see the man who called?' I asked.

Jess shrugged. 'She didn't say. I know the mistress took on something awful when I told her. Called Master Robin an unfeeling brute and lots of other things far worse. After a while, I stopped listening. Then Mistress Hollyns knocked on the bedchamber door. Said she was going out and asked

196

if she could fetch anything for the mistress at the apothecary's. Mistress got all petulant and threw a pillow at her.'
Jess giggled. 'So that was that. Mistress Hollyns went off in
a huff and left me to it. Course, Mistress Avenel should have
an attendant of her own, but like I said, the master was a
tight-fisted man in some respects. We four girls, we're maids
of all work.'

I was listening with only half an ear by now. What Jess
had told me confirmed Edgar Capgrave's information. Rowena
had not left with Elizabeth Alefounder in the morning, but
had been with her when she returned later in the afternoon.
She had quit the house not long after Robin. So, before
leaving, had he instructed her to follow him as soon as she
could? Had he confided in her the reason for his hasty departure? I suspected that he must have. She was certainly privy
to whatever had been going on and as deeply involved in it
as Master Avenel and his sister. She, too, must have gone to
the Bell Lane stable for a mount and then made her way to
Rownham Passage. But how had she managed to evade
Edgar Capgrave's vigilant eye at the Frome Gate? If she had
left by the Redcliffe Gate, at journey's end she would have
found herself on the wrong side of the Avon, in the manor
of Ashton-Leigh and been forced to take the ferry across the
river. Too much time would have been wasted. And I could
vouch for the fact that she was in the 'murder' house when
I made my ill-fated appearance at midday. So somehow or
another she must have left the city using the Frome Gate
without being spotted by the gatekeeper. I must have another
word with Edgar Capgrave.

I was suddenly aware that Jess had finished speaking and
was regarding me indignantly as the realization dawned that
I had not been listening – at least, not for the last few
minutes.

'Have you heard a word I've said?' she demanded angrily.

I leaned forward and kissed her gently on the cheek. 'Of
course,' I protested. 'The important part. And that's all that
matters.'

I delved into my pack and brought out a fine ivory comb
that I had been saving as a Midsummer present for Adela,

but had somehow forgotten to give her. Guiltily, I handed it to Jess, whose glow of pleasure in some measure compensated for the fact that I was becoming a neglectful husband. But then, I always had been. I thanked God that Adela was an understanding wife.

'I must go,' Jess said as we heard the kitchen door open and an urgent voice call softly, 'Jess! She's coming!'

Jess swung hurriedly on her heel, but as she did so, I grabbed her arm.

'Does Mistress Hollyns have a blue brocade gown and a pair of red leather shoes?' I asked.

Jess freed herself with an impatient gesture and reached the kitchen door in three long strides. But with her hand on the latch, she turned.

'No, not her. Mistress had a blue brocade gown but it got mislaid. No one seems to know what happened to it. She blames us, of course. But she's never had a pair of red leather shoes. They belonged to the master.'

'I tell you, Mistress Hollyns, or whatever she's called, did *not* leave by the Frome Gate that morning.' Edgar Capgrave was adamant. 'I know which morning you're talking about, chapman, and I didn't see her, I tell you.'

My luck was still in and I had found Edgar at his post when I had gone looking for him on leaving the Avenel house in Broad Street.

'Try to remember,' I pleaded, ignoring the fact that I was holding up four increasingly irate carters and a shepherd with a flock of sheep who, most unusually, seemed to have wills of their own and were wandering all over the street, fouling the cobbles. 'Mistress Alefounder went out very early . . .'

'Just after curfew was lifted,' Edgar agreed, 'like I've already told you.'

'And then about two hours later – ten o'clock, would that have been? – Robin Avenel left.' Edgar nodded. 'And very soon afterwards, Mistress Hollyns.'

The gatekeeper shook his head.

'No,' he said firmly. 'I keep telling you, no! I would remember. She came back with Mistress Alefounder about an hour after Robin returned. But I've already told you that, as well. Now, will you please get out of the way, chapman? You're holding up the traffic.'

Eighteen

By this time, it was getting towards mid-afternoon and the heat was brazen. It had returned with renewed vigour after the rain of the previous day and I was sweating profusely. I needed somewhere cool to sit down and think things out where I would not be distracted by the aimless chatter of my fellow men (and women). That ruled out the Green Lattis, or any other of Bristol's numerous hostelries. Moreover, I had drunk more than enough, for a while at least: a potent brew at the Wayfarer's Return and a mazer of elderflower wine with my dinner. My head was swimming and its cause was not just the warmth of the city streets.

My conscience, too, was beginning to trouble me. I hadn't earned as much as a groat for nearly two days, having spent the time in searching for clues to prove Burl Hodge's innocence. Adela would soon be complaining of a lack of money and I should have nothing to offer her. It would mean breaking into my secret hoard – and I was saving that for an altogether different purpose. All the same, pounding the hot cobbles or even walking out into the countryside at present held no allure. My mind was focused on winkling out the real murderer of Robin Avenel.

I was conscious of a feeling I had so often experienced in the past; an awareness of being in possession of some fact, some knowledge, that I had either overlooked or was unable to extricate from the deeper recesses of my mind. I cursed myself roundly, as I always did, for one of these lapses. Carelessness and inattention to what was being said or done by the people around me undid all God's efforts to set me on the short and easy path to the truth.

I was by now finding the heat – and my thoughts – so oppressive that I decided to stroll down to the banks of the Frome near the Dominican friary in the Broad Meads, where the river curved around the base of the castle and formed a part of its moat. I therefore left the city by the Pithay Gate and bridge and walked across the parched fields to my favourite spot, opposite the castle mill and weir, where I pulled off my boots and jerkin and lay supine among the sweet-smelling grasses and flowers that bordered the water's edge. But when sleep threatened to overwhelm me, which it very soon did, I forced myself to sit upright and plunged my feet, hose and all, into the river. The shock of the cold water did the trick. It was time to take stock and sort out what I knew. And what I didn't.

To begin with, I felt certain that Elizabeth Alefounder's appearance and continued sojourn in Broad Street was no mere family visit to her brother, but had had, from the outset, a much more sinister purpose. Robin Avenel had been under suspicion of being a supporter of the Lancastrian, and therefore of Henry Tudor's, cause since the previous summer. But in my estimation he had never been decisive enough to hold any opinions of his own without having them formed for him by someone of far more positive views. His father, Peter Avenel, was a straightforward man who, I suspected from the little I knew of him, would always support the ruling faction in the interests of a quiet and prosperous life. He would change his political coat as often as he changed his everyday apparel and shy away in horror from any hint of treason. But somebody had persuaded Robin to dabble his toes in the murky waters of sedition, and that person, I felt sure, was his strong-minded sister.

So, I had established to my own satisfaction that Elizabeth Alefounder had arrived in Bristol with some nefarious purpose in mind; some purpose which involved Robin Avenel renting the old Witherspoon house at Rownham Passage for a night at the beginning of June. He had told the apothecary that the accommodation was needed for two men, although when, the following day, I had made my own ill-fated entrance upon the scene, I had only been aware of the presence of

201

one man – a man I now thought, from his speech, might have been a Scot.

But that, I had to admit, was no more than guesswork. There had indeed been trouble in Scotland, according to the Dominican friar who had stopped to refresh himself at the Full Moon. King James III had quarrelled with his brothers: one, the Earl of Mar, had died in suspicious circumstances; the other, the Duke of Albany, had fled, no one knew whither. But supposing he was here, in Bristol . . . Yet what possible connection could there be between Lancastrian supporters of Henry Tudor, such as Elizabeth Alefounder and Robin Avenel, and a royal duke of Scotland escaping his brother's wrath?

To add to my confusion, I was also faced with an Irish slaver who – it seemed likely – had been about to double-cross the Avenels and who had been summarily murdered for his pains by a pair of ruthless women, who had at first mistaken me for him. And now Robin Avenel himself was dead, but by whose hand? And why had he risked breaking into my house a week and more ago? What had he been hoping to do or find?

My head was beginning to ache, and not just because of the sun's relentless glare, but I did my best to ignore it and continue with my train of thought. Although Edgar Capgrave had observed Rowena Hollyns returning with her mistress from Rownham Passage, her gown muddied and wet, he swore that she could not have left by the Frome Gate earlier that same day without him having seen her. Or, rather, without him *remembering* to have seen her. There was a difference, and it might be that his memory was not as infallible as he thought it.

All the same, had not Jess, the kitchen maid, told me less than an hour since that the blue brocade gown belonged not to Rowena, but to Mistress Avenel? And that her mistress complained of not being able to find it? If that were so, had it merely been mislaid or had it been taken by someone else? And if so, by whom and why? Jess had also denied Rowena's ownership of a pair of red shoes. Indeed, I already knew that Robin Avenel had possessed red shoes; one of them still reposed in my secret hiding place, along with the ring I had found in the 'murder' house. But I was still uncertain of the significance of either item . . .

I was beginning to nod off by now, and made a determined effort to keep myself awake, sucking in great gulps of air and agitating my feet in the river. But it was no good. Fatigue and heat won the unequal contest, and I was vaguely aware of my chin falling forward on my chest before I was lost in a scene that seemed to have no connection with any of the myriad thoughts milling around inside my head.

I think I have said somewhere before in these chronicles that my mother was gifted with the 'sight', something that I have inherited but which visits me very rarely and then only in the form of dreams . . .

Now, I was standing in the crypt of Saint Giles, but the rows of shelves and coffins had disappeared and I was at the bottom of the steps leading down from the nave. But it was not the present staircase; indeed I knew – although how I knew was a mystery – that the church was a different building. It was not even a church any more.

Above my head, I could hear a mob baying for blood, hammering and battering at the outer door, screaming filth and imprecations in the mindless way that only a crowd can do. I have seen it happen too often: people lose their souls; all vestige of human dignity and kindness desert them and they turn into ravening beasts. I could feel the hair rising along my scalp, even though, in the strange way of dreams, I knew I was not their quarry.

I moved forward effortlessly, weightlessly, skimming the ground along the length of that great cellar. From somewhere overhead came the sound of rending wood and the crash of the door caving in. Blood-curdling shouts of triumph preceded the rush of feet towards the cellar stairs and my heart started to beat so fast that I could scarcely breathe. People were in danger and I had to reach them before their persecutors did . . .

I could see them now, faint shapes in the darkness, illuminated by the flickering glow of rushlights and candles. There were about a score, all men, and wearing – judging by some ancient illustrations I had seen – the Jewish gabardine.

'What are you doing? Why are you still here?' I yelled, but although my lips moved no sound came out. 'The others have all gone! Why haven't you gone with them?'

But they couldn't hear me any more than I could hear myself. They turned and looked straight through me, foreknowledge of death already written on their faces.

'Why did you wait?' I demanded again. 'Why didn't you leave with the others?'

But they took no notice, blowing out the candles and all pressing hard up against the furthest wall. Then, in a great rush of noise and movement, the mob was upon them, slaughtering them like beasts in the shambles until the floor and walls ran red with blood. One of the crowd set fire to a man's gabardine with his torch, another dashed someone's head in with his club. And yet a third took hold of me by the shoulder and shook me violently, urging me to move. I spun round, fetching him a blow across his cheek, and found myself flat on my back on the river bank, staring up stupidly into the cowled features of one of the Dominican friars.

'Riding the night mare, Roger?' enquired a familiar voice ruefully as the man rubbed his face where my hand had caught him. 'If all that snorting and threshing of limbs is anything to judge by, you must be suffering from a very bad conscience. Or I suppose, knowing you, it might just be too much ale and victuals.'

'T–Timothy?' I stuttered, my brain still feeling as if it were stuffed with feathers, and trying desperately to shake off the clinging remnants of my dream. 'Timothy Plummer?'

He sat down beside me on the grass, tucking surplus folds of the habit, which was far too large for him, around his knees.

'The very same,' he grunted.

My mind was beginning to clear and I sat up with such force that I almost knocked him over.

'Where have you been?' I roared. 'I've been looking for you everywhere for days. And what in heaven's name are you doing dressed up as a Dominican friar?'

'I'm staying with the brothers in the friary,' he answered mildly. 'I'm less conspicuous if I blend in with my surroundings. And could you try not to be so rough? That's the second time in minutes that you've attacked me. What's making you so angry?'

'You are,' I replied in a more subdued tone, but with enough venom to let him know that I was still not mollified. 'Finished playing the beggar now, have you? Now that your testimony has got a friend of mine arrested and charged with a murder he didn't commit.'

'Ah!' Timothy paused to wipe his nose on the sleeve of his habit. 'So that's it. I thought if I started that particular hare, our good friend Richard Manifold might go chasing after it. It seems I haven't been disappointed.'

'Burl Hodge did not kill Robin Avenel,' I hissed furiously. 'You know he didn't.'

Timothy laid a restraining hand on one of my arms, and it was only then that I realized my own hands had balled themselves into fists.

'How do you know your friend is innocent?' he asked softly. 'Have you any proof?'

'Not yet,' I snapped. 'But I mean to find some.' I turned to look at my companion, scrutinizing him narrowly. 'I'm sure you have a very good idea as to the name of the real murderer.'

He lowered his hood and shook his head. 'I'm afraid I haven't. I wish I had. It might indeed be your friend, this Burl Hodge, for all I know.'

'And you think I'll believe that?' I sneered.

Timothy shrugged. 'You must believe what you will. It happens to be the truth. I didn't want Robin Avenel dead. At least, not until . . .' He broke off, looking vexed.

'Until what?' I asked, feeling daunted. I had counted on being able to prove Burl's innocence once I had found the Spymaster General. But now *he* had found *me* and I was no further forward. My mind was still clogged with my dream, trying to interpret its meaning, and I wasn't really thinking about what I was saying. I just made a stab in the dark. 'You were hoping he would lead you to the Duke of Albany, I suppose.'

The effect of my words on Timothy was as unexpected as it was startling. Taken unawares, I found myself lying once again flat on my back with my companion's fingers around my throat.

'What do you know about the Duke of Albany? Where is he?'

I made a gurgling sound, unable to speak, and felt the blood pounding inside my skull. Recovering from my surprise, I took hold of Timothy's skinny wrists in a grip of steel and prised his hands from my neck. Then I rolled over, coughing violently and pinioning him beneath my weight.

'Don't,' I said, bringing my face as close to his as I dared without being asphyxiated by his breath, 'ever do that to me again. I don't like it.'

I held him down until I could see that he was struggling for air, then freed him. He sat up, every bit as furious as I had been.

'Don't threaten me with what you like and don't like, Roger! I could have you arrested and tried for treason as easily as I could spit in the river there. I hold a warrant and a token of credence from the King. There isn't a sheriff in the country who wouldn't acknowledge their authority and do my bidding. So if you've any sense, which I sometimes doubt, you'll answer my question. What do you know about the Duke of Albany, and how do you know it?'

I rubbed my throat and hawked and coughed a bit more, just for appearances' sake and to make him wait, as well as to impress upon him that he had done me serious injury. But I could tell he was growing impatient and so, without further ado, I explained how I had come by such knowledge as I possessed.

When I had finished, I could sense rather than see his disappointment. He sighed.

'You don't really know anything,' he said. 'You've just been bumbling around in your usual incompetent fashion, nosing out a fact here and a bit of gossip there, then adding a rumour or two and a few lucky guesses to the brew until it's all bubbling away inside your head like a bad cook's mess of pottage.'

I knew that when Timothy began insulting me, I was closer to the truth than he liked. I squeezed the water out of the feet of my hose and turned to look at him.

'Stop waxing poetical and just tell me what's going on. You ought to know by now that you can trust me.'

He thought about this, staring at the sunlight sparkling on the river, brilliant discs of gold like newly minted pennies. Then he heaved another sigh, this time of resignation.

'Very well,' he agreed. 'But I can't tell you who murdered Robin Avenel, because I don't know. That is the truth. Of course,' he added, puckering his thin lips judiciously, 'my guess, if I had to make one, would be Silas Witherspoon.'

'*Silas Witherspoon?* In God's name, why?'

Timothy shot me a sideways glance. 'I'm trusting you as you requested, Roger – interfering, disobedient fool though you are. I gave you strict instructions not to get involved in this.' He gave a short bark of laughter that sounded almost affectionate. 'I might have known I was wasting my breath!'

'In the name of Gabriel and all the angels, just get on and give me the facts,' I begged. 'Why Silas Witherspoon?'

'He's a Tudor agent. Has been for years.'

'You know this for a fact?' My companion nodded. I tried to make sense of what I was hearing. 'But in that case, why haven't you got rid of him? Even if there's no positive proof, don't try telling me you couldn't manufacture some if you put your mind to it.'

Timothy leaned forward and trailed a hand in the river, frightening a moorhen who had rashly ventured forth from her nest among the reeds.

'Don't underestimate me, Roger, by supposing that I don't know how to do my job. Of course I can tighten the noose around Silas's neck any time I please. But what would be the point, have you thought of that? Another agent would only be sent from Brittany to take his place; a man who would be unknown to us and whose identity would have to be discovered all over again. As it is, Apothcary Witherspoon is closely watched by the Sheriff and his men and is even, on occasions, given false information to confuse our

Lancastrian friends across the Channel. One day his time will come, but not just yet.'

I rubbed my forehead, trying to adjust my mind to this new vision of Silas Witherspoon as an agent of Henry Tudor.

'So,' I said at last, 'he and the Avenels are bedfellows?'

Timothy dried his wet hand by shaking it, the iridescent drops flying in all directions like a miniature rainstorm.

'They were,' he conceded, 'until lately. But not, I fancy, any more.'

'Go on,' I encouraged, when he seemed disinclined to continue.

He rubbed his chin thoughtfully. 'We–ell, I fancy it's a matter of loyalties. There have been rumours coming out of Brittany for some months past – you may even have heard them yourself – that Henry Tudor has been ill. He's always been of a sickly constitution, but recently there have been, or so I'm told, serious worries amongst his followers concerning his general health. In short, there are fears that he might die before he can make old bones. So you see the Lancastrian dilemma.'

I did indeed. The direct male line of Henry of Bolingbroke had come to an end, first at Tewkesbury, with the death in battle of his great-grandson, Prince Edward, and then, subsequently, with the death in the Tower of London of his grandson, the boy's father, King Henry VI, who had died, we were informed, of 'pure displeasure and melancholy'. (And if you believed that you had to be the most credulous fool in Christendom.) The Lancastrian cause was in decline, as were its contenders for the English crown. Henry Tudor, who, through his mother, Margaret Beaufort, was the great-great-grandson of John of Gaunt and his third wife and former mistress, Katherine Swynford, was the best that supporters of the Red Rose could find. But his claim was thin and tarnished by the Bend Sinister. If he were to die, who could be found to replace him?

'You mean . . .?' I began, but hesitated.

Timothy nodded. 'There are certain Lancastrian supporters who have been casting around for another claimant to the throne. The Scottish king and his siblings are all grandchildren of James I's queen, Joan Beaufort, who was herself a grand-child of John of Gaunt and his paramour, Lady Swynford. So you see, this quarrel between King James and his brothers set some of Henry Tudor's disaffected supporters thinking.'

'They could offer one of his brothers the chance of the English throne?'

'Precisely. Now, whether Albany's flight from Scotland was really because he thought his brother, the Earl of Mar, had been murdered and feared the same fate, or because he received an offer from across the water, no one's yet sure. My guess would be both.'

'But surely,' I protested, 'no one would give up a royal dukedom for the life of a puppet at the court of Brittany with no serious chance of ever inheriting the English throne? Everyone knows that King Edward has two sons to succeed him. Not to mention several daughters in a land that has no Salic law.'

Timothy smiled. 'Probably not, if the offer of the crown was the sole inducement. But if Albany really is in fear of his life . . . That's why I said my guess would be that he's influenced by both considerations.'

There was silence for a minute or two, broken only by the chirping of a cricket hidden somewhere in the grasses. The white flowers of water hemlock nodded like stars at the end of their long, coarse stems.

'Are you telling me,' I asked eventually, 'that you believe the Duke of Albany to be in hiding here, somewhere in Bristol?' Timothy inclined his head. 'But in Jesu's name, why? Why would Tudor agents bring him west instead of taking him south or east? Plymouth, Dover, Southampton would be understandable. But here? It doesn't make any sense.'

'It makes perfect sense if one of the most reliable agents you have – and one, moreover, who is an ardent supporter of the faction now anxious to replace Henry Tudor with a healthier specimen – lives nearby. Elizabeth Alefounder not only resides at Frome, but also has – or, rather, had – a brother in Bristol with whom she could stay without raising any conjecture. As for Bristol itself, it's a port, isn't it, like any other? Ships from many countries sail up the Avon and anchor here with every tide. And it has the added advantage of throwing Albany's pursuers off the scent. King James's men, as I happen to know, are even now looking for him all along the east coast, thinking him bound for France.'

'But the ship that came to fetch him away was Irish-owned, the *Clontarf*. Its captain, Eamonn Malahide, was an Irish slaver.'

Timothy looked annoyed.

'Is there anything you don't know? Anywhere where you haven't poked that long nose of yours?' Again, he shrugged. 'I have no idea why Mistress Alefounder made that decision. Maybe because she found it easier to make arrangements with someone who spoke the same language. Well, spoke it after a fashion, that is! Then again, perhaps not. But whatever her reason, she seems to have picked the wrong man.'

I nodded. 'So it would appear. He had a reputation among his own kind for avarice, and in pursuit of money would sell his services to two sides at once.'

Timothy heaved an even deeper sigh than before.

'And how did you learn that?' he asked resignedly.

'I visited the Wayfarer's Return in Marsh Street.' Even Timothy knew enough about Bristol by this time to need no interpretation of this remark. 'My guess is,' I went on, 'that Eamonn Malahide was to pick up his passenger – in all probability this Scottish duke – from the house at Rownham Passage, where Elizabeth Alefounder would pay him his money to carry the man to Brittany. But in fact, Malahide would have made him a prisoner as soon as he was far enough out to sea, and then sailed with him to Scotland where he would have returned the duke to his brother and collected a fat reward.'

Timothy stretched and yawned. 'As fair an assessment of events as I could have made myself. You know, you really are wasted as a pedlar, Roger. You're an educated man and have all the makings of an excellent spy. One who could even become Spymaster General when I decide to retire.

You should accept Duke Richard's offer of employment, then I could oversee your training.'

'You work for the King.'

'Not for much longer. I have asked permission to rejoin the duke's household and His Highness has been pleased to grant my request. I shall ride north to rejoin Prince Richard as soon as this particular task is brought to a satisfactory conclusion.'

'But you hate the north,' I protested, 'and I understand that His Grace rarely comes south since Clarence's execution. They say his hatred of the Queen's family is as strong as ever.'

'True,' Timothy admitted. 'But I love that man and I miss him. I'm even willing to live amongst barbarians in order to serve him. So . . .' He spread his hands and gave me a sheepish grin.

I knew what he meant. Richard of Gloucester had always exerted the same fascination over me. But, unlike my companion, I was not prepared to sacrifice either my independence or my passionate affection for my own strip of ground for the duke or for any other man. All the same, I was glad to know that the King's brother would soon have one of his most loyal and ablest servants with him again.

'So, what would be a satisfactory conclusion to this case?' I asked.

'To find the Duke of Albany and take him to London as a hostage for the English crown. Our spies in France tell us that King Louis is busy inciting King James to break the truce with England and begin raiding across the border again, which, of course, could eventually lead to a full-scale war. The Duke of Albany could prove to be a valuable bargaining counter in this dangerous game.'

'And you're sure that the duke is somewhere in Bristol, unlikely as that may seem?'

Timothy scratched his nose. 'When Robin Avenel and his sister learned – from whatever source – that this Irish sea captain was going to betray Albany and carry him back to Scotland, they were left with the duke on their hands until they could arrange for another ship to take him to Brittany. They must have hidden him somewhere.'

211

'Why didn't they leave him in the Witherspoon house at Rownham Passage?'

Timothy pulled down the corners of his mouth. 'That's what makes me think that Silas Witherspoon is not of their way of thinking. That he's still loyal to Henry Tudor. They didn't dare risk him discovering the true identity of the man they were trying to get to Brittany.'

'So, you assume they brought the duke back here and have kept him hidden ever since?'

'Yes, until they can arrange to smuggle him aboard some other ship. And that could happen any day.'

'How do you know it hasn't happened already?'

'To be honest with you, I don't. Some of the Sheriff's men have been keeping close watch on all the foreign ships tying up along the Backs, but there are so many of them, it's impossible to stand guard over each one every minute of every day. But as long as I'm not certain that Albany's gone, I have to stay and do what I can to intercept him.'

'And if you were sure he'd gone?'

Timothy eased his thin buttocks against the hard ground. 'I'd have to return to London and admit defeat to the King.'

'Would he be angry?'

'He may not be pleased,' was the cautious reply. 'But as I'm to leave Westminster soon, perhaps I'm not as afraid of His Highness's displeasure as I might otherwise have been. Besides, my own guess is that Albany will himself tire of this charade. He must know very well that his chances of ever becoming King of England are extremely slight, if they exist at all. He's probably just using Elizabeth Alefounder and her friends to find a way abroad that will fool his brother and all King James's agents who are hot on his trail.' Timothy got slowly and, I thought, a little painfully, to his feet. I realized suddenly that in the eight years since I had first met him, he had aged considerably. He stooped and laid a hand on my shoulder. 'So if you hear anything you think I should know, Roger, I rely on you to tell me.'

'And the murder of Robin Avenel?' I asked. 'What do you know of that?'

'I've told you, no more than you do. My one concern is

212

to keep his name separate from my search for Albany. Let matters alone there, lad. Your friend won't be the first innocent man to swing. In the interests of the State, it's better that this death is resolved simply and cleanly.'

He pressed my shoulder once again and strode off in the direction of the friary. I sat where I was, watching him until he entered the gate and disappeared from view.

Nineteen

I was conscious of an overpowering feeling of rage and resentment against the Spymaster General. I had never before actually disliked Timothy Plummer – I had found him pompous, irritating, self-important, yet nothing that was not eventually forgivable, if not exactly lovable – but now I was overwhelmed with hatred, not just for him, but also for his masters. The State? What new concept was this that could so dispose of innocent lives as if they were worms to be crushed beneath our feet? In the old days, men served their liege lords; living, breathing people who listened to pleas for help and clemency, who were open to reason and charity. But *I* had been threatened, my wife and family had been threatened, and now Jenny Hodge was likely to find herself a widow – and all because of this heinous, faceless new monster: the State. The wheel of fate and fortune revolves, my friends, but not necessarily for the better.

I realized that I was hot and very thirsty, but judging by the sun it was not yet time for supper. If I went home now, Adela would want to know where I had been, what I had been doing, and, above all, how much I had sold and what money I had earned. So, like many an erring husband before me – and no doubt like many who will come after – I decided to drown my grievances against the world in drink. I dragged myself to my feet, dried my wet hose as well as I could in the long grasses bordering the river, put on my boots and jerkin, shouldered my pack and set off back the way I had come.

The Green Lattis was full at this time of day, and although I recognized most faces, there were one or two strangers

214

among the people crowded around the tables and seated on benches along the walls. I managed to catch the pot-boy's eye and ordered a cup of ale before beating a local pieman to a stool that had just that second been vacated. The other occupant of this narrow trestle eyed me approvingly.

'You're nippy on your feet today, Master Chapman.'

I stared at him, trying to place the thin, tired-faced man who addressed me as if he knew me. There was something familiar about him, but for the moment, recognition eluded my grasp.

He smiled. 'My name's John Longstaff. We met at Rownham Passage a week or so back. You questioned my son, Henry, about two women you said had attacked and tried to drown you . . . Friday's the day I sell my vegetables in Bristol market,' he added, seeming to feel that his presence in the alehouse needed an explanation.

'Of course! I remember now.' The pot-boy set my cup of ale before me, slopping its contents as he did so, and departed to serve someone else with an equal lack of grace. 'How is your mother?' I asked. 'She was none too well as I recall.'

Master Longstaff sighed. 'Much the same, I thank you. Always dying, but never quite dead.' He looked ashamed of this remark as soon as he had uttered it and continued hurriedly, 'She's looking after Henry for me. Or he's looking after her, I'm never quite sure which.' He set down his own beaker and wiped his mouth on the back of his hand before continuing, a little self-consciously, 'By the way, there was an odd sequel to your interrogation of my son.'

I raised my eyebrows and waited. He appeared to be faintly embarrassed, although I couldn't think why, and twisted the half-full beaker of ale between restless hands.

'When we got home,' he said, 'that day, I naturally quizzed Henry further about what he'd seen, just to make sure he hadn't been making it up.'

'He hadn't,' I interrupted.

'No, no! I realized that. His story didn't vary, however many times I made him repeat it. But a day or so later we were visiting my mother yet again and I had to help her to the chamber pot. Henry was in the room at the time, and

215

afterwards he asked me why his grandmother wasn't made the same as other women. I told him that of course she was. I didn't understand what he was talking about.' Master Longstaff took another swig of ale. 'Finally, I winkled out of him that one of the two women he'd seen pushing you into the river – the one who'd hoisted her skirts up around her waist – had . . . had . . . well . . . had the same thing as you and I and every other man conceals in his breeches. Naturally, I told him this was impossible and that he must have been mistaken, but he swore – and continues to swear – that it's true. Says he saw it plainly.' My companion finished his drink in one gulp and rose to his feet, flushing deeply. He really was surprisingly shy. 'I . . . I just thought you might be interested to know. I mean, I thought it might have some significance for you. I do hope you won't take offence at my plain speaking. Well, I must be off, back to my stall. God go with you, Master Chapman. If you're ever in the manor of Ashton-Leigh, come and see us. Everyone knows where we live.'

He eased his way out of the Green Lattis, now crowded to the point of discomfort, and left me sitting at the table, my mind reeling, while so much that had been a puzzle fell into place. Of course! *Of course!* What was wrong with me that I had been unable to work out such an obvious truth for myself? My wits had gone wool-gathering, atrophied by my brush with death, by my weeks in bed and by the unrelenting heat.

Elizabeth Alefounder's companion on Saint Elmo's Day – that person whom Edgar Capgrave had seen riding beside her as she entered Bristol by the Frome Gate, that person in a wet and muddied blue brocade gown – had not been Rowena Hollyns, had not in fact been a woman at all. I ordered another stoup of ale from the harassed pot-boy and ignored all attempts by the pieman, who had seized upon Master Longstaff's empty stool, to enter into conversation with me.

I knew now that there never had been a third assailant in that room in the 'murder' house. The man's voice I had heard belonged to my attacker in the blue brocade gown. *She* was a *he*, and I had no hesitation in assigning him a name. This surely must have been King James's brother, the Duke of Albany.

I recollected a question I had meant to put to Timothy Plummer. Who or what was the Midsummer Rose? Now, with my new knowledge, I never doubted but I had the answer. It was the name by which Robin Avenel and his sister referred to their guest in case they were overheard by inquisitive eavesdroppers such as Jess. How Timothy had learned of it, I was unable to guess, although I doubted that anything remained a secret from him and his fellow spies for very long. His network of informers must be formidable. I swallowed some more ale and set my mind to working out what must have been the likely sequence of events.

How, or by whom, the suggestion that he might replace Henry Tudor as the Lancastrian pretender to the English throne had been put to the disaffected Albany, I had no idea, and probably never would have. Nevertheless, I was certain that someone in Brittany had instigated this proposal. While King James' agents had conducted a vain, and what they hoped was a secret, search for the refugee along the eastern and southern English coast, that someone had accompanied Albany south to Rownham Passage. There, Robin Avenel, alerted to the plan and obviously approving, had hired a night's lodging for the duke and his escort in the abandoned Witherspoon house on the Avon shore. ('A couple of friends . . . both men,' Robin had told the apothecary.) Meantime, a deal had been struck with Eamonn Malahide for the Irishman to sail an unnamed gentlewoman to Brittany in his ship, the *Clontarf*. But the captain, running true to form, had somehow managed to discover his passenger's true sex and identity, and promptly offered to sell the duke back to his brother. He would take him not to Brittany, but to Scotland.

Here, plot and counter-plot, discovery and counter-discovery began to play their part in the story. The nest of double traitors – those originally disloyal to King Edward and now to their master, Henry Tudor – had, by some means or another and at the eleventh hour, been made aware of Malahide's intentions. Robin had been warned, but not until the very day itself, and after his sister had already left for

Rownham Passage, taking with her, I suspected, a blue brocade gown and cloak belonging to Marianne and a pair of Robin's shoes, red and sufficiently fancy to be worn by a woman. (His wife's shoes would have been too small to fit a man.)

But *why* was Albany to be disguised as a woman? As with so much else, I could only guess (but my guesses so far seemed, to me at least, to make good sense). It was more than possible – more than probable – that Henry Tudor's most loyal adherents, like his Uncle Jasper, had by now heard rumours of disaffection in their midst. Whispers could have reached their ears that Albany, another descendant of Gaunt's bastard Beaufort line, was the chosen rival, so agents of the Tudor court would be on the watch for his appearance in Brittany – and no doubt his murder had already been arranged. Moreover, Duke Francis himself might well find it embarrassing to harbour yet another aspirant to the English crown on Breton soil, and Albany's return to Scotland would win him the gratitude of King James. So Breton agents, too, could be on the lookout for the Scot. But in the guise of a woman, it might be possible to keep his arrival in Brittany a secret until his claim gained greater support amongst the exiled Lancastrians.

But the plans for Albany's immediate escape across the Channel had all gone awry with the discovery of Eamonn Malahide's treachery. Robin Avenel had arrived at Rownham Passage with the news and had then left almost at once to return to Bristol. Why had his sister and Albany not accompanied him? Why had he not waited for them? The second question was perhaps easier to answer than the first. There were urgent arrangements to be made for Albany's concealment until such time as another ship could be found to carry him abroad. But that posed the question: where had Albany been hidden these past few weeks?

As to the rest of the events of that Saint Elmo's Day, they were easy enough to piece together. Elizabeth Alefounder had probably hoped to follow her brother, accompanied by the fugitive, back to Bristol before the arrival of Eamonn Malahide, but when I, poor fool, had come knocking at the door of the 'murder' house, she had mistaken me for him and had tried to kill me. Albany had been upstairs, but the commotion had brought him running down to her assistance. In the middle of their debate on how to dispose of me, the real Eamonn Malahide had walked in, and Albany had despatched him with a swift, unerring thrust of his dagger, like the accomplished soldier he no doubt was . . .

'You're a miserable bugger to try talking to, ain't you?' the pieman demanded angrily as, with a snort of disgust, he stamped out of the Green Lattis, but not before he had emptied the remaining contents of my cup over my head – to the great amusement of my neighbours, all of whom laughed heartily at my discomfiture. Cursing and drying my hair and face on my jerkin sleeve, I grabbed my pack and followed him outside, but he had disappeared. Which was probably just as well. It was still too hot to pick a fight. Besides, I had other things to think about.

The church bells were ringing for Vespers. I judged it was time to go home for supper.

For the first time in our two years of marriage, Adela and I were not speaking to one another. Her annoyance at discovering that I had still not sold any goods – or, more exactly, her annoyance at finding that I had not even *tried* to do so – had spilled over into a torrent of abuse that ended with me threatening her, at the top of my voice, with the scold's bridle. After which, there was nothing more to be said.

Supper was the quietest and most uncomfortable meal I could ever remember eating. Even the children, who never took any notice of my antics and tantrums, were reduced to silence by their mother's unaccustomed anger. As for me, I knew Adela had right on her side, but I felt aggrieved and mulishly refused to apologize. 'Master in my own house' were the words that kept buzzing around my head while I ate my vegetable pottage and drank my small beer. But in the end, even they were drowned out by more clamorous thoughts and by the urgent need to know where Elizabeth Alefounder and her brother had hidden their unexpected guest.

Irrationally, I entertained the belief that if I could only locate the Scotsman I would find out who had killed Robin Avenel.

And then, quite suddenly, while I was scraping the last spoonful of stew from the bottom of my bowl and wondering with one part of my mind if I dare ask for a second helping, three memories surfaced and finally converged to give me a possible answer to the riddle.

The first memory was of my dream that afternoon, on the river bank. I had not yet worked out its meaning, but where I had been and what I had 'seen' was obvious. I had been in the cellars under the synagogue in Jewry Lane nearly three hundred years ago, when the last members of the city's Jewish community had been massacred by a mob of bloodthirsty citizens. But why had some Jews remained behind when most of their friends and families had already fled? And what were they doing in the cellars? Conjuring up the scene of my dream yet again – almost, you might say, being drawn back into it – I realized what had eluded me before. They had not been trying to get *out* of the cellar, but had all been crowding up against the furthest wall, just as if . . . Just as if what? Just as if they had been trying to get *through* it! Yes, that was it! Through it! And at least two men had been bending down as though searching for something.

At very nearly the same moment, Luke Prettywood's voice echoed inside my head. 'My grandfather used to tell me that *his* grandfather, as a boy, came down here looking for a way into the secret vault that people swore had been built by the Jews in order to house their hoard of gold and silver.' And another voice, this time Edgar Capgrave's, joined in chorus with the first. He was describing his meeting with Silas Witherspoon on the evening of Midsummer Day. 'He was keeping close to the wall of Saint Giles's and the rest of the buildings, and taking very precise, evenly paced steps . . . He seemed to be concentrating on his feet.'

Precise, evenly paced steps and concentrating on his feet – what did that suggest? That the apothecary had been counting, perhaps. But what had he been counting? The answer came pat. He had been measuring in paces the distance from the beginning of Saint Giles's Church to Saint John's

Arch, and had no doubt, at some other time, paced from one end of Saint Giles's crypt to the further end of the cellars. But had he found a significant discrepancy between the two distances?

Timothy had told me that Silas Witherspoon was a Lancastrian agent, and he could well be one who retained his loyalty to Henry Tudor. If he had discovered, or been warned, what Robin Avenel was up to – or if, equally likely, Robin had tried to recruit him to the cause – then Silas would have been as anxious as anyone to find the missing Albany, probably with orders to kill him on the spot. So, could that make the apothecary the possible murderer of Robin Avenel?

I gave my head a little shake. I was going too fast. First, I had to find out if my newly formed suspicion was correct; that there was indeed a secret hiding place somewhere in the old synagogue cellars and that it was where Albany was being hidden. One other circumstance persuaded me I was right. I had never been able to locate the bed which Jack Nym told me he had taken, on Robin's instructions, to store in the crypt. But even if I could convince myself of the secret chamber's existence, I still had to discover how to open it. Had Silas Witherspoon already done so? Was the Scotsman already dead or spirited away? I didn't know, and only time would tell.

I scraped my stool back from the table and stood up, stretching and yawning.

'I have to go out again, sweeting,' I said. And it was only when I met Adela's outraged gaze that I recollected our quarrel.

I knew that I should stop and make things up between us, but I didn't have time just then. I was filled with a sudden urgency to put my theory to the test. I would have kissed her, but she ducked away.

'I won't be long,' I promised.

In the bright evening sunshine, I, too, paced the distance of Bell Lane and of Jewry Lane from the Fish Street end of Saint Giles's to Saint John's-on-the-Arch. Then I entered the church and descended to the crypt, where I walked its and

221

the two cellars' length. I did it a second time. And a third, just to make sure. But there was no doubt about it. The interior was shorter than the exterior by a good ten paces.

Once again, I conjured up my God-given dream (although the 'sight' can be an instrument of the Devil, as my mother had taken care to warn me) and as far as I could recall, the two men bending down had been in the far right-hand corner of the last of the three chambers. It was too dark to see anything in detail, so I went back upstairs to the church and lit a candle, then descended once more, sheltering the flame with one hand.

I knelt down, holding the candlestick as close to the wall as I was able, but saw nothing except damp stones and spiders, the latter scurrying away in high dudgeon, angry at being disturbed. In spite of the heat outside, the chill struck up through my knees, making me shiver. At least, I persuaded myself it was the cold and not fright that had this effect. I shifted the light again and the shadows assumed new shapes. Still I could see nothing but slime and mould. Then I had an inspiration. I drew my knife from its sheath and began to scrape away the patches of lichen that mottled the wall.

How long I had been down in the cellars, I had no idea. I seemed to be losing all track of time and I was growing sleepy. Deciding to stretch my legs and walk around for a while, I picked up the candle, which I had placed on the floor beside me, but as I did so, something caught my eye. I moved the flame closer to the wall, my heart pounding with excitement. And there it was: a tiny six-pointed star carved into one of the stones where I had recently removed a circle of moss no bigger than a thumbnail. I sat back on my haunches, staring at it and wondering what to do next. Tentatively, I put out my right hand and pressed my fingers to the star . . .

There was a muted rumble, a slight rattle like a hiccough, and a section of the wall, just about big enough for two men to enter abreast, swung inwards on well-oiled hinges to reveal the chamber beyond. I took a grip on my knife and cautiously stepped across the threshold.

There was some unidentifiable source of fresh air in the chamber, but it was not enough to counteract the strong smell of urine and human excrement that met me, and my eyes were at once drawn to the chamber pot that stood near the end of a bed that occupied most of the room's cramped space. But there were also a chair, a stool and a table, on which stood the remains of a meal. Three or four lighted candles and a flint and tinderbox stood on a shelf above the bedhead, a chessboard and chessmen were scattered over the floor, as if their owner had thrown them down in a fit of pique, while a green velvet-covered book, its laces all tangled, lay alongside them. And seated on the edge of the bed, eyes wide and staring in alarm, sat a man dressed in a soiled white shirt and dark-red hose. A blue brocade gown, together with a woman's coif and hood, lay beside him.

Several moments of complete silence followed my entrance while we stared at one another. Finally, the figure on the bed rose slowly and stretched to its full height, which was about as high as my chin, but still no word was spoken. I decided I must break the deadlock.

'Am I addressing His Grace, the Duke of Albany?'

He replied formally, 'Alexander Stewart at your service,' and inclined his head. Then formality was thrown to the winds as he demanded violently, 'And who in the Devil's name might you be?' I saw one hand grope behind him, searching for his dagger, which was lying on the counterpane.

I gave what I hoped was a disarming grin.

'Thomas Bourchier, Archbishop of Canterbury,' I said, hoping to make him laugh and, much to my surprise, succeeding. Well, he smiled – quite broadly as a matter of fact.

'Has Elizabeth sent you?' His Scots accent was thick, but, as I had remembered from our first encounter, sufficiently anglicised as to be comprehensible to my west country ears.

'No,' I answered bluntly. There was no point in beating about the bush. 'I'm the man you've twice tried to murder; firstly in the house at Rownham Passage when you thought I was the Irish sea captain, and secondly when you broke into my house two weeks ago. And don't try to tell me it wasn't you. You left a shoe behind – a shoe I now know was lent to you by Robin Avenel.'

He had stopped smiling and was looking grim. He had at last found the dagger, and I saw his fingers close around the hilt. I moved swiftly to hold the point of my own knife at his throat, although somewhat hampered, I have to admit, by the candlestick in my other hand. Reluctantly, he released the dagger.

'Proceed,' he said. 'What do you want? Or is that a stupid question? I'm sure there's a price on my head.'

'Not that I know of. In any case, I don't deal in blood money,' I assured him, but without lowering my knife. '*Why* did you try to murder me a second time? And how did you know where I lived?'

He blinked rapidly. 'The answer to both questions is Mistress Alefounder. She asked me to do it and she told me where to find your house. She's afraid of you. She said you can't keep your nose out of other people's business and were better disposed of. Sooner or later, she thought, you'd puzzle out what was happening. It seems she was right.'

He was smiling again, so I took a chance and removed my knife from his throat. He made no move to attack me.

'I'm not the only one who's been looking for you,' I said. My anger with Timothy Plummer had still not abated. 'There's a government spy in the city, desperate to discover your whereabouts and take you hostage for our king. A bargaining counter to use against your brother, King James. There's also the apothecary, Silas Witherspoon, who owns the house at Rownham Passage and is one of Henry Tudor's agents. I have reason to believe that he has also joined in the search. Now, the motives of both these men bode ill for your future good. I, on the other hand, just want to prove the innocence of a friend of mine who's been arrested for murdering Robin Avenel.' With a jerk of my arm, I brought up my knife again and pricked the skin of his throat. A bead of blood appeared on his neck. 'So, what can Your High and Noble Mightiness tell me about that?'

'I? N–Nothing,' he stammered. But his eyes shifted sideways and downwards to try to locate his dagger.

I pressed the knife further into his thin flesh and a second gout of blood joined the first.

'By my reckoning, Master Avenel was killed right outside this door. If you didn't kill him, you must know who did. I just want to know the name of the murderer, that's all. Then as far as I'm concerned, you're free to go to Brittany or France or wherever you wish. I shan't try to stop you, I promise.'

The sweat was standing out on his forehead in great drops.

'I don't know,' he said. 'I really don't know, I swear by Christ and all His saints.' He made to push aside the point of my knife, but I held it steady. 'Look,' he said desperately, 'in return for your help, I'll tell you all I do know.'

'And what help can you possibly need from me?' I sneered.

'I need to get away. To escape. I need a ship to carry me to France as soon as possible.'

I frowned, sensing a trap. 'Isn't that what you're doing? What Mistress Alefounder is doing for you? Trying to arrange your passage to Brittany?'

The duke sat down again on the bed, emitting a little moan and burying his etiolated face in his long, thin hands.

'I don't *want* to go to Brittany,' he said in defiant, but muffled tones. Then he raised his head, a desperate expression in the sapphire-blue eyes, and proceeded to explain.

'When Sir Thomas St John – he's a disaffected Lancastrian supporter of Henry Tudor – came to me at Stirling and made his proposal, I have to admit that I was excited by it. I promised I'd consider the scheme. However, before I'd had time to think about it carefully, word reached me that my younger brother, Mar, was dead, probably murdered, and I was advised to get out of Scotland before I suffered a similar fate. Sir Thomas's offer at once took on the appearance of divine intervention. It also meant I would have protection on my journey and that my passage abroad would be arranged without any extraordinary exertion on my part. So, Sir Thomas escorted me south to this house near Bristol, where we slept the night. The next day he left me in the care of Mistress Alefounder, who would see me safely aboard the Irish ship which was to carry me to Brest, and there I should be met and cared for by others of the conspirators.' He shrugged. 'But it all went awry, as you know only too well. Instead of being transported to Brittany, I've been mewed up here for over three weeks.'

'And you've had time to think,' I suggested.

The duke laughed grimly and said something in broad Scots which I didn't understand, then reverted to English.

'I've done little else but think in between Mistress Alefounder or that pretty friend of hers bringing me my meals. I shall go mad if I have to stay walled up here much longer. And after Master Avenel's murder, his sister's been as jumpy as a cat on cinders – and with good reason, I suspect. Especially now you tell me that there is not only an agent of Henry Tudor living in the town, but also one of King Edward's spies.'

'Not "one of",' I corrected him. 'The best.'

Albany cursed fluently, again in broad Scots. It sounded splendid. I wished I knew what he was saying.

He continued. 'As I said, I've had time to think these past weeks and it's brought me to my senses. I realized I've been deluding myself that I could ever usurp Henry Tudor's place as the Lancastrian pretender to the English crown. Within days, hours even, of landing in Brittany, I'd be as dead as yesterday's meat. But more than that, the whole mad scheme has as much substance as a puff of air. Henry Tudor is *never* going to be King of England. *I'm* never going to be King of England. King Edward's hale and hearty according to all the reports I've ever had of him, and he's the father of two male heirs.' Albany gave a smile of great cunning. 'Besides, I'd much rather be king of Scotland, and if I play my cards aright – well, who knows? Stranger things have happened. So you see –' he paused and spread out his hands – 'what I need is an accomplice who might be able to help me escape to France.'

I considered him for a moment or two, still holding him at bay with my knife. Was he genuine, or was this a ploy to put me off my guard? I had to make up my mind.

'And in return for my assistance, you agree to tell me what you know of Robin Avenel's death?' I asked.

'Everything. Although in fairness I should warn you, it isn't as much as you would wish.'

I hesitated before slowly lowering the point of my knife. 'I'll have to take that chance,' I said.

Twenty

I sat down beside him on the bed, but at a distance. I still wasn't wholly convinced that I could trust him. He was a dark, swarthy creature of about my own age, but there was a shifty look in his eyes that somehow called his probity into question. It was an expression I had seen in the past in the eyes of George, Duke of Clarence, another dissatisfied younger brother.

'Very well,' I said. 'Tell me what you can.'

Before replying, however, he got up and walked over to the open section of wall, which, with an effort, he pushed shut. Catching sight of my face, he laughed.

'You're quite safe. It can be opened from this side, too.' He resumed his seat on the bed, slewing a little to his right, so that we were almost face to face. 'It's a marvellous piece of machinery, don't you agree? The Jews are a very clever people. Which is why we are so afraid of them, I suppose. Now, before I tell you anything, you tell me how you will get me across the Narrow Sea to France. I need to be gone as soon as possible. Tomorrow. Tonight if it can be arranged.'

'What will you say to Mistress Alefounder?' I enquired.

He shrugged. 'Nothing, unless it's necessary. She won't come again until the morning. She's already brought me my evening meal.' He grimaced, intimating that he had not enjoyed it. 'Since yesterday and her brother's death, she has had much to occupy her mind, as you might expect. So, Roger – am I right? Is that your name? – what makes you think you can find me a ship's captain willing to carry me to France, when Robin Avenel and his sister have so far been unsuccessful?'

'There's an Irish slave trader with whom I've had some

228

dealings in the past. At present, his ship is moored along the Bristol Backs. He's an honest rogue who knew of Eamonn Malahide, but had nothing but contempt for his double-dealing. He'll take you, I feel certain, provided you can pay him what he asks.'

'Ah!' The duke gave me a quizzical glance. 'Money! I'd forgotten about money. I'm afraid I don't have any. Do you?'

Typical! These noblemen are all the same. They never pay for anything if they can help it; they're too busy leeching off everyone else.

'No, I don't,' I answered shortly. 'Not that sort of money, at any rate. I'm a pedlar. Don't you have any rings or a jewelled collar or something of that sort that I could offer Briant?'

Albany sighed and shook his head. 'Not here. I left Scotland in such a hurry, I had to leave most of my belongings behind. I did have one ring, my signet ring, but I lost it – the Virgin only knows where.'

I caught my breath. 'A heavily chased gold band and a roundel engraved with two letter As, is that the one?'

He stared at me, nodding. 'Two As and the Lion of Scotland.' He shook my wrist. 'What do you know about it? Do you know where it is?'

'I found it lodged in the mattress of the bed at Rownham Passage when I went back there to have a look around. I think you must have slept in that bed and got your hand caught between the ticking and the feathers. The ring worked loose.'

The Scotsman clapped his hands. 'Of course! Why didn't I think of that? Mistress Alefounder was right on yet another count. You are a nosy fellow, Roger! God bless you for it.' A sudden thought struck him. 'You still have it?' he demanded anxiously. It was my turn to nod. 'Then we can offer it to this Irishman of yours. Tell him that when I get safely to France and my good cousin, King Louis, grants me a pension, I'll buy it back from him at three times its price. He'll be well recompensed for all his trouble.'

It might work. I reckoned the signet ring was of sufficient weight and value to satisfy Briant. And he was shrewd enough to see that it could have an importance in Albany's eyes beyond its simple monetary worth.

'Very well,' I conceded. 'But I'll have to go home and fetch it.'

'And take it to this Irishman now, this evening, without delay. If he agrees to the transaction, I'll be aboard his ship tonight. I can return to Ireland with him, if necessary, and wait there until he's able to carry me to France.'

I could tell he was used to issuing commands that he expected to be obeyed instantly. But there again, that's royalty for you. Never a thought for what might be inconvenient – or dangerous or even difficult, come to that – for other people. My young lord entertained not the slightest doubt but that I would do as he bade me, in spite of the fact that he had twice tried to kill me. I guessed I was meant to be grateful that he hadn't quite succeeded.

When I didn't move from the bed, he gave me an imperious look.

'We had a bargain,' I reminded him. 'I'll fulfil my part of it when you've fulfilled yours.'

He glowered. 'But if I do, how can I be sure you'll do as you've promised?'

'Because you have my word.'

He snorted with laughter at that. 'The word of a pedlar! What guarantee is that?'

I rounded on him. 'It's as good as the word of a fugitive prince who can't even keep friends with his own brother.' I sprang to my feet. 'But if you don't agree, I'm off!'

He held out a placatory hand. 'No, no! Don't be so touchy! I'm sorry. Forgive me. That was unpardonably rude. Sit down again, please, and I'll tell you what I know about Master Avenel's murder. But, remember, I did warn you that it isn't much.' He patted the bed beside him.

I feigned reluctance, but eventually allowed myself to be persuaded. In any case, I had suddenly realized that I didn't know how to open the secret door from inside the chamber.

'So? What can you tell me?' I asked.

He nodded towards the wall where I knew the door to be, although nothing was visible, not even the faintest hairline crack. Albany was right. Its original designer had been an engineer of genius.

'There's a small peephole over there, to the left. Not much good for seeing anything – it isn't really big enough and it's too dark on the other side – but at least you can occasionally hear things through it. Noises drift in from time to time. People come down here to store unwanted furniture, or they use it as a trysting place. Once, I came out too soon to stretch my legs and you were there, rummaging around.'

'Yesterday morning,' I said. 'You were dressed as a woman. I saw you, but when I couldn't find any trace of you, I decided you were a figment of my imagination.'

He looked slightly bemused. 'Was that only yesterday? Time plays strange tricks on a man with no one but himself for company . . . Yes, yes, I remember now. I thought I'd risk going out for a while, so I put on my woman's garb. But your presence thwarted my plans. Another time, you saw me in the street and shouted to me. You thought I was Mistress Alefounder's maid. But I ran down here and hid myself.' He chuckled to himself before proceeding. 'So! To Master Avenel's murder. It must have been . . . Let me see . . .'

'The night before last,' I prompted. 'Midsummer Eve.'

He nodded. 'The lady I was just speaking of, the lovely Rowena –' he smiled lasciviously – 'had brought me my supper. Now there's a woman ripe for the plucking, but unfortunately, something of a prude.' He rubbed one cheek reminiscently, and I guessed Rowena had rejected his amorous advances in no uncertain fashion. After another pause he went on, 'Well, some while after I'd finished my supper – just how long, I've no idea – I heard the sound of men's voices, raised in anger, come floating through the wall. One, I immediately recognized as Robin Avenel's, but the other I didn't know. And yet it sounded vaguely familiar, as if I'd heard it a couple of times before. I put my ear to the hole, but I was unable to hear exactly what was being said. There was a lot of shouting and also a noise like scuffling, which suggested to me that the two men were having a fight, a suspicion that was borne out by the fact that the voices got

231

even louder and angrier until, suddenly, they ceased. Then there was silence.'

'And?' I was growing impatient.

He chewed his nails for a moment before continuing. I noticed that they were bitten down to the quick.

'Well, after waiting for what seemed like an age, I opened the secret door – with the greatest caution, I might say – and almost at once saw Robin Avenel lying in the middle of the cellar floor. I knew it was him even though his face was turned away from me, but I fetched a lighted candle just to make sure. He was dead. He'd been stabbed through the heart.'

'What did you do?'

'What *could* I do in my position but wait for Mistress Alefounder to come looking for her brother? Normally, she wouldn't have visited me again until early the following morning, when she brought me my breakfast, but I guessed that when Master Avenel failed to return home that night, she would grow anxious and begin to look for him immediately. Which, of course, she eventually did. I don't know what hour it was when her search finally brought her down here, but it was very late. At first, Elizabeth accused me of murdering Master Avenel – *me!* – and was ready to tear my eyes out. Not, it transpired, because she thought I'd killed her brother, but because I'd jeopardized my chances of remaining hidden and, in due course, of being spirited away to Brittany. By the time I'd managed to convince her of my innocence, the night was even further advanced. It must be nearly midnight, she told me. And the following morning, of course, Robin's disappearance would become public knowledge. She would have to inform the Sheriff, who would organize an official investigation. Sooner or later, Master Avenel's body would be found, and the last thing she wanted was for the Sheriff's men to come nosing about down here.'

Albany stopped to draw breath. 'Let me guess,' I interrupted him. 'You and Mistress Alefounder carried Robin up into the street and left his body in Jewry Lane, where it was found by the Watch patrol, just after midnight.'

The duke shrugged. 'What else could we do? I'm ignorant of the other details. But, wait a moment!' He clapped a hand to his forehead in the manner of one who had just recollected something vital. 'I forgot to tell you that while I was waiting for Mistress Alefounder to arrive, I naturally shut myself in here, out of sight. But, suddenly, I heard a woman's scream. Naturally, I thought it was Elizabeth, but when no one came to the peephole to speak to me, I grew suspicious and stayed where I was. Which was just as well, as it turned out, because Mistress Alefounder later assured me that, whoever it might have been, it wasn't her.'

'And was she worried about this stranger who had accidentally stumbled across her brother's body?'

Albany frowned.

'Now you mention it,' he said slowly, 'no, she wasn't. It didn't strike me at the time, there was too much else to think about . . . How very odd.'

'Maybe not,' I said. 'Perhaps she knew, or guessed, who it was. How soon after you found Master Avenel's body did you hear this scream?'

His frown deepened. 'Not very long.' He pondered the matter for a moment or so, then glanced sharply in my direction. 'I can see by your face that that is the answer you wanted. That it means something to you. Am I right?'

'Maybe,' I agreed, as pieces of the puzzle began falling into place, and I realized what it was that had been troubling me ever since this morning and my visit to Saint Giles's. 'You say the murder took place sometime during the evening, after you'd eaten your supper?'

The duke pursed his lips. 'Two, maybe three hours afterwards, as far as I was able to judge. Maybe longer. I tell you, time is not itself down here. Now, are you satisfied? Has what I've told you helped in any way to disprove the charge of Robin Avenel's murder that has been laid against your friend?' I nodded and he again clapped his hands, like a child who had been given a sweetmeat. 'Then *en avant, mon brave*! There is nothing more to wait for. Fetch my ring from wherever you have hidden it and take it to this Irish slave master of yours.' He clicked his tongue mockingly.

233

'For a respectable man, Roger, my friend, you know some very strange people.'

'Isn't that the pot calling the skillet black?' I retorted, sliding off the bed. I indicated the apparently solid wall. 'You'd better let me out. But before I go, I'd be interested to know what it is you've done to be branded a traitor by your brother.'

His face lost its recent good humour and assumed a sullen expression. I thought he wasn't going to answer me. But then, suddenly, he began to laugh, displaying an upper row of surprisingly healthy teeth, with a single blackened one to spoil their general appearance.

'My younger brother, Mar, and I were urging James to resume hostilities against England; to break the peace and start raiding across the border once again. He refused, so we began to plot with some of the other lords to bring about his downfall. Unfortunately, one of the bastards betrayed us to the King. The rest you know. Mar is dead, and I have been forced to fly for my life.'

Still chuckling to himself, Albany crossed to join me by the wall, where I was shown first the tiny peephole and then a stone similar to the one on the other side, bearing the faint indentation of a six-pointed star. The duke pressed it and yet again the same section of wall swung inwards with the familiar slight rumble and hiccough.

'When you've arranged everything,' he said, 'come back here. Whisper through the hole and I'll open the door from this side. I'll be waiting, ready.' He laid a hand on my arm. 'Don't fail me, Roger. I'm relying on you.'

By curfew, everything was arranged, but I waited until it was properly dark before returning to shepherd Albany through the Bristol streets and handing him over to the tender mercies of Briant of Dungarvon. When, finally, I rolled into bed, I was well nigh exhausted.

I had first been home to collect Albany's signet ring and fend off Adela's indignant enquiries as to where I had been and where I was going – it seemed she had decided to speak to me again, but only to point out my shortcomings as a husband. Then I visited Marsh Street, where my reappearance in the Wayfarer's Return had been greeted with the sort of suspicion that makes a man want to stand with his back to the wall and a long, pointed knife in his hand. By the greatest of good fortune, Briant had not returned to his ship, and although undoubtedly drunk, he was able to hold his whisky well enough to grasp what I was saying. He listened to my story in silence, and although he had some difficulty in understanding the political machinations that formed its background, he was more than willing to assist a fellow Celt in trouble, especially one who might possibly prove an embarrassment to the English crown. His animosity made me wonder yet again what exactly had happened to Padraic Kinsale.

So, having delivered my charge safely into Briant's hands, and having been assured of Albany's undying gratitude and patronage should I ever have need of it, I staggered home to a darkened house and a sleeping family, stripped off my clothes and fell into bed beside Adela, expecting the waters of Lethe to close over my head without delay. But sleep proved elusive as the enormity of what I'd done gradually began to sink in.

I had allowed my anger with Timothy Plummer and his political masters to cloud my judgement to such an extent that I had committed what was tantamount to treason. When, earlier that evening, I had left Albany, the man who had urged his brother, the King, to re-invade the northern shires of England, I should have gone, not to Marsh Street and Briant of Dungarvon, but to Timothy Plummer at the Dominican friary. Instead, I had assisted an enemy of my country to escape to France. A great knot of fear started to form in my stoamch.

I tossed and turned, fell into an uneasy doze and dreamed that I was being marched to the gallows by Timothy Plummer, woke with a mouth as dry as tinder and had to creep downstairs to the kitchen to get a cup of water from the barrel. Adela moaned and grumbled in her sleep, but, thankfully, didn't wake. Finally, as dawn was rimming the bedchamber shutters, I came to the conclusion that regrets were useless. What was done was done, and provided Albany kept his mouth shut, which he had promised me most faithfully he would do, no one need be any the wiser. Elizabeth Alefounder was unlikely to raise the hue and cry, and as for the miscarrying of her plans, I felt not the slightest shred of guilt.

All that remained for me to do now was to concentrate on clearing Burl's name by pinning Robin Avenel's murder on the real killer.

It was during breakfast – another silent meal, although I could feel the frostiness in Adela's manner beginning to thaw – that I suddenly realized it might prove difficult to lay the blame where it truly belonged without revealing what I knew about the moving of Robin Avenel's body. I cursed silently and sat, my spoon halfway to my mouth, frozen into immobility. The children found this very funny and began to point and laugh. Adela enquired sharply if I were well.

'Perfectly well, my love, thank you.' I laid down my spoon and started pulling on my boots. 'I have to go out.'

'Then why aren't you taking your pack?' my wife demanded as I laced up my jerkin and made hurriedly for the door. 'And also that dog of yours! Roger!'

But I pretended not to hear her and fled the house, making my way through the already busy streets to Redcliffe and avoiding Broad Street, although glancing along its length as I passed the turning, I thought I saw a flurry of activity outside what had once been Alderman Weaver's residence.

I hurried across Bristol Bridge, dodging acquaintances and friends who wanted to stop and talk, and hiding under a shop's awning until Jack Hodge had passed. He looked ill and drawn, and I guessed he was on his way to visit Burl in the bridewell.

I went straight to Margaret Walker's cottage and knocked on the door.

'Where does Luke Prettywood live?' I asked when she answered my peremptory summons. Her two friends, Bess Simnel and Maria Watkins, peered over her shoulders. They were evidently paying her a morning visit.

'And God be with you, too, Roger,' she snapped, affronted by my lack of greeting.

She would doubtless have treated me to a lecture on manners had I not protested that I was on an urgent mission to prove Burl Hodge's innocence.

Her eyes brightened. 'You know who really killed Master Avenel?'

I nodded. 'I believe so. But proving it might be another matter.'

Margaret's lips set in a determined line, as did those of Goody Simnel and Goody Watkins. 'Not if I can help it.' She glanced at me suspiciously. 'But why do you want to know where Luke Prettywood lives? What's *he* got to do with it? You know very well he can't be guilty. He'd assaulted Jack Gload and been taken into custody by the time the body was discovered.'

'Just tell me where he lives,' I pleaded. 'I know it's somewhere in Redcliffe, but not which street.'

Her sharp-featured face was suffused with doubt, but eventually she directed me to a cottage near the rope walk, where the former brewer's assistant lived with his parents.

'And don't go upsetting Goody Prettywood,' Maria Watkins admonished me. 'She's a friend of mine.'

I reflected grimly that in a close-knit community like Redcliffe, everyone was a friend of everyone else. That was the trouble with murder; it harmed more lives than just those of the killer and his victim.

As I approached the Prettywoods' cottage, I could see the ropemakers in their stout leather aprons and caps, two at either end of the walk, their roughened, red hands twisting and re-twisting the lengths of hemp into the thick ropes necessary for binding bales of goods, before they were hoisted aboard ship for despatching overseas.

The summer heat showed no sign of abating, and the cottage's single window was wide open to the air. As I passed, I could see Luke sitting at a table in the despondent manner of someone who no longer has employment to go to, playing idly at fivestones, one hand pitted against the other. He seemed to be alone, so, without knocking, I lifted the latch and went inside.

He glanced up as I entered, but the dead-eyed look with

which he greeted me altered when he saw who it was, to be replaced by a wariness and a tensing of his body that told me he was suddenly afraid.

'What do you want, chapman?' he demanded, his voice cracking.

I said quietly, 'I've come to tell you that I know it was you who murdered Robin Avenel.'

His hands closed tightly over the fivestones. I could see sweat glisten suddenly across his forehead. But he had recovered his composure sufficiently to try a little bluster.

'That's ridiculous and you know it.' He managed a convincing laugh. 'I'd been arrested by the time the Watch found the body. And before Edgar Capgrave closed the Frome Gate and went home.'

I walked over to the table, pulled another stool from underneath it, and sat down.

'But Robin Avenel wasn't murdered in Jewry Lane, was he? He was killed downstairs, in the furthest one of the old synagogue cellars. I showed you the bloodstain, and you tried to convince me that it was two hundred years old, remember?' It was my turn to laugh.

'So? I was teasing you. There's nothing in that to make me a murderer.'

'You and Marianne Avenel are lovers. You admitted it to me yourself. You meet secretly in Saint Giles's crypt, and I've seen the pair of you down there with my own two eyes. It's the sort of secret that everyone knows about, or at least suspects – except, of course, the poor, cuckolded husband.'

Luke reddened, but jutted his chin defiantly. 'All right. I was a fool to confide in you, of all people, I can see that now. But it doesn't mean I killed Master Avenel.'

'It gives you a very strong motive.'

He shrugged and began tossing the stones again, his confidence returning. 'I've told you, I was in custody when the murder took place.'

I let that go for the minute and regarded him straitly.

'I did wonder,' I said, 'why you became involved in an apprentices' riot. You're no longer one of them. You don't share their grievances. And why pick on Jack Gload, a

Sheriff's man? What stupidity! Unless, that is, you were anxious to be arrested.'

'Why would I want that?' he sneered.

'Because you'd killed a man, a man you were cuckolding, as quite a lot of people knew. You were sharp enough to realize that if you drew attention to yourself in some other way – in a big enough way – no one would then think to connect you with Robin Avenel's murder. You couldn't have known, of course, that his body would later be moved, making this deception of yours unnecessary.'

He looked up sharply at that, about to ask a question, but thought better of it. He was a clever lad. He knew better than to admit curiosity.

'Go on,' he said. 'This is quite amusing. My mother won't be back for a while – she's gone to the market – and my father's working in the rope walk. You may have seen him as you passed. Tell me some more of this fairy tale of yours. It helps to pass the morning.'

'Very well.' I rested my elbows on the table and stared hard at him. He dropped the fivestones and stared back. 'Here is what I think happened. You arranged to meet Mistress Avenel in your usual trysting place in Saint Giles's crypt during the Midsummer Eve's celebration. Everyone would be occupied; eating, drinking, playing games. It's easy to get lost in a crowd. No one knows for certain where anyone else is. A simple excuse by Marianne that she wanted to use the privy and she could leave the trestle where she was sitting with her husband and Mistress Alefounder. I doubt if they even noticed her absence. They both had a lot on their minds.

'You and she had arranged the meeting that same morning, during the herb-gathering in Redcliffe fields. I saw the pair of you, heads together, near Saint Mary's Church. But things went wrong, didn't they? In your eagerness, you arrived early: Marianne wasn't there. Then you thought you heard her approaching. Only it wasn't her, was it? It was Robin Avenel! You jumped to the conclusion that he must know all about you and Marianne, especially when he drew his knife and started shouting. He went for you, and in the ensuing struggle, you killed him, probably accidentally. Then you ran. The more you thought about it, the more you saw that you could be the chief suspect. People knew where you and Mistress Avenel met. Later, Marianne caught up with you. She'd found her husband's body by that time and guessed what must have happened. What were you going to do? She must have been frantic. But when the apprentices' riot broke out, you suddenly saw your chance to divert suspicion away from yourself.'

I paused, reflecting that, of course, I hadn't been quite frank with him. Robin Avenel hadn't gone down to Saint Giles's crypt because he knew of Luke's tryst with Marianne. He had gone down there to speak to Albany – maybe to inform him that he had failed yet again to arrange a sea passage for him to Brittany. But when he saw Luke, his first thought must have been that, somehow or another, his treason and the secret hiding place had both been discovered. He wouldn't have stopped to reason things out or to reckon up the likelihood of such a discovery. He simply lost his nerve, drew his dagger and attacked Luke with the intention of killing him before he could reveal what he knew.

My companion still made no comment, but I could see his left cheek had developed a twitch. His hands were clenched.

'And I'll tell you why I'm sure of your guilt,' I went on, continuing to hold his eyes with mine; a rabbit staring into the eyes of a stoat. 'When I told you yesterday morning, in the Green Lattis, of my belief that Robin Avenel had been murdered in Saint Giles's Church, I made no mention of the crypt, or where I'd seen the bloodstain on the floor. Yet when you insisted on my showing it to you, you didn't hesitate, but took a candle and descended at once into the old syna-gogue cellars, going straight to the very spot.' I reached across the table suddenly and gripped his wrists with my hands. 'Now, how do explain that, if you didn't kill him?'

240

Twenty-One

He sprang to his feet, wrenching himself free of my grasp. 'You can't prove it!' he shouted.

'I just have,' I answered steadily, speaking with a confidence that I did not really feel.

He was frightened now, and frightened people do foolish things. If he had stopped, just for a moment, to think about it, he had the perfect reply to my accusation. If it were true, how had the body come to be discovered in Jewry Lane? Who had moved it? But Luke was already scared; appalled by what had happened. But, I guessed, he was more afraid that another man, an innocent man, would be found guilty of the crime and hanged for something he had not done. He had been congratulating himself on how well he had covered his tracks and diverted attention away from his friendship with Marianne Avenel, only to find that Burl Hodge had been accused in his stead. How long had he been trying to convince himself to say nothing, to let events take their course? Perhaps he had already decided to maintain his silence. But now here was I telling him that I was privy to his secret.

Maybe it tipped him into a sort of madness. Or maybe it was simply relief at being able to share his guilty knowledge with someone else. Whatever the reason, he blurted out, 'All right! All right! Yes, I killed Robin Avenel, but, like you said, it was an accident.' He was breathing hard as though he had been running. His eyes glittered feverishly. 'I didn't mean to stab him, but he started shouting at me like a man possessed. Don't ask me what he was shouting about; nothing he said made any sense. Then he came at me with his dagger, cursing and swearing, and I could see he was serious. He meant to kill me if he could. I was yelling

241

too by this time, frightened half out of my wits. I managed to grab him around the waist and we struggled for a while. I can't really remember what happened next; it's all such a muddle inside my head. I only know he suddenly stopped shouting and slumped to the ground . . . And when I looked . . .' Luke's voice caught on a horrified sob. 'When I looked, his dagger was sticking out of his chest. It had pierced him right through his heart.'

Luke began to laugh hysterically, rocking himself backwards and forwards on the balls of his feet. 'And do you know what, chapman? The silly part of it is, that if I'd set out to do just that, I couldn't have done it. I would have botched it. People like us don't learn how to use weapons such as swords and daggers, now do they?' He continued with his rocking and inane laughter for a few more seconds, long enough for me to rise from my stool and come round the table towards him. But then he snapped to attention, his face transformed into a mask of hatred. 'Still, now I've killed a man once, maybe I can do it again.'

Before I had time to realize what he would be up to, he spun round and reached up to a shelf fixed to the wall behind him. When he turned back, he was holding one of his mother's long-bladed kitchen knives in his hand.

He smiled. 'If you're dead, then who's to know what really happened?'

I hastily put the width of the table between us.

'Put the knife down, Luke,' I said gently, trying to stop my voice from shaking. 'Don't be so foolish! How are you going to explain killing me?'

The smile broadened. 'I'll say you attacked me. I'll say you tried to force me into confessing to the murder of Master Avenel so as to save your friend, Burl Hodge.'

He was talking wildly now, not considering what he was saying, and I regarded him warily. In normal circumstances, I was a good deal stronger than he was, but a desperate man, teetering on the edge of unreason, can often display a disproportionate strength. I moved cautiously in the direction of the door. He laughed and made a sudden rush at me, leaping the table.

I turned sideways on to him and felt the knife slash the top of my arm. I was unaware of any pain, only of the need to protect myself. I flung out both hands and grabbed the knife blade as it swooped once more towards me. I was vaguely aware of a cut hand and blood trickling down my left wrist and into my sleeve.

Help arrived in a most unexpected guise, as what appeared to be the three Furies burst through the cottage door and flung themselves on Luke Prettywood, taking him by surprise and bearing him easily to the ground. Bess Simnel and Maria Watkins then sat astride his chest while Margaret Walker, panting a little after so much exertion, clambered to her feet to see if all was well with me.

'You're bleeding like a stuck pig,' was her comment once she had finished her examination, 'but it's nothing serious. You'll live. Now run and fetch that useless lump, Richard Manifold. We three overheard everything that passed between you and this murderer here.' Noting my puzzled frown, she deigned to explain. 'When you left my cottage, we followed you – Maria and Bess and myself – to see what you were up to, and we've been listening outside the window ever since we arrived. We'll confirm what was said.' She gave the struggling Luke a venomous glance. 'You may not have meant to kill Robin Avenel,' she spat at him, 'but you were quite prepared to let Burl Hodge take the blame. You'd have watched him hang just to save your own worthless skin. And no one in Redcliffe will ever forgive you for that.' She collapsed heavily on to the hapless youth's legs and glowered up at me. 'For heaven's sake, get on your way, Roger! Go! Don't just stand there like the great, gormless idiot that you are.'

I stooped suddenly and kissed her, a big, smacking kiss full on her lips. She looked astonished, but not displeased.

I kissed her again and went.

There is not a lot more to tell.

Richard Manifold, who, I think, was beginning to have doubts, if not about Burl's culpability, then certainly about his chances of making the case against him stick, was grateful

243

for my proof of Luke Prettywood's guilt and the three goodies' testimony, which corroborated my story. Not that anyone would have known it from the surly way in which he behaved, berating me for withholding evidence and upbraiding Margaret Walker and her friends for putting themselves in danger. But he got short shrift from my three avenging Furies.

'You'd have had another murder on your hands if we hadn't followed Roger here,' my former mother-in-law informed him roundly. 'Luke was about to kill him.'

'Kill him! Kill him!' echoed Maria and Bess, wagging their heads vigorously and showing their blackened stumps of teeth.

The sergeant made a valiant attempt not to look too downcast by the fact of my survival as he marched his prisoner away under guard, flanked by Jack Gload and Peter Littleman. The former could barely contain his satisfaction at the outcome: he still bore the scars of Luke's Midsummer Eve attack.

I went home, accompanied by Margaret Walker, to confess all to Adela, to be scolded, exclaimed and fussed over and made to feel a hero – which I wasn't. I was also made to promise – although this was done so subtly that I hardly noticed it at the time – to concentrate on my work as a pedlar now that Burl's innocence had been happily established. The cuts on my upper left arm and hand were bathed and bandaged with sicklewort leaves, in order to staunch the flow of blood. Then I was sent to bed with a potion of lettuce juice to help me sleep, while my womenfolk kept the children quiet and no doubt discussed my latest antics with pursed lips and much sad shaking of their heads.

By the time my younger son woke me, using the simple expedient of yelling at the top of his voice in my right ear, it was almost suppertime and I was ravenous. I sat up, my head ringing from Adam's stentorian effort, hauled him on to the bed, tickled him mercilessly until he was almost choking with laughter, then, carrying him on my shoulders, went downstairs.

The news of Burl's release from prison and of my part in the arrest of Luke Prettywood had spread like wildfire, and the house seemed to be overflowing with people. Half the denizens of Redcliffe, including the Hodge family, had crossed Bristol Bridge and were crowded into the Small Street hall, parlour and kitchen, helping themselves liberally to my ale and eating the food intended for my dinner. Jenny Hodge flung her arms around my neck and burst into tears of gratitude – I could feel myself flushing with embarrassment. Jack and Dick patted any part of my anatomy they could manage to reach, and even Burl himself, pale and sunken-eyed from his brief sojourn in prison, muttered a few awkward words of thanks. He couldn't stop his envious glance from darting here and there, taking in every detail of a house he was sure I didn't deserve, but he embraced me before departing.

'Friends?' I asked, thrusting out my hand.

'Friends,' he agreed, somewhat reluctantly, then suddenly grinned. 'Oh, damn you, Roger!' He thumped me in the chest. 'How can folk stay at odds with you, when you go around pulling them out of trouble all the time?'

'That's enough of that sort of talk,' Jenny admonished him sharply. 'Just be thankful that there's somebody who can!'

Eventually, my well-wishers dispersed, including Margaret Walker, who was borne off in triumph by Bess Simnel and Maria Watkins to recount their adventure and be fêted in turn by those Redcliffe neighbours who had not ended up in Small Street, eating and drinking me out of house and home.

Adela, the children and I settled down to a belated supper of mutton stewed with lentils and garlic and a much-depleted bowl of cherries, my favourite fruit (and, by the look of things, the favourite fruit of many of our uninvited guests). But we were not to be left alone for long. The arrival of Richard Manifold, to ask more questions, put paid to our peace.

He was not our only visitor. Accompanying him was Timothy Plummer, who had at last shed his various disguises and was restored to the full importance of his royal livery. His apparently sudden appearance had plainly disconcerted the sergeant, who was regarding him morosely. And my innocent revelation that the King's Spymaster General had been in the city for several weeks, first as a beggar, then as a Dominican friar, only added to his resentment.

I ushered them both into the parlour and folded my arms, waiting to hear what they had to say.

'Well, we have Luke Prettywood's confession,' Richard began. 'And we also have Mistress Avenel's evidence that her husband attacked Luke first and that the killing was done in self-defence. Of course, that's borne out by the fact that Master Avenel was stabbed with his own dagger.'

'Mistress Avenel was present when her husband was killed?' I asked.

Something in my tone must have betrayed my stupefaction because Timothy Plummer glanced sharply at me. Richard Manifold, however, heard and saw nothing out of the ordinary.

'Of course. She was down in Saint Giles's crypt with Luke when Master Avenel found them. Why else would he have attacked the lad, if not because he was her lover? He must have suspected what was going on between those two and followed them. It also explains how the body came to be moved into Jewry Lane. But for some reason or another that I can't quite fathom, they both deny shifting it. However, it's obvious to me why they did it. If people knew where their trysting place was, they ran less risk of being suspected of the crime if it was thought Master Avenel had been killed in the street. Then, to make doubly certain, Luke assaulted Jack Gload and was taken into custody. Oh, yes! He's a very cunning young man.'

Across the little room, I met Timothy Plummer's unwavering gaze.

'And is that what you think happened, Roger?' he asked.

'Well . . . Yes, of c–course. It makes perfect sense,' I stuttered.

'And you can offer no other idea as to who might have moved Robin Avenel's dead body? Or why?'

'I don't know why you suppose I should be able to,' I answered blandly, recovering my poise. I turned back to Richard Manifold, who was regarding the pair of us with a slightly puzzled expression. 'What does Mistress Alefounder have to say concerning her brother's movements on Mid-summer Eve?'

The sergeant shrugged. 'She has no knowledge of them. He'd said nothing to her of his suspicions, and there was so much confusion during the feast. She's returning to Frome as soon as possible. It's been a terrible time for her. First her brother's death, and now this revelation of her sister-in-law's perfidy.' He braced his shoulders, his natural self-importance reasserting itself. 'Well, I must be off. There's work to be done. I just thought you'd like to know what's happened, Roger. Once again, you've done the Law a service.'

Heaven knows what the admission cost him. He had to grit his teeth and his features were set in a rictus smile. Besides, he must have guessed that I had been aware of Timothy Plummer's presence in the city and given him no warning. But still, he managed it with sufficient grace to make me disclaim modestly that I wasn't worthy of such high praise. The Spymaster General looked as though he agreed with me, and I wasn't surprised when he declined Richard's invitation to dine with him at the castle.

'I need to speak to the chapman, Sergeant, if you don't mind. Privately.'

All Richard's suspicions were reawakened, I could tell, but there was nothing he could do but leave us alone.

'I'll make my adieus to Adela, if I may,' he said stiffly, and I nodded.

'You'll find her in the kitchen.'

When the parlour door had closed behind him, Timothy let out a sigh of relief.

'That man's a fool,' he remarked, stretching and seating himself, uninvited, in the window embrasure. 'If he were capable of placing events in an orderly sequence, he'd see at once that that adulterous pair couldn't have moved her husband's body. So, Roger, who did?'

'Why should you think that I know?'

He laughed mirthlessly. 'Because you knew what was going on. Because you worked out where Albany was hidden and you found him. It was somewhere down in that cellar beneath the church. It has to be. And don't insult my intelligence by trying to persuade me otherwise. So where's our precious renegade now, eh? Mistress Alefounder obviously doesn't know any more. She's lost him or she wouldn't be going home to Frome. That leaves you, Roger. You realize I could charge you with treason?'

'I should deny all knowledge of any Scottish duke. I should also deny speaking to you on the river bank when you told me far more, I'm sure, than you ought to have done. For which you should be thankful, or it might be you who is charged with treason. All I'm guilty of is clearing the name of an innocent man who you were quite prepared to see die on the gallows. You thought that Albany had killed Robin Avenel, didn't you? So you found a scapegoat and threw him to the wolves.'

Timothy sighed. 'You are bitter, aren't you? Is that why you did it? Why you helped Albany get away?'

'I don't know what you're talking about,' I answered coldly.

The Spymaster got to his feet.

'Ah well! I shall just have to return to the King and report failure in this case. Don't worry, I shan't mention my suspicions concerning you. I'm riding north, anyway, as soon as I can, to rejoin my lord of Gloucester. I think I told you. Shall I say you commend yourself to him?'

I shook my head. 'No. I love him, but I'd rather you said nothing about me. Out of sight is out of mind and I'd just as soon he forgot me.'

Timothy laughed, but I realized later – too late – that he'd made no promise not to mention me. Politely, I held open the parlour door, intimating that he should take his leave. He laughed again as he passed me. But then he turned and tapped my arm.

'I shan't go back to Westminster entirely empty-handed. I shall be taking the Tudor spy, Silas Witherspoon, with me as a peace offering and to prove that my time here has not been altogether wasted. It's a pity, of course. It means Sergeant Manifold will have to be on the lookout for his replacement from Brittany, and it won't be easy. He'll probably suspect entirely the wrong man. But there you are. Needs must when the Devil drives. My salutations to Mistress Chapman. I won't trouble her with them in person.' He scratched one armpit. 'A most unsatisfactory affair. Most unsatisfactory!'

He was gone and I drew several deep breaths, unconsciously straightening my shoulders. I hadn't been arrested. I was free to return to my family and my life. But it wasn't until I was in bed that night that I remembered two things.

The first was Albany's valedictory salute. 'You've been more than good to me, Roger Chapman, Sassenach though you are. I shan't forget you. I shall know who to call upon if ever I need a friend among the English.' At the time, it had seemed no more than the parting words of a grateful man. Now, lying in the dark, it suddenly had a sinister ring. It held the seeds of future trouble.

The second was the realization that I would never now possess the sheath that Apothecary Witherspoon had been making for me. Adela and I would have to go on relying on the old, untrustworthy methods of child prevention. And, as I snuggled up to her, I wondered if there was any cabbage in the house.